The Wendals

Austin Kennedy

Cover art by McCain Kennedy

To my children, Emma, Sadie, Bryant, and Delaney.
May your life be one great adventure.

And to Steve, the original Wendal, and the
best friend a guy could ask for.
I miss you, buddy.

CONTENTS

THE WENDALS

Wendals Publishing

Chapter 1

Fall of 1998

Austin scanned the crowded shelves of candy inside the small convenience store, indecisive on what to buy. All of his favorite treats were right in front of him—Sour Warheads, Abba-Zabas, Bubblicious, and Now and Laters—but to his dismay, he only had enough spare change for one item. Glancing at the digital watch on his wrist, he saw that it was 7:12 a.m. School started in a little over an hour, and still having more that he wanted to accomplish before heading back into town, he knew there wasn't much time for lollygagging. He grabbed a small pack of Swedish Fish and made his way to the front of the store.

Austin Kenney looked like your typical Southern California boy of the late 1990s. Slightly taller than the average fourteen-year-old, his dirty blonde hair was casually parted down the middle and styled into a carefree, just-got-out-of-bed, surfer look. He wore a tightly-fitted blue Hurley T-shirt, and like most boys his age he had on a pair of jeans that were a little too baggy and that sagged a little too low around his waist.

After he arrived at the store's register, he put the bag of candy on the counter, and the worker, an older man with tan skin and dark hair, punched a few buttons on the register's keypad. The store was vacant except for Austin and the lone employee, and a small TV played the local news behind the counter. "Seventy-five cents," the man said unenthusiastically, and with a thick accent.

Austin guessed that the man was from somewhere in the Middle East, but that was solely based on accents he had heard from characters on his favorite cable TV shows. Digging through his pockets, he found three quarters and placed them next to the bag of Swedish Fish.

A breaking news story popped onto the TV screen behind the counter, catching Austin's attention. A handsome man in a sharp suit excitedly gave the report: "The local bank robber that authorities have nicknamed 'Bart the Burglar' has now committed his third bank robbery in just a matter of weeks. His latest heist was at the Anaheim branch of Bank of Southern California, where he once again wore his now-trademark Bart Simpson Halloween mask. Although authorities seem to be making very little progress in the case, police did receive a witness tip that the burglar may have been seen driving a Green Ford Escort."

A low-quality black-and-white image of the bank robber, with his face hidden behind the Bart Simpson mask, was displayed in the corner of the screen.

Austin gave a sigh of disappointment when the news segment ended, having hoped that the police would have found some better information on the case by now. He was wildly interested in these robberies for two reasons: one, he was abnormally curious and inquisitive for a young man his age and was keenly obsessed with the faintest bit of excitement that happened in his small—and generally boring—town of Ocean View, California; and two, his dad was the local police sergeant in town, and he wanted very badly for his father to lead the charge in cracking a cool case such as this one.

Austin looked at the older man behind the register, and spoke matter-of-factly, "He's not a burglar." The man stared back at Austin in confusion. Pointing at the TV, Austin continued, "They call him Bart the Burglar, but he's not a burglar. He's a robber. There's a difference." It bothered Austin that not even the local media could get the two terms straight.

The man at the register was clearly uninterested in what Austin had to say, and he asked, "Can I do anything else for you?"

Austin grabbed his candy from the counter. "There used

to be a dirt trail, further up the highway, that led to some bike jumps. Is it still up there?"

"Isn't it a school day?" the man responded dryly.

"I've got time," Austin shot back with a hint of attitude.

Easing up a little, the man replied, "The brush has gotten too thick in that area. No one goes back there anymore."

With a look of disappointment on his face, Austin turned and headed out of the convenience store. Once outside, he picked up a black backpack from off the ground, shoved his new candy inside one of the side pouches, and threw the bag over his shoulders. Then he hopped onto his red BMX bike and started to pedal back up the main road as fast as he could. It was clear and sunny outside, and other than a strong wind, it was a near-perfect morning.

The highway Austin traveled along was the famed PCH, and was the longest road in California, spanning nearly the entire coast of the Golden State. Just far enough away from Los Angeles and San Diego to avoid the hustle and bustle of the big cities, Ocean View was one of the quieter beach towns situated along PCH—at least by Southern California standards. But this was part of the reason why Austin thought his town was lacking in excitement.

The view on his ride up the empty road was breathtaking. The land had yet to be developed here in the northern outskirts of town, and both sides of the highway were covered in nothing but massive trees and wild vegetation. To his left, after several hundred yards of dense brush, were huge cliffs that dropped down to the Pacific Ocean below, and Austin could see the glistening blue of the water in the distance as he charged ahead to his destination. He loved it in the outskirts. It was quiet and secluded, and the air seemed to smell just a little fresher to him than it did back in town.

After some time riding, Austin finally pulled his bike over to the side of the road and stopped at a spot along the western shoulder where he hoped to find the entrance to the trail that led to the bike jumps. However, seeing only heavy brush barricading any path to the wilderness inside, he quickly became discouraged. Riding his bike slowly along the perimeter of the brush, he watched carefully as he went until he eventually arrived at a spot in the growth that seemed to be slightly less impenetrable than it was anywhere else. After examining the spot for some time, he finally decided it was worth a shot.

With his bike at his side, he pushed his way right into the dense brush wall. As he fought through the heavy vegetation, he was stabbed and scraped by sharp branches and spiky thorns, and his baggy jeans were snagged by the bushes' wooden claws. The ground was sopping wet from an early September rain that had come down the night before, and Austin's white skater shoes sunk deep into the mud with each step. But he kept moving forward.

Finally, he broke through the thickest part of the brush and popped out into an area that was much more open. *Thank goodness*, he thought, as he dusted the leaves and dirt from off of his clothes. He looked at his white shoes, now covered in thick brown mud, and he worried what his mom would say when he got home later that afternoon.

Taking a moment to evaluate his surroundings, he saw a trail in front of him that cut through the brush and was wide enough to easily ride his bike down. However, this trail didn't appear to be the same one that led to the bike jumps he was looking for.

Then Austin noticed something strange—thick tire tracks pressed deep into the mud in front of him, following all the way down the trail— and he contemplated the scene for a moment. *What was a car doing out here?* he wondered. The tire tracks looked fresh, and he figured that the car must have passed through very recently, considering the fact that the rain had just come down the day before. He thought about the situation briefly, and then looked at his watch. It was 7:44 a.m. If he left right away, he could probably make it to school just in time. But as it usually did, his curiosity got the best of him, and he hopped back on his bike and headed down the dirt trail, following the tire tracks.

This new trail took him on a steep and windy path that descended down the cliffs and towards the ocean below. It was a rough ride, and for most of the trip, he was blind to where he was heading because of the tall brush that surrounded him on both sides of the trail. Every time he arrived at a fork in the road, he had to make his best guess as to which path would lead him out of the arduous maze.

Just as he was thinking about turning back, he saw a beautiful glassy blue color piercing through the thicket ahead of him. He continued towards the blue, and a few moments later, he finally broke out of the heavy vegetation and arrived at the edge of a cliff that overlooked the wide-open scenery below. The wind was beginning to blow with such force that it almost knocked him off of his bike, but after regaining his balance on top of the cliff, he looked out and admired the beauty of what was around him.

In the distance straight ahead of him he saw the magnificent glassy blue of the Pacific Ocean, stretching out as far as the eye could see. Large waves rolled forward with majestic power and crashed gently onto the secluded beach cove below, looking like a scene out of *Robinson Crusoe*. The image was like nothing Austin had ever seen before.

The beaches in this part of the coast were so remote that they stayed almost completely devoid of human visitors, mostly due to a lack of any convenient public access. Austin imagined that eventually there would be some kind of road built to allow beachgoers an easy path down to the water, but for now there was nothing out here but untamed wilderness and untouched sand.

Below him, he could see that the crude trail he had been following continued to wind back and forth down the rocky cliffside terrain, until it eventually dead-ended at a clearing in the brush on a flat spot of dirt ground, not far from where he was standing. On this dirt clearing, Austin was very surprised to see two parked vehicles.

The first vehicle was an old, rundown, travel trailer RV—the kind of RV that you would hitch to a large truck to comfortably trek across the country. However, this RV definitely hadn't traveled anywhere in quite some time, and it didn't look very comfortable either. It was dirty, rusty, and looked so run down that Austin thought it must have been abandoned and left desolate since before he was born. The yellowish-orange color used to accent the trailer's off-white paint job was faded, and the tires underneath were completely flat, with large tears in the rubber. Dirty and ragged shades were pulled down on the inside of each window, making it impossible to see inside.

Then Austin looked at the second vehicle, which was a green four-door sedan. The car also appeared dirty and beat-up, and the tires were worn and muddy, but it looked to him like it might still be in working condition.

Austin couldn't get over his curiosity of what these vehicles were doing in such a secluded area, all alone. He grabbed his backpack from off of his shoulders and steadied it on the bike handles in front of him. After unzipping the backpack, he searched through the contents inside, and finally pulled out a pair of small black binoculars. He hung the binocular strap around his neck, and then looked through the sights. First, he got a better view of the old RV. Then, he spied the sedan, which appeared to be empty.

The wind started to pick up again, and a strong gust knocked Austin's backpack off of his bike handles and onto the dirt. This startled him a little.

Crash! came a loud noise from the clearing below. Austin jumped so hard that he dropped the binoculars out of his hands and almost fell off his bike.

Frozen with terror, he stared down at the RV, wondering where the loud noise had come from. Eventually, he realized that the strong burst of wind had slammed shut a small compartment door at the back of the RV, making the terrible sound. The compartment door now swung back and forth in the breeze, creaking eerily as it did. Austin's heart was beating fast in his chest. He took a deep breath, trying to calm himself down. *It was only the wind,* he told himself. But as he stared down at the old RV, the whole scene started to give him the creeps.

Then something caught Austin's eye about halfway down the trail between the RV and where he was standing. An object that looked like a small green piece of paper was slowly being blown up the path by the wind. The small object continued to tumble towards him until another gust of wind eventually blew it deep into the thick bushes next to the trail.

Giving in to his powerful urge to investigate anything that seemed out of place, Austin glanced back at the quiet RV below and then cautiously moved down the trail, straight toward the bushes. He walked slowly, his head wild with curiosity, and his heart beating faster and faster with each step. He wasn't sure why he felt so nervous about the old RV, but something inside of him suddenly told him to get out fast—a feeling he promptly ignored.

Once he reached the spot of brush where the paper had been blown, he got down on his hands and knees and peered into the bushes. There was something lying on the dirt underneath the shrub. He reached in and pulled it out, then dusted it off to examine it. It was a crisp one hundred dollar bill.

At first, Austin was excited about finding so much money. But his excitement quickly turned to apprehension, and then to confusion. *What on earth was this doing out here?* he wondered. Other than being dusty from its journey up the trail, the bill looked brand new, like the kind you could only get from a fresh batch at the bank.

This new discovery sent Austin's above-average youthful paranoia soaring. He looked down at the creepy old RV, immediately feeling like something was seriously wrong. *But what was it?* he wondered. Then he looked at the green car parked next to the RV, and it suddenly hit him like a ton of bricks. *The breaking news story,* he remembered. He thought back to the man in the suit reporting the news on the television, and the latest tip the police had received on Bart the Burglar: *The burglar may have been seen driving a green Ford Escort!*

With a pang of terror in his chest, Austin clutched the binoculars that hung around his neck and slowly pulled them back up to his eyes. A deep knot in his stomach tightened as he peered through the lenses. Focusing his sights straight onto the left side of the back of the green car, just above the bumper, he saw the silver and blue Ford logo. Then he anxiously panned to the same spot on the right side of the car, just above the bumper, and saw the silver metallic letters that spelled out the model of the car: Escort. *It was a Green Ford Escort.* Austin froze in complete shock, and his mind raced as the binoculars slipped from his grip again.

Then he heard a noise coming from inside the RV. He wasn't sure if it was real, or if it was just his imagination, but he wasn't sticking around to find out.

Austin sprinted back to his bike as quickly as he could, almost tripping over his own feet as he went. As he anxiously threw his backpack over his shoulders, he suddenly realized that in all of his excitement he had dropped the hundred dollar bill—the only evidence of what he had seen. But unwilling to go searching for the money now, he took off on his bike as fast as he could, without so much as looking back.

Chapter 2

Two Weeks Later

Austin sprinted down the outdoor courtyard of Ocean View High School, checking his watch as he ran. The bell that signaled for students to get to their first period classes had already rung several minutes earlier, and he knew that the tardy bell wasn't far behind. He also knew that if he was late to Mr. Gonzales' science class again, he would get a note sent home to his parents, and he desperately wanted to avoid that. After flying past a group of long-haired boys kicking around a knit hacky sack, he turned the corner to the science halls.

Clang! Austin let out a sigh of disappointment as he heard the tardy bell ring loudly in his ears, but he kept on running. Three girls in spaghetti strap tank tops and choker necklaces giggled as they watched Austin pass them by. As he got further down the hall, he could see that the door to Mr. Gonzales' classroom was already closed. He came to an abrupt stop in front of the class, wiped the sweat off of his forehead, and then cracked the classroom door open as quietly as possible and snuck inside.

Standing at the front of the classroom, Mr. Gonzales paused the opening lines of his daily class introduction, stared at Austin as he entered the room, and then announced his arrival to the rest of the class. "So glad you could join us, Mr. Kenney," he exclaimed loudly. Mr. Gonzales was short and lean and had a terrifyingly icy glare. The entire class turned around in their seats and stared at Austin. Some students snickered, while others looked annoyed. "That's three tardies in a two-week period," Mr. Gonzales said with insincere enthusiasm. "Let's all give Mr. Kenney a round of applause for being the first student this year to reach that mark." The students clapped their hands together in mock celebration, and not knowing how to react, Austin smiled and took a bow to his fellow students, eliciting even more laughter from the class.

Mr. Gonzales did not look amused. "Of course, that means you'll have to pick up a tardy notice after class, which must be signed by your parents," the teacher said. Austin's smile quickly faded away, and his face turned red. "Now, please take your seat," Mr. Gonzales continued. "You have already stolen valuable time away from today's presentations."

Austin squeezed through a row of desks and found his seat near the middle of the classroom, next to his best friend, Steve.

Steve Andretti was tall, athletic, and ruggedly handsome for a fifteen-year-old boy. His dirty blonde hair was bleached at the tips and spiked wildly all around with hair gel. He kept the two top buttons of his blue checkered shirt wide open, exposing his white tank top shirt underneath, and he wore a tight-fitting puka shell necklace around his neck. There was a small gap between his front two teeth, which only added to his rugged look.

Steve was just ending a conversation with a cute brunette girl behind him when Austin sat down. With a charming smile, he gave the girl a flirtatious wink and then turned his attention to his friend.

Austin nodded to Steve and, as discreetly as possible, the two boys gave each other a special handshake that involved a finger snap and ended with both boys softly whistling the same two-syllable sound in unison. They called this the Wendal handshake.

"Three tardies?" Steve whispered. "You're getting worse than me. Where you been?"

Austin noticed Mr. Gonzales shooting his icy glare in their direction, and he shook his head at Steve. "We'll talk later."

Steve nodded. "Ryan's giving his presentation first, so you got here just in time." Both boys looked towards the front row of the classroom, where Ryan anxiously gathered his presentation materials from his backpack and headed to the front of the room.

Ryan Hartman was fourteen years old, short, and had black hair and a dark complexion. He also spiked his hair, but his spikes shot straight up and were styled much more neatly than Steve's. He wore a white Red Hot Chili Peppers t-shirt, baggy cargo shorts, and puffy DC skater shoes.

After picking up a giant homemade replica of a carbon atom from the corner of the classroom, Ryan placed it on Mr. Gonzales' desk in the front of the room. The teacher smiled in awe as he stared at the detailed model. Large red and blue styrofoam balls were clustered in the center of the replica, representing the protons and neutrons, and two thick styrofoam rings were mounted around the nucleus, representing the inner and outer shells, with painted green balls carefully placed for the atom's electrons. It was obvious that Ryan had gone above and beyond with the assignment. He was proud of his finished product. However, as he looked out at his peers, who stared back at him coldly, his body went numb and he was unable to speak.

Steve leaned over and whispered to Austin, "He seemed pretty nervous before class."

"He'll be alright, he's a Wendal," Austin whispered back.

The Wendals was the name that the boys had given to their small group of friends, and as far as Austin was concerned, they were the most tight-knit group of boys you would ever find on the face of the earth. The group meant absolutely everything to him.

"True," Steve said with a smile, and then turned back to watch Ryan.

The long silence that followed was very uncomfortable for everyone in the room, and Steve and Austin looked on at their clearly petrified friend anxiously, praying for him to begin his presentation.

In the back of the room, three rough-looking boys sat together, laughing cruelly as they whispered to each other. Tyler, the obvious leader of the group, was big and thick and looked much too old to be a high school freshman. His hair was buzzed almost to the scalp, his ear lobes were pierced and had large black plugs inside of them, and he wore a black motocross t-shirt with a large skull printed on the front.

Both smaller and uglier than Tyler, the other two boys fell over themselves as they tried to impress their ringleader by laughing at his every joke as if he were the most clever fifteen-year-old alive. It was obvious to most of the class that their teasing was directed at Ryan.

While making a coughing noise, Tyler blurted out, "Loser," loud enough for half of the class to hear, and his two friends laughed even harder, along with a few other students sitting close by. Austin glanced back at Tyler in anger, and then looked up to the front of the room to see Ryan's face turning completely red. He very badly wanted to do something but had no clue what he could do.

Finally, Mr. Gonzales stood up. "Quiet down and show some respect, people," he said as he walked over to Ryan and put his arm around him. "The project looks great, and Ryan is doing his best. Just wait until it's your turn, and you'll realize this isn't as easy as it looks." He turned to Ryan, whose head was now buried in his chest. "Take your time and begin your presentation whenever you're ready."

Tyler balled his fists and put them up to his eyes, pretending to cry. "Maybe he needs his mommy here with him," he said in a mocking tone, quiet enough to only be understood by the students close by. More laughter came from all around him.

"Excuse me, Tyler?" Mr. Gonzales shot his angry glare at the bully.

Sitting straight up in his seat, Tyler reported, "Oh, I just said that Ryan's mom must be very proud of him." His friends could barely hold back their laughter as Mr. Gonzales looked on suspiciously.

Fuming with anger, Austin turned to Steve, who was calmly drawing on a sheet of paper inside of his three-ring binder. He never understood how Steve stayed so calm in times like these.

Steve finished drawing, folded the sheet of paper in half, and passed it to Austin. After quickly unfolding the sheet, Austin looked at the page. In the center of the sheet was a crudely drawn stick figure boy with an angry scowl and dark beady eyes. A thick red X mark was crossed over the stick figure, and above the drawing, Steve had written in all caps, "TYLER WILL PAY." Then, at the bottom of the page was written, "Wendals 4 Life!"

Austin's anger subsided, and he laughed as he stared at the drawing. He turned back to Steve and saw a cocky and mischievous look on his friend's face—which was a look that Austin had come to know and to love—and he felt better instantly.

Chapter 3

As he thought over what they were about to do, Ryan was even more nervous than he had been on his first day of high school. "We don't have to do this, guys. It's not a big deal, honestly," he pleaded with Steve and Austin, who were with him in an outdoor hallway of the school campus. The grounds around them were mostly empty now that school was over, but a few students still passed by them sporadically.

"He messed with a Wendal," Austin replied as he pulled a yellow elastic water balloon launcher out of his backpack. This three-man water balloon launcher was one of the Wendals' favorite toys for causing mischief, and they took it with them everywhere they went. To fire the launcher, two boys would take hold of the handles and spread out wide into a firing stance, while a third person was stationed in the middle and was in charge of launching the balloon.

The launcher position was by far the most important job out of the three. After loading a balloon into the center pouch, the launcher would pull the pouch back as far as he wanted the balloon to travel and would then aim the balloon as precisely as possible before firing. Aiming was extremely difficult and took a lot of skill and practice, and Steve was easily the best launcher out of the Wendals. With Steve launching the balloons, the boys had gotten proficient at hitting targets from over a hundred yards away.

Ryan reluctantly took one of the handles of the launcher from Austin.

As he carefully loaded a water balloon into the launching pouch, Steve said, "You've gotta hit back, or these guys will never leave you alone. I mean, just look at the morons now."

About sixty yards away, in an open area of the campus, Ryan could see Tyler and his two henchmen playing keep-away with a smaller boy's *Power Ranger* backpack. Tossing the backpack back and forth to each other, the three larger boys mocked the smaller boy, who looked like he was about to cry. They were so distracted by their current game that the bullies didn't even notice the Wendals prepping for their launch.

Watching the pitiful scene made Ryan upset. "Yeah, I guess you're right," he said. But his anger quickly turned back into uncertainty. "What happens if we hit them, though?"

"I don't know," Austin said, shrugging his shoulders. "But isn't that the exciting part?"

"You mean *when* we hit them," Steve said confidently. "Don't worry about it, Ry, I'm not afraid of Tyler." He pulled the water balloon pouch backward. "Just hold those handles steady. I want a clean shot." Ryan and Austin spread out into their launch positions, with their legs wide and their knees bent, and they stretched their arms out in the direction of the bullies. Together, the three boys looked like water balloon launching professionals.

Steve continued to pull the balloon pouch backward, building tension in the elastic bands.

"Better get 'em on the first try," Austin said, struggling to keep his handle still.

"You know my aim is impeccable," Steve responded confidently, as he made small adjustments to the balloon pouch. "I never miss." Then, after one more final adjustment, he let the pouch go, and Austin watched excitedly as the water balloon sailed through the sky. Unable to handle the intensity of the moment, Ryan closed his eyes tightly and clenched his jaw.

Tyler must have heard the loud *snap* as the launcher was fired because he turned around just in time to see the water balloon connect perfectly with the middle of his chest. The impact of the balloon on his rib cage made a thunderous sound that echoed through the campus and made Ryan cringe even more.

Tyler fell to the ground hard, and his two goon friends stared back up at the Wendals in total confusion and disbelief.

Jumping up and down in utter excitement, Austin cheered, "What a shot!" Then he watched as Tyler's friends helped the bully back up to his feet, and his excitement ebbed. "Okay guys, it would probably be a good idea to get out of here now," he exclaimed. But when he turned around, he saw that Ryan had already taken off running, and was now halfway across campus.

Steve didn't move. "You go ahead," he said to Austin. "I told you; I'm not scared."

Seeing that the bullies were now in an all-out sprint, heading right for them, Austin grabbed Steve by the arm, and spoke sternly, "Wendals stick together."

Steve looked at Austin, and after a moment, realizing his friend meant business, he nodded in surrender. Side by side, the two boys turned around and ran hard, away from the bullies, who were hot on their tails. It wasn't long before they arrived at the bike racks at the main entrance of the school campus.

Ryan was already on his bike and ready to ride. "Let's go," he shouted nervously.

Breathing heavily, Austin and Steve worked quickly to unchain their bikes. Austin hopped on his bike as soon as it was free of the rack, and followed after Ryan, pedaling away from the school fast, and assuming that Steve was right behind them.

But as Steve finished unchaining his bike, he saw Tyler and his goons coming around the corner, looking like a pack of angry wolves. He lowered his bike back down to the ground, dropped his backpack behind him, and fearlessly took a step towards the bullies.

Austin and Ryan had turned several corners in the neighborhood across from the school before they finally stopped their bikes to catch their breath. Looking behind, Austin immediately began to panic. "Where's Steve?" he shouted.

"I don't know," Ryan replied, exhausted, and afraid. "I

thought he was right behind you."

After exchanging terrified glances, the boys quickly turned around and started back in the direction of the school.

"Pick him back up," Tyler shouted to his friends. "I'm not done with him yet."

Steve was on his hands and knees, in obvious pain, as the three bullies surrounded him. Tyler's two friends grabbed Steve by each arm and lifted him up onto his feet.

"Let's finish him off fast," one of Tyler's friends said with a cynical cackle. "I've gotta work the drive-thru window today, and I'm already late for my shift."

Blood dripped from Steve's nose, and his shirt was torn at the shoulder, but somehow, Steve was laughing. "Try hitting me again, I might feel it this time," he jeered. "Actually, maybe you should let one of your girlfriends here have a chance. I bet they hit harder than you."

Steve's arrogant attitude enraged Tyler even more, and he balled his fists tightly and grabbed Steve by the shirt collar. Pulling his right arm back for a disdainful punch, Tyler paused, looked at Steve, and cracked a smile. "It's not my fault that your *Wendal* friends ran away and left you all alone," he said smugly. "Maybe it's time for some new friends."

As Tyler was about to unleash a fury-filled haymaker on Steve, a white Dodge Durango SUV came flying around the corner of the school parking lot and slammed on its brakes just a few feet away from the confrontation. Startled, the bullies released Steve, letting him fall back down to his knees, and then turned around to see who it was that had arrived so hastily.

The driver's door of the car opened, and out stepped a tall and muscular older boy, with a round face and a pronounced chin. His dark hair was slicked straight back, and he wore a black t-shirt with the letters *N.W.O.* printed in white on the chest, and *new world order* in smaller type underneath. The sleeves were torn off of the shirt, revealing his strong arms.

"Oh shoot, it's a junior," one of Tyler's friends said to the group, as he backed up quickly.

When they saw the muscular boy walking fast towards their leader, both of Tyler's friends immediately took off running in the opposite direction. But Tyler stood his ground and got into a fighting stance, ready to defend himself. When the older boy got close enough, he threw a hard punch. The older boy easily dodged Tyler's swing and quickly retaliated by kicking Tyler in the stomach. Tyler hunched forward in pain, and the boy grabbed Tyler's head, shoved it in between his legs, took ahold of Tyler's sides, and lifted him into the air. Then the muscular boy *power bombed* Tyler, like a professional wrestler, throwing him into the nearby bushes.

Tyler rolled out of the bushes and laid on the ground, stunned and confused.

Satisfied with his victory, the boy smiled and headed over to Steve. "You alright?" he asked as he helped Steve up. Then he grabbed Steve's face, trying to assess the damage.

Wincing in pain, Steve said sarcastically, "I had him right where I wanted him."

The boy responded with a smile, "Yeah, but this was a tag team match, buddy."

"I owe you one, Dylan," Steve said as the two boys did the Wendal handshake.

Ryan and Austin had arrived back at the school entrance just in time to witness Dylan's heroics, and they quickly hopped off their bikes and ran to their friends. "D-man for the win!" Ryan shouted enthusiastically as he gave Dylan the Wendal handshake.

"Thanks, D-man," Austin said, and he and Dylan did the handshake as well. "We really needed your backup there."

"No problem, little bro," Dylan replied, soaking in the praise. Then he grabbed Austin, put him in a headlock, and playfully rubbed the top of his head, messing up his hair.

Austin half-heartedly fought back against his brother's harmless assault, which just made Dylan assert himself even harder. With a two-year age difference, Austin was used to getting manhandled by his older, and much larger, brother. But considering what Dylan had just done for Steve, Austin was willing to let him have his fun. After finally letting his brother go, Dylan said to the group, "Throw your bikes in the back of the car, I'll give you guys a ride home."

As the boys loaded their bikes in the back of the SUV, Austin glanced back at the bushes and saw that Tyler was gone.

Chapter 4

"Turn the music up!" Steve shouted to Ryan, who was sitting in the front passenger seat of the SUV. Dylan drove while Austin and Steve sat in the back, singing along to the radio at the top of their lungs. The song on the radio was from Blink-182, a popular skate-punk band of the late nineties, and one of Austin and Steve's absolute most favorite bands. Ryan turned the small knob on the car stereo until the music was so loud that the vehicle's dashboard began to shake, and Dylan and Ryan joined in on the singing.

"I never wanted to hold you back... I just wanted to hold on... But my chance is gone..." Singing even louder, Austin and Steve played the air guitar while banging their heads back and forth. "I know... Just where... I stand... A boy... Trapped in the body of a man and..."

Driving fast through the downtown streets of Ocean View with their windows down, the boys' music filled the otherwise quiet late afternoon sky. They passed shops and restaurants of every kind while the sun setting over the ocean horizon, just a block to the west, made the sky a pretty shade of pink and yellow. Austin looked out his window and saw tired beachgoers heading back to their cars after a long day in the sun.

The song ended and Ryan turned the radio back down.

"I would kill to see Blink-182 at Warped Tour this year," Steve said emphatically, his eye still red and swollen from his earlier tussle. "This year's lineup is going to be ridonculous."

"I could get a ticket with my leftover birthday money," Austin replied excitedly.

"I'll be getting money from my Dad when report cards

come out," Ryan joined in.

Steve looked disappointed. "I'd have to mow lawns or something, to afford a ticket," he replied. "Things are a little crazy at home right now."

Steve's home life had always been a little hectic, but it was becoming more and more volatile with each passing year. His parents had separated when he was young, and his dad had moved out of state and hardly ever came to visit, leaving Steve feeling abandoned and more than a little resentful. His mom meant well, and Steve knew that, but in his eyes she was so busy working long hours and dealing with her own personal issues, that she didn't have the time to be the kind of mother that he wanted her to be.

"Wasn't your mom getting a new job at the bank?" Ryan asked.

"She had an interview, but she's still at that dump of a diner for now," Steve said. "She's so unpredictable. It feels like we're always one bad decision away from having to pack our bags and leave town again."

Hearing Steve say this sent an unpleasant jolt up Austin's spine. Steve had only moved to Ocean View a few years earlier but had already become the best friend that Austin had ever had. In his mind, Steve was the heart and soul of the Wendals, and he didn't want to hear any talk of him moving away. Austin opened his mouth to respond but was cut off by his brother.

"Hold on, guys," Dylan exclaimed. "They're talking about Austin's man-crush on the news." He turned the radio up, and the boys quieted down.

The eloquent voice of a radio news anchor came through the speaker: "Bart the Burglar has struck again this afternoon at a bank in Corona, California. This is the latest in a string of robberies by the Southern Californian masked outlaw. More of this story at the end of the hour."

Dylan turned the radio back down.

"Remind me why you're so obsessed with this guy again?" Ryan asked.

29

"I'm not *obsessed* with him," Austin responded defensively.

Steve chimed in. "He thinks he saw the guy hiding out by the old bike jumps last week."

Dylan laughed as he drove. "I'm so sure, man. Just like all the other fantastical stories you've told us over the years," he said, rolling his eyes. Then he looked at Ryan with a sly smile, and he continued, "He's got a whole secret detective file on the burglar at home. I found it in his underwear drawer, behind his tighty whities."

Ryan laughed hard.

Irritated, Austin sat up in his seat. "First off, he's a robber, not a burglar," he exclaimed. "A burglar is someone who breaks into your house without you knowing." Dylan wasn't appreciating his brother's condescending tone. "At a bank, it's considered robbery because the money is taken by force or threat of force," Austin said, shaking his head. "Why can no one else get that straight?"

Dylan stared at his brother blankly as Austin continued. "Secondly, I thought I told you to stay out of my room," Austin said angrily. "You're so dang nosy."

"I'm nosy?" Dylan asked in complete shock. "I'm not the one who carries around binoculars everywhere I go. Seriously, who does that? You're always in everyone else's business. You assume everyone around you is up to no good."

"Leave him alone," Steve stepped in. "So what if he likes to investigate stuff? Maybe he'll be a cop some day, like your old man."

Austin smiled. One of his favorite things about Steve was that he always had his back when he needed it. However, Austin was too embarrassed to admit to the other boys, including Steve, just how much he had been out to the old RV since his first trip down the cliffs in an effort to figure out what was really going on out there. Although he still hadn't found any other hard evidence to prove what he believed, Austin had seen the man who was living in the RV, and his suspicions of foul play were only growing.

The first morning that Austin had returned to the spot, he waited until about 7:35 a.m., when a disheveled looking man with shaggy brown hair and an unkempt beard finally exited the RV. No older than forty, the man wore a dark blue baseball cap and a t-shirt and jeans that were dirty and tattered. Something about the man's appearance screamed trouble to Austin. The man grabbed a large empty-looking duffel bag out of the trailer, along with a dirty shovel, threw them both into the Ford Escort, and hopped into the car and drove up the hill.

Returning to the spot as much as he could over the next couple of weeks, Austin witnessed almost the exact same thing, at about the exact same time, every morning he was there. The only variation being that the man sometimes had the duffel bag and shovel with him, and sometimes he didn't.

Austin had gone to the spot several times in the evening as well, witnessing a similar occurrence. Each night he was there, at around 8:00 p.m., the Ford Escort would return down the hill to the campsite, and the same unkempt man would get out of the car and head to the RV—sometimes with the duffel bag and shovel in hand, and sometimes without. It all just seemed a little too fishy to Austin.

One night, he saw something extra strange happen. After the disheveled man had arrived back at the RV, the man went straight into the trunk of the car and pulled out a black garbage bag. Through the binoculars, Austin thought he saw something moving wildly inside of the bag, and though the sound of the wind passing through the brush made it extra hard to hear that night, he could have sworn he heard the hissing sound of an angry cat coming from the campsite below. He had no idea what to think of that.

"If you really think you found this guy, why haven't you told your dad?" Ryan asked, sounding confused. "He could go down there with a squad of cops and arrest the guy."

Austin sunk back down into his seat, and replied sheepishly, "Well I'm not one hundred percent sure it's him yet. I've still got some more digging to do."

Dylan turned to Ryan with a smirk. "The truth is, he knows that if my parents find out he's been ditching class in the morning to chase a burglar, he'd be grounded for life."

"Ah, now it all makes sense," Ryan laughed.

"How about you just leave the poor hermit alone," Dylan berated. "I'm sure he's not a criminal, and frankly, whatever reason he has for being out there is none of your business."

Austin shrugged his shoulders as he responded, "I just like to know what's going on in my town. Where's the harm in that?" Dylan had no rebuttal. "Did you know that he's already stolen two million dollars in cash?" Austin asked, trying to hide his enthusiasm.

"Say what?" Dylan said, suddenly very interested. He was in awe as he thought more about it. "Imagine what you could do with that kind of money."

Ryan suddenly got excited. "Girls would *have* to take me seriously if I had that much cheddar," he said with a large grin across his face.

Steve's eyes went wide. "I would never go to school again, that's for sure."

"Mrs. Barr would be okay with that," Austin joked. Ryan started laughing so hard that he couldn't speak, so he nodded his head in agreement, while Steve smiled mischievously.

Dylan was confused. "What did you do to my favorite English teacher?"

"Ah, she hates me for no good reason," Steve said, clearly leaving something out.

Ryan fought back his laughter as he tried to recap what Steve had done. "He used a sharpie...to draw a female body...on her favorite stuffed pig," he said, barely getting it out.

Dylan now burst into laughter. "No, you didn't! She loves her stuffed animal piggies. They're like her classroom mascots," he said, laughing so hard that he momentarily stopped paying attention to the road. The car swerved to the left, and he quickly readjusted the steering wheel and focused back on his driving.

Austin grabbed onto the seat in front of him, steadying himself from his brother's complacence. "She almost got him expelled," he said with a chuckle.

Steve shook his head, and said gravely, "She still won't even look at me during class." Steve was quickly becoming known as quite the nuisance to the teachers at their school, although his antics were typically never anything too severe—nothing more than childish fun.

Ryan became serious. "She's a really tough teacher though. I had a hard time on her last exam. I hope I did alright," he said.

"You better be careful, Ryan. Last time you got a B on a test, I thought I'd never see you again," Austin joked.

Ryan nodded, and almost looked scared. "Yeah, my parents grounded me for a month. I was afraid they were going to disown me for a while there," he said, with a voice completely free of sarcasm. Coming from a very strict and highly accomplished household—his Dad was a successful businessman and member of the city council, his Mom ran a local nonprofit organization, and his brother was studying engineering at MIT— he wasn't given much leeway for messing around.

"Oh come on, man, you'll get an A in her class regardless, and you know it. You're like *Good Will Hunting*," Steve responded, slightly annoyed. "Meanwhile, I'm doomed to fail."

Dylan tried to be encouraging. "You just gotta start applying yourself, buddy."

Austin rolled his eyes. "Says the guy whose only A comes from fifth-period weightlifting," he said snarkily. Steve and Ryan burst into laughter again, and Dylan let go of the steering wheel with his right arm and flexed it proudly for the boys to see. Then he kissed his bulging bicep muscle with a smile, and the boys laughed even harder.

"On that note, I'm starving," Dylan said, and without any warning he took a sharp right turn, forcing the other boys to brace themselves. The car burst into a busy parking lot with several restaurants and small stores and then headed towards the drive-thru lane of a Burger King.

A thought came to Steve's mind as he saw the lit-up sign in front of the fast-food restaurant, and he grabbed Dylan's shoulder. "Stop the car!" he shouted, and Dylan slammed on the brakes, stopping abruptly in the middle of the parking lot. "Tyler's flunky friend works at this Burger King," Steve said with a sinister grin.

Ryan became worried, and quickly cried out, "Shouldn't we go somewhere else, then?"

"Nah, I've got a better idea," Steve replied. Then, poking his head up next to Dylan's, he asked, "How full is your window wash fluid?"

Dylan suddenly realized that Steve was up to no good, and he begged, "Oh come on, man, I really just want to eat a good burger in peace right now."

Thinking he knew exactly what Steve had in mind, Austin became excited and he stepped in to help his friend out. "Relax, bro, In-N-Out is just down the street," he said enthusiastically. "We'll get you a four by four after we do this."

The promise of an In-N-Out burger satisfied Dylan, and he put the car in park. Steve quickly hopped outside and carefully adjusted the little black windshield washer spray nozzles on the hood of Dylan's car. Since Steve had shown him this trick before, Austin knew that if you turned the washer nozzles sideways, instead of spraying the windshield, you could shoot the washer fluid to the side of the car like a super soaker squirt gun, blasting unsuspecting victims as you passed by them. Ryan was now giddy as Steve crawled back inside of the car.

"Did you angle them right?" Austin asked.

"Don't worry, it'll be perfect," Steve replied confidently.

With the windows down, the white SUV slowly rolled up to the Burger King drive-thru speaker, and Ryan, Steve, and Austin all fought to hold in their laughter. Dylan kept his composure and signaled for the other boys to calm down as a voice came through the speaker.

"Welcome to Burger King. What can I get for you today?" said a slightly muffled, and extremely lackadaisical teenage voice.

"That's definitely him," Ryan whispered to the others, laughing quietly. Then he leaned over Dylan and yelled towards the speaker, trying to keep a straight face, "Can I get a Big Mac, please?" Austin had to put his hand over his mouth to keep from laughing.

The voice from the speaker responded, already annoyed, "This is Burger King. We don't have Big Macs here."

Steve leaned forward into the front of the car. "Can we get a stuffed crust pizza, then?" he asked casually, pretending like he didn't see what the problem was.

"*Wrong restaurant, guys.*" The voice was sounding more upset. "There's a pizza place down the street."

"Okay, okay," Austin jumped in. "What about four double-decker tacos, then?" he asked through the back window, and unable to control himself any longer, he burst into laughter.

The voice that responded now sounded extremely angry, "Very funny, you little turds. If you're not going to order something off of our menu then please quit wasting my time."

Austin, Ryan, and Steve nearly fell out of their seats with laughter, but Dylan tried hard to show some restraint. Since he was the only one able to speak, he replied, "I'm sorry about my friends, we'll just pass through the line and go somewhere else."

Dylan put the car back into drive and headed down a narrow partitioned lane, stopping at the drive-thru window. Inside the window, the boys could see Tyler's bully friend, dressed in fast-food employee attire, and busily punching numbers into a small computer as he spoke into his large black headset. After a few moments, Tyler's friend realized that the boys were parked outside his window. At first he was surprised to see the Wendals there, and then he quickly became angry.

Visibly flustered, Tyler's friend opened the window and leaned outside. "What are you dweebs doing here? Didn't you learn your lesson when you messed with us at school?" he asked viciously. Then he looked over his shoulder, and, seeing his manager helping a customer not far behind him, he quieted down as he continued, "I'm busy right now. You can't come into my place of business acting like a bunch of..."

But before the boy could finish his sentence, Steve quickly leaned forward into the front of the SUV and pressed a button next to the steering wheel, which unleashed the car's window washer fluid. A sharp stream of liquid blasted out from the black nozzles on the hood of the car and hit Tyler's friend straight in the face, while Steve continued to relentlessly hold the button down. Frantically trying to protect himself, the boy threw his hands in front of his face, causing the water to bounce off of his arms, and to splash all over everything inside the small window. Soaking wet, the bully finally reeled backward and closed the window as he wailed in agony.

The Wendals were completely hysterical. Steve finally let go of the spray button and jumped back into the back of the car. Then Dylan slammed his foot down onto the gas pedal and shot through the rest of the drive-thru line and away from the restaurant.

Parked in a busy In-N-Out parking lot, the boys sat quietly in Dylan's SUV, stuffing their faces full of burgers and french fries. While Steve, Austin, and Ryan chomped down on Double Double burgers, Dylan shoved a huge Four by Four into his mouth, which was four beef patties, topped with four slices of cheese. It was the perfect meal for a boy like Dylan, whose diet consisted of protein, protein, and more protein. Dylan finished his burger and tossed the wadded up wrapper at Austin in the back seat of the car. While the other boys continued to eat, he put the car back into drive and headed out of the parking lot.

Austin spoke from the back seat with a mouth full of fries. "Our parents are gonna be out late tomorrow night, so let's all hang out."

Steve sipped on his soda. "I told Josie I'd take her to see the new Austin Powers movie tomorrow," he said hesitantly, knowing how much Austin hated when girls, or anyone else, took time away from the Wendals. "You guys can tag along if you want."

Ryan got excited. "You're going out with Josie, the sophomore?" he asked. "How do you do it, man? You gotta teach me your moves." Ryan wrapped his arms around an imaginary body in front of him and started kissing the air.

"Well, the first thing you'd need to do, Ry, if you really want to get a girl...is to get that belly button of yours checked out," Steve replied. "The smell of that thing is heinous." Dylan and Austin burst into laughter. It was a regular joke with the Wendals that Ryan's belly button had a stench that was similar to that of toe jam, and no one could figure out why.

While the other boys laughed, Ryan lifted up his t-shirt slightly, swabbed the inside of his belly button with his index finger, and then shoved his hand right under Dylan's nose. Dylan jerked his head back and slapped Ryan's hand away—but it was too late. Covering his mouth with his hand, Dylan started to gag. "I'm gonna barf!" he shouted.

Now Ryan laughed mischievously. "I don't know what else to do about it," he said. "I've been sticking deodorant in it every day, like Steve recommended."

With a look of disgust on his face, Austin steered the conversation back to the subject of Steve's date. "Sounds like you and Josie are getting pretty serious."

Steve could sense Austin's disapproval. "Not at all," he brushed it off. "Although, I think she wants me to ask her to Homecoming," Steve said, shaking his head. He wasn't sure if he was ready for that kind of commitment with Josie.

It was pretty clear that Austin was annoyed. "Either way, we need a Wendals night tomorrow. No girls. Can you just cancel with her?" he asked.

Knowing that it was more of an expectation than a request from Austin, Steve was unsure of what he should do. "She'll kill me if I ditch her again," he said.

"Well, we better make it worth it then," Austin exclaimed, smiling.

"Yeah, man, come on. I'm sure you'll have another girl-friend by the weekend," Dylan joined in. "We could go play some b-ball at the sports park tomorrow night."

"Nah," Ryan said disapprovingly. "No one ever passes me the ball there. Let's go to the movies instead. We could see *The Phantom Menace* again?"

"Dude, you made us watch that twice already," Dylan said with irritation.

"Yeah, because it's one of the best movies of all time," Ryan smiled.

Austin looked at Steve, pleadingly. "What about pizza and a Laker game?"

"Lakers suck," Steve shot back. Dylan turned around and reached back in the car, playfully trying to smack Steve in the face for what he had said, but Steve dodged his punches. "Alright, alright," Steve said laughing. "If I'm ditching Josie again tomorrow night then we better have some real fun. And since I know that you nerds can never think of anything cool, I'll make the plans."

A huge smile came over Austin's face. "I knew you'd come through," he cheered. "What do you have in mind?"

"You'll see tomorrow. Just bring the balloon launcher," Steve responded.

Austin and Ryan looked at each other excitedly, for, in their minds, no one came up with plans that were as fun or exciting as Steve's.

The white SUV pulled into the driveway of a small, one-story tract home—Steve's house. It was dark and quiet in the suburban neighborhood, where cookie-cutter style homes were stacked side-by-side in all directions, as far as the eye could see. Even in the dark, it was obvious that Steve's house wasn't as well cared for as the other homes. The grass looked like it hadn't been cut in quite some time, the driveway was covered in dead leaves, and the outside walls were in desperate need of a coat of paint.

"Thanks for the ride, D-man," Steve said as he grabbed his belongings and got out of the car. Austin hopped out right behind him and headed to the back of the SUV, where he unloaded Steve's bike and rolled it alongside him, following Steve up to the house. The boys stopped at the doorstep, and Austin leaned the bike against the wall.

"How's your eye?" Austin asked. "Your face might look bad in the morning."

"It'll still look better than yours," Steve jested with a smirk. He gently touched below his eye. "I'm sure it'll be alright. I've been hit harder."

"Well, good. Because I'm sure Josie would be ticked if you were all swollen and bruised for the big homecoming dance," Austin said, mockingly.

"Shut up," Steve laughed.

"Hey, seriously though," Austin said with a change of tone. "What were you thinking earlier, taking on Tyler and his goons by yourself?"

Steve rolled his eyes. "Come on, relax, man," he said, brushing it off. "I'm fine."

"You could have gotten yourself killed," Austin said emphatically. He realized he was probably being overdramatic, but didn't care.

Steve paused for a moment, and his demeanor changed completely. "Yeah, well it's not like I've got a lot to lose anyway," he said, his tough exterior seeming to melt away, and a deep insecurity surfacing.

Austin was shocked at the vulnerability he was seeing from the boy he thought to be invincible. "What are you talking about? You've got the Wendals!"

Steve bit his bottom lip. "You guys were fine before I moved into town, and you'll be just fine after I'm gone," he said in frustration.

"No way, you completed the group," Austin responded, not knowing what else to say. It was obvious that his friend was seriously struggling, but the whole situation was foreign to him, and he felt completely caught off guard and unprepared. "And what do you mean, 'when you're gone?' Why are you talking like that?" Austin was getting upset now.

"It's just that…" Steve also struggled to get out what he wanted to say, never having talked about this stuff with anyone before. "I don't know. You know my Mom. I know she's doing her best, but I just have a feeling like things are getting bad again, and that she's not telling me everything…Maybe I'm just being ridiculous."

"You're not being ridiculous at all." Austin's frustration fizzled out and he was left feeling sorry for his friend. "Things will work out. They have to," he said. Austin paused and then smiled. "Life is perfect right now, just the way it is," he said light-heartedly. "We can't let anyone mess it up."

Steve cracked a smile. "Alright, alright. Whatever you say." The somber mood started to ease, and the boys simultaneously reached out to give each other the Wendal handshake.

A car horn honked loudly from the driveway—Dylan was getting impatient.

"Hey, can you pick me up for school in the morning?" Steve asked quickly. "My mom's gotta work early."

"Yeah, of course," Austin said enthusiastically. "I guess I'll see you bright and early then." He smiled, and then turned and started jogging back down the walkway. But before he got far, he stopped and turned back to Steve. "Don't worry about it," he said confidently. "You're my best friend. I won't let anything happen to you."

Nodding his head, Steve smiled. "Thanks, man. See you tomorrow."

Chapter 5

Austin stared out the passenger side window of the Dodge Durango, watching the sun in the cloudless sky as it rose up over the hills to the east. "Semi-Charmed Life," by Third Eye Blind played on the radio, and Dylan sang along quietly as he drove. Although everything appeared to be right in Austin's world, he had spent most of the night with a pit in his stomach, worrying about his best friend. He had never seen Steve act the way he had acted the night before, and it had left him with an unsettling impression that made it hard for him to fall asleep. But, feeling much better this morning, he was looking forward to another day with the Wendals.

"So, what do you think Steve has planned for us tonight?" Dylan asked as the song on the radio ended.

Austin hadn't mentioned his conversation with Steve to his brother. "I don't know, but I'm sure it will be awesome," he replied.

"Of course you would say that. Steve can do no wrong in your eyes," Dylan said laughing. "You're so infatuated with him."

"Wow, that's a big word for you, bro. Congratulations," Austin replied sarcastically.

"It's okay, man, don't hide it. You feel about Steve the same way that I feel about Sable," Dylan smiled big. Sable was a WWF professional wrestler Diva that Dylan had a huge crush on. He also had a large poster of her on the wall above his bed. "You probably think about spooning Steve at night, the same way I imagine cuddling up with Sable?" Dylan mocked.

Austin cringed at the thought of his brother cuddling anyone. "Shut up, man, don't be ridiculous. You're just jealous of our friendship," he said snobbishly.

Arriving at Steve's house, Dylan parked the car in the driveway next to an old white Dodge Neon. Austin hopped out of the car first and headed up to the front door quickly. He was just about to ring the doorbell when he noticed a white sheet of paper, that looked like some kind of legal document, taped to the middle of Steve's front door. The paper was folded on the door in such a way that Austin couldn't read what it said, but something about the sight of it immediately brought back his uncomfortable feeling. He stared at the paper for a moment, and then, unable to help himself, he pulled it off the door, unfolded it, and began to read.

Dylan came walking up behind his brother. "What's that?" he asked. "You being nosy again?" Shaking his head and not waiting for an answer, he rang the doorbell.

Austin ignored his brother and read the paper quietly to himself:

"This is an official 30-day notice to the homeowner, to either pay the current balance of late mortgage payments, or else the home will be foreclosed on, and Bank of Southern California will take possession of the property."

Austin didn't need to read any further. A million thoughts began to swirl around in his mind, and he felt panicked—not yet fully understanding what the letter meant, but assuming the worst. *Could this really be happening now?* he wondered. Even with what Steve had told him the night before, he never imagined anything like this could happen so soon. If this really was what he thought it was, it was literally his worst nightmare.

The front door opened and Steve stood in the doorway wearing nothing but his boxer shorts. His hair was a mess and he shielded his eyes from the sunlight that flooded into the house, making it obvious that he had just woken up.

Dylan let out a sigh of disbelief. "Dude, you were supposed to be ready by the time we got here. Now we're going to be late for school," he cried, as he hastily pushed Steve backward into the house. "Go get ready!"

Rubbing his eyes, Steve said groggily, "Okay, okay. Calm down," and he turned and headed back into his bedroom.

Dylan walked through the door, headed straight into Steve's kitchen, and started to raid the fridge. After pulling out a carton of milk and a box of *Peanut Butter Crunch* cereal, he poured himself a bowl.

Austin read the eviction notice a second time as he stepped into the entryway of the house.

Steve's hair was still a mess when he returned from his bedroom, but he was now dressed in a yellow Volcom t-shirt and baggy jeans. He grabbed a silver Pop-Tart bag out of his pantry and his backpack from off the couch and then headed towards Austin. As he got close, he could see the look of concern on his friend's face. "What's wrong?" he asked casually.

Instead of responding, Austin silently handed Steve the paper. Steve gave Austin a funny look, and then grabbed the sheet and started to read. He didn't get very far before his casual demeanor quickly changed to one of frustration.

Before Austin could say anything, Steve's mom, Linda, entered the room in a hurry. Linda was tall, blonde, and young for having a son Steve's age. She wore a blue waitress uniform, had her hair up in a tight bun, and looked tired and slightly stressed out.

"Oh, hey boys," Linda said. "Thanks again for taking Steve to school today. I'm late for work already." She headed to the kitchen and grabbed her purse from off the counter, and after opening the bag, she started fishing through it frantically.

"Mom," Steve said, trying to hold back his irritation.

"Yes?" she replied softly, her head still in the purse. Whatever she was searching for inside her bag seemed to be eluding her.

Steve waited a moment to see if his mom would look up from her bag, but then finally lost his patience. "Mom!" he shouted forcefully.

Linda finally looked up. "What, sweetie?" she asked, surprised by her son's tone. Dylan took a large bite of his cereal in the kitchen, and casually watched the interaction, ignorant as to what was going on.

Anticipating an unpleasant confrontation, Austin stayed silent and listened.

Steve held up the sheet of paper. "What is this about?" he asked accusingly. Linda squinted her eyes at the sheet, and then walked over to Steve and snatched the paper from out of his hands. As she read through it, her smile began to fade away.

"You said you were taking care of this," Steve said as his anger was building.

Linda was quiet as she finished reading, and then quickly folded the paper and shoved it into a pocket on the front of her uniform. "I know, I know," she said quickly and dismissively. "They called me again last night. They won't leave me alone." She sounded as if she was trying to play it off. But as she looked at Steve and saw the frustration on her son's face, she quickly realized that she wasn't going to get off that easy. "I was going to talk to you about it tonight," she said.

Steve took a couple of steps towards his mom, confused and bothered. "You said the extra shifts at work would be enough to cover the mortgage payment."

"Well, I thought they would be. But with so many bills, I've had to choose between paying on the house and putting food on the table," Linda said, looking more and more distressed.

Steve tried to calm his tone down. "How much do we owe?" he asked.

"Don't worry about that; I'm handling it," Linda responded quickly.

Steve's frustration came right back. "They're going to take the house from us, Mom. How much do we owe?"

Walking over to the couch and sitting down, Linda put her head into her hands, clearly trying to fight back tears.

Dylan felt uncomfortable listening in on the extremely personal conversation, but not knowing what to do, he stayed in the kitchen and awkwardly ate his cereal, as if nothing unusual was happening. Austin, on the other hand, watched the interaction intently and unabashedly.

Speaking through her tears, Linda said, "About twenty-five thousand between late payments and back taxes," as her crying intensified. "Then we're behind on the car payment, credit cards, the utilities...I don't know how it all got so bad again." She now cried hysterically.

Steve was in shock, but he managed to take a deep breath, and he walked over to the couch and sat down next to his mom. Still very frustrated, he put his arm around Linda, trying his best to push away his anger and to comfort her. "It's okay, Mom. We'll figure it out. We always do," he said, sounding as sure as he could.

Linda slowed her crying and sat up. "I called your dad last night," she confessed.

Dylan almost dropped his cereal bowl when he heard what Linda had said, and Austin listened with even more intensity, both boys worrying about what would come next.

Steve looked at his mom incredulously. "What for?" he asked softly.

The makeup around Linda's eyes was blurred from her tears, but she stopped crying for the moment. "You're going to go live with him in Utah for a while," she responded.

"What?" Steve couldn't believe what he had just heard his mom say, and he lost it. "You can't do that. There's no way I'm gonna live with that jerk!"

"The decision is final," Linda responded, almost coldly. "I obviously can't take care of you right now. Your Dad is coming down Sunday afternoon to pick you up."

Steve's face turned a deep shade of red as he sat next to his mom, contemplating this new revelation. After a few moments of silent anger, he finally stood up, grabbed his backpack from off the floor, and stormed out of the house—passing right by Austin without saying a word. Linda put her face back into her hands and began to cry again.

Dylan hesitantly took one last bite of cereal, put the bowl in the sink, and then swiftly headed for the front door. He looked at Austin as he passed him by, and shrugged his shoulders. Staying in the house for a moment, Austin tried to come to grips with what had just happened. He watched Linda, crying on the couch all alone, and he wondered if he should try to console her. Instead, he turned and slowly headed outside to the car.

The song "Creep," by Radiohead played from the car stereo while the boys headed to school. Not saying a word, Dylan planted his eyes firmly on the road ahead of him as he drove. Steve sat in the back seat in silence, spiking his hair with green gel from a small tub that he kept in his backpack, for just such occasions.

Austin sat in the passenger seat, wrestling with thoughts of their now uncertain future. *What would happen to his friend?* he wondered. *What would happen to the Wendals?* He thought about how much his life had changed in the years since Steve had moved into town, and he thought about how much Steve had brought the boys together in a way that no one else could have.

He wasn't going to let this happen. He had to do something, and he had to do it fast. Austin stared out the car window, racking his brain to come up with a solution.

Chapter 6

Sitting in the school library, Austin worked at his computer while his teacher lectured the class on a research project that was coming due in a couple of weeks. Each student was stationed in front of their own personal library computer, which consisted of a large, white, cube-shaped analog screen monitor, a huge brick-shaped computer tower, and a wired keyboard and mouse. Some of the students listened intently to the teacher, while others browsed the internet, researching their chosen topic.

Austin, however, was searching for news and updates on the recent activity of Bart the Burglar, now that his interest in the local robber had grown immensely. This was not just because of his love for local crime investigation or because his suspicions had grown every time he had returned to watch the hermit at the RV. But he now had a new motivation to figure out what was really going on at that campsite, and it involved keeping the Wendals together.

Thinking more and more about his stakeouts at the RV, Austin's brain was busy trying to put all of the pieces together. He hadn't found any new evidence that would link the hermit at the RV to the local robberies, but he had seen the dubious hundred dollar bill that had appeared to be fresh out of a bank vault, and he knew that the man at the RV drove the same type of car that Bart the Burglar had been seen driving. Was this enough evidence for his case?

The only other bit of intel that Austin had gathered from his trips to the RV was the hermit's daily schedule. Based on what he had seen, the hermit left the RV at the same time every morning and returned to camp at the same time late every night. He wasn't sure yet why this was important, or how it could help him, but he had a hunch that it would turn out to be useful. Even with his limited information, Austin was starting to formulate a plan as to how it could all benefit the Wendals.

His internet search in the library that morning had also yielded some very valuable information. Austin learned that the criminal had robbed another bank that very morning—which made six in total—and that once again the robber had worn the same Bart Simpson rubber mask that he had worn at every robbery he had committed. The mask was obviously the reason why local authorities were referring to him as "Bart the Burglar," and even though the term *burglar* was being misused, Austin realized that the nickname had a much better ring to it than "Bart the Robber" did.

During his library search, Austin had also read that every bank that had been robbed thus far was a different branch of the local bank chain Bank of Southern California. And while he didn't know why the robber was favoring that particular bank chain, he had figured out by his own calculations that every branch that had been robbed was located within an hour's drive of the old RV campsite. There were just too many connections for him to believe that it was all a coincidence.

Browsing through a local news website, Austin used the bulky library mouse to click on a link that pulled up a digital wanted poster of the criminal. The poster featured a large photo of the thief in action, which was taken from a bank security camera. The black-and-white picture was a grainy shot of the masked robber fleeing the inside of the bank and carrying two filled duffel bags. Below the photo was a caption asking for the public's help in bringing forward any information about the robberies. Austin clicked on the menu bar at the top of the computer screen, scrolled down to the bottom, and selected *Print*.

Finally looking up from his computer, Austin saw that his teacher was no longer lecturing the class but was sitting at a desk in front of the computer stations, sorting through papers.

Without the teacher's close attention, most of the students were now using their computers to goof around on Yahoo or to play Minesweeper.

Austin glanced down the aisle of computers to his right, and to his surprise, he saw Tyler snarling at him from the end of the row. Without taking his gaze off of Austin, the bully clutched a pencil with his right fist and then snapped it in half with his thumb. Austin cringed slightly but then smiled back at Tyler and gave him a thumbs-up, knowing that Tyler couldn't do anything to him in the safety of the school library.

Austin got up from his computer and casually walked over to the printing station, which happened to be right next to where his teacher was sitting. He grabbed the wanted poster sheet from the printer and turned to head back to his seat.

"Mr. Kenney," the teacher said enthusiastically, stopping Austin in his tracks. "It's good to see that someone is taking this assignment seriously. Are you printing up information to re-view at home?"

Knowing he couldn't admit to what he was doing, Austin spoke with a phony smile, "Well, yeah, I just want to make sure I spend as much time on this as possible."

"Well done," the teacher said. "I'm sure you must have chosen a topic you feel strongly about, then?"

Austin took a step backward. "You're exactly right," he said as he folded the paper in half so that the printed side was not visible. "I'm very passionate about what I have right here."

An even bigger smile came over the teacher's face. "Well, why don't you let me see what you've got then? Maybe I can give you some advice on the topic."

Austin laughed nervously, worried not only because he didn't want the teacher to know that he wasn't working on the research assignment, but also because he didn't want anyone else to know about his interest in Bart the Burglar. He clenched the paper in his hand, and his palms started to sweat.

Clang! The bell rang, signaling the end of the class period. Austin had literally been saved by the bell, and he let out a sigh of relief. "Oh well, I guess you'll just have to wait and see when I turn the project in," he said, pretending to be disappointed.

His teacher gave him a suspicious look but didn't press the issue. Austin smiled and quickly headed back towards his seat to grab his belongings and head to lunch.

Sitting at a table in a busy outdoor area of campus, Austin and Ryan ate their lunches in silence. Close by, a group of boys wearing matching black and red varsity football jerseys tossed a ball back and forth to each other, and a half dozen girls stood in a circle by the water fountain, laughing loudly as they gossiped.

Meanwhile, Austin sat somberly, nibbling on a slice of cold cafeteria pizza. Ryan hadn't touched his healthy home-packed meal—a turkey sandwich, carrot sticks, and milk. Instead of eating, Ryan was watching Steve in the distance. Steve was at the other end of the lunch area, flirting with a tall blonde girl and a short brunette girl, who were each wearing matching red and black cheerleader outfits and giggling excitedly after everything that Steve said.

"It's not fair," Ryan complained. "If Steve moves, it kills all my chances of hanging out with hot girls."

Austin pushed his lunch to the side, slightly annoyed. "Is that all you can think about?"

Ryan immediately felt ashamed. "No, of course not," he responded. Continuing to watch Steve, he started thinking hard, and then looked at Austin inquisitively. "You ever wonder why he even decided to be friends with us in the first place?" he asked. "I mean, he could hang out with anyone in this school. Everyone loves him."

Looking over at Steve, Austin nodded his head in agreement. He knew that the only guys at school who didn't want to be friends with Steve were the ones who were jealous of the fact that he got all of the girls.

"You really think he's going to Utah?" Ryan asked.

Austin thought for a minute, not yet sure how much he was ready to divulge about his plan. "He has to go to Utah," he said. "Unless we make a big move."

Ryan's eyes got larger as he looked at Austin. "Oh no," he responded skeptically. "You're not scheming up another big Austin plan, are you?"

"What's that even supposed to mean?" asked Austin, acting like he didn't understand. Ryan stared at him impatiently, until Austin finally continued, "Okay, look. I've been thinking about this a lot. And I think I know what we can do to…"

Ryan cut his friend off. "This is way over our heads, man. Forget it already," he said intensely. Ryan had always been the most risk-averse of all the Wendals, and over the years he had been burned by more of Austin's schemes than he would have liked to admit.

Quickly becoming defensive again, Austin asked harshly, "Really? You wanna give up that easy?"

Ryan didn't want to lose his friend either, but he didn't think it was something they had any control over. "Well no, of course not, but…"

Cutting him off again, Austin said, "Let me ask you something, Wendal to Wendal." Ryan could see the intensity in Austin's eyes, so he stopped his arguing and listened. "How far would you go to save your friend?" Austin asked, his gaze fixed firmly on Ryan. "How far would you go to save the Wendals?"

Ryan didn't know how he could possibly give a good answer to that loaded question, but he felt unjustly challenged by it. "You know I would do anything for you guys, but…"

Austin wasn't having it. "But nothing. Unless you've got a better idea, then you should at least hear me out," he said. Ryan went quiet again and returned his focus back to his friend. Reaching into his backpack, Austin pulled out the sheet of paper he had printed in the library.

But Ryan's attention was quickly interrupted when he noticed someone approaching in the distance, and a boyish grin came over his face.

Turning around, Austin saw Josie walking straight towards their table. Josie was tall and blonde and had tan skin from a summer full of laying out on the beach with her friends. She wore a denim skirt, a white spaghetti strap tank top, and white and pink Etnies skate shoes. Austin and Ryan both thought she was one of the prettier girls in school.

Arriving at the table, Josie smiled at the boys and hugged her pink school binder close to her chest. "Hi, guys!" she said in a cheerful tone.

Ryan tried to respond, but his ears turned red and he looked down at his lap instead.

"Hey, Josie," Austin replied unenthusiastically, as he quickly folded up the wanted poster, and shoved it into his back pocket.

Josie noticed the awkwardness at the table but didn't call attention to it. She looked over in Steve's direction and a frown came over her face. "He's been talking to those girls all lunch," she said disappointedly. "Do you think he's into them?"

"I don't know," Austin said. "Have you been watching him all lunch?" He didn't intend to sound so disdainful in his response, but it came out that way regardless.

Josie looked surprised by the response, but then quickly reclaimed her cheerfulness. "So... has Steve asked anyone to homecoming yet?"

Austin realized that Josie didn't know about Steve's situation. "He hasn't asked you?" he responded, trying to hide the fact that he couldn't care less about the homecoming dance.

"Not yet," Josie pouted, looking down at the floor, as her confidence wavered. "I really thought he was going to ask me tonight at the movies, but he canceled our date." Then she quickly looked back up at Austin. "He's not going out with another girl tonight, is he?" she asked, unabashedly paranoid.

Suddenly, Ryan was able to speak. "He's hanging with the Wendals tonight," he blurted out loudly and anxiously.

Austin kicked his friend's foot hard underneath the table, and Ryan immediately became embarrassed and looked back down at his lap.

The fact that Steve had canceled their date for no good

reason made Josie upset, but she hated even more that she was constantly getting snubbed by their little boy's club, which was the disdainful term that she often used with her friends to describe the Wendals. "What is a Wendal anyway?" she asked condescendingly.

Ryan and Austin looked at each other, both at a loss for words.

Austin couldn't possibly describe to her what a Wendal was in just a few words, and he didn't really care to try. Not knowing quite how to explain it either, Ryan shrugged his shoulders, and said, as if it were obvious, "A Wendal's a Wendal."

Austin smiled and backed his friend up. "Yeah! We're Wendals," he said matter-of-factly.

Josie looked confused and bothered. "Okay, whatever you say." She tried her best to act friendly again. "Can you guys talk to him for me though? He's been ignoring me all day. I don't get it," she said.

"Well, he's had a lot going on today. Maybe he just doesn't want to talk to you," Austin replied insensitively. Josie suddenly looked very offended.

Clang! The bell rang loudly, signaling the end of lunch.

"Gee, thanks for the help," Josie said sarcastically, shaking her head in disbelief.

A sudden commotion filled the surrounding area as crowds of students were now starting to head back to their classrooms. Two other popular-looking girls that Austin had seen around campus approached the group and stopped next to Josie. One of the girls was tall with short dark hair, and the other was a skinny redhead girl. They looked Ryan and Austin up and down.

Standing up straight, Austin smiled at the girls. "Hey, ladies, how's it going?" he asked in his most suave voice. The girls smiled back at him. Then Austin looked at Ryan, who was now standing next to him, frozen stiff. With his mouth gaping open, he stared at the girls silently. Austin casually nudged his friend with his elbow, but Ryan didn't budge. One of the girls whispered something into the other girl's ear, and they both giggled. Then the taller girl grabbed Josie by the arm and tugged at her, slowly pulling her away from the two boys.

Josie gave them one last look of desperation. "Just tell Steve to call me after school. I really need to talk to him. He's supposed to be going to the lake with my family this weekend," she shouted, and then she and her friends disappeared into the crowd of students.

Ryan stood next to the lunch table with a huge smile on his face, slowly waving goodbye to the girls, who were already long gone. "You see," Ryan said to Austin disappointedly. "Those are just the kind of interactions I'm gonna miss out on when Steve's gone."

Austin looked at Ryan in disbelief. "You're going to miss out on having pretty girls standing in front of you, and not being able to say a word to them?" he asked.

"Well at least I was around them," Ryan replied, still smiling.

Putting his arm around Ryan, Austin said in all seriousness, "You choked, man. But it's alright, we're gonna work on that."

Ryan shook his head, snapping out of his trance. "I'm going to be late for science class!"

Hurrying, the boys began to gather their belongings back into their backpacks, when suddenly they were startled by a loud *whack* on the table next to them. Both boys jumped in surprised alarm and dropped everything they were holding. Leftover food items and sheets of paper from their binders dropped onto the table and scattered everywhere.

The boys looked up to see Tyler standing in front of them with his two goon friends, laughing hysterically. They realized that Tyler had snuck up behind them, and slammed his three-ring binder on the top of the table next to them, intentionally trying to scare them. The bullies found the outcome of their little prank to be extremely comical.

"Hey, guys," Tyler shouted enthusiastically. "How are my

favorite losers doing?" The look in Tyler's eyes made Ryan's heart begin to beat quickly.

Austin finished gathering his belongings from off the table and casually threw his backpack over his shoulder. "We're great," he exclaimed sarcastically, and then he looked at Tyler's friend. "How'd the rest of your shift go last night?" he asked with a devious grin. The goon quickly and angrily stepped toward Austin, but Tyler immediately held his friend back. Then Austin looked back at Tyler and started to laugh. "And how's your back after meeting my brother yesterday?"

His face turning red with anger, Tyler let go of his friend and got right into Austin's face. "Careful. Your Wendal dweeb protectors aren't here to take the punch for you right now," he said snarling. Tyler's friends became excited as they looked forward to the potential confrontation.

Austin looked Tyler in the eyes, unflinchingly. "We can handle ourselves just fine," he said confidently.

When Tyler realized that Austin wasn't backing down, he took a step back. The red in his face faded and he began to laugh. "You're actually in luck today," he said, in a less aggressive tone. "Mr. Johnson just told me that if I get in one more fight at school this year, I'll be expelled." He seemed to be proud of the fact. "So I guess you guys are safe for now, as long as you stay on school property."

With more than a little sarcasm, Austin exclaimed, "Thank our lucky stars. I was really scared for a minute there."

"That doesn't mean you're completely off the hook," Tyler shot back. "There's plenty of other places outside of school where I can give you nerds the payback you deserve." The intensity in his voice was returning. "I mean, what's to stop me from following any of you home after school today?"

"Yeah, we know where you guys live," one of the bullies shouted from behind Tyler.

Ryan looked pale, but Austin kept his composure.

"I'm in a negotiating mood today though," Tyler said. He turned to Ryan and adopted a more passively aggressive manner, similar to a mob boss intimidating a local shop owner. "I just heard we have a big assignment due in chemistry this period, and I'm really close to failing."

Ryan could have guessed what was coming next.

"So, here's the deal. Give me your assignment and I'll forget about the cheap shot you guys pulled on me yesterday," Tyler said with a sinister smile.

Austin stepped closer to Ryan to show him that he had his back. "You don't have to do that," he responded quickly.

Ryan looked at Tyler, and then at Austin. Both boys stared back at him, and he felt a considerable amount of pressure as he weighed his options. On one hand, he knew he would disappoint the Wendals if he gave in to Tyler's bullying. On the other hand, he knew that if he didn't give in to Tyler's demands, he would be putting a bigger target on their backs. Having dealt with bullying for most of his youth, Ryan longed to conquer this facet of his life once and for all. But at the time being, all he could think about was his desire to make it to the end of the school day alive. "I'll give it to you... If you promise that you'll leave the Wendals alone," Ryan finally answered.

Austin immediately looked disappointed.

Tyler smiled. "I can promise to leave you and your precious Wendals alone for the rest of the week," he said as sincerely as he could, while his goon friends laughed like Hyenas next to him.

Positive that Tyler was full of it, Austin shook his head. He knew that the water balloon incident had really hurt Tyler's ego and that the bully wouldn't stop until he had his full revenge on the Wendals.

Ryan had doubts about Tyler's promise as well, but he figured he didn't have much of a choice at the moment. And a week of peace seemed worth taking the chance, especially since this was most likely the last week the Wendals had together anyway. He hesitated, but then slowly unzipped his backpack, pulled out a thick sheet of stapled together papers, and handed them over to Tyler.

With great satisfaction, Tyler took the papers. "You definitely are the smartest of the group," he said, laughing. His bully friends smiled fiendishly at their victory.

From seemingly out of nowhere, Steve arrived at the group and intentionally bumped hard into the back of Tyler as he made his way to join his friends. The science packet fell out of Tyler's hands and onto the ground, and a few of the pages broke from the binding and scattered about.

"Oops," Steve said, standing tall in between Ryan and Austin, ready for an altercation. "You guys back for round two?"

Tyler's face went red again, and he took in a deep breath, trying to play it cool. Without hesitation, his two goon friends jumped onto the ground and gathered the science project papers together. Steve and Austin laughed as they watched the boys pander to their bully boss. One of the bullies finally handed Tyler the messy packet of papers, and the two goons popped back up and rejoined their leader.

Raising his outstretched index finger to the Wendals, and restraining himself the best he could, Tyler said, "You get till the end of the week." Then all three bullies turned around and walked away together.

Steve looked at Ryan and Austin, confused. "What was that about?"

"It's a long story," Austin said, frustrated as he watched the bullies walk away. He was sick of Tyler and his friends getting the best of the Wendals, and he was tired of Ryan giving in to their demands.

"You didn't give them your homework, did you?" Steve asked Ryan.

There was no need for Ryan to respond because he gave away the answer with the look of shame on his face.

Showing more patience than Austin, Steve put his arm around Ryan. "Don't worry about it," he said. "I still have faith you're gonna stand up to those guys someday. And then you'll realize there was never really anything to be afraid of all along."

A sheepish grin came over Ryan's face. "Or, I can just keep

hiding behind you guys, can't I?" he asked, only half-joking.

Steve laughed. "We're not always gonna be there when you need us."

"Well, that really sucks," Ryan said glumly. He knew that Steve was right though, and he knew that if he didn't start standing up for himself soon, that he might end up going his whole life allowing people to walk all over him.

The three boys started towards the classroom halls together, and Ryan tried to lighten the mood. "Are we still on for tonight?" he asked.

"Absolutely," Steve replied, and then looked over to Austin.

"Yeah, for sure," Austin agreed but sounded slightly distracted—as if he was working something out in his head. "I'll be a little late though. I've got something I have to do first."

Ryan and Steve gave Austin a skeptical look.

"It's just some research for a project I'm working on," Austin replied. "But I wouldn't miss tonight for the world."

Chapter 7

It was a cold evening and Austin was starting to wish that he had worn a jacket as he rode his bike speedily up the Pacific Coast Highway. The visibility around him was getting worse by the minute, both because he was moving farther away from the lights of the city, and also because the sun was getting lower and was now almost completely lost behind the horizon. Turning a dark shade of blue, the ocean would soon look like a pitch-black chasm at the edge of the world. As Austin watched the water lose its color, his mind wandered, and he thought about how terrifying it would be to be stranded alone in the middle of the sea, in the dead of night. The horrifying thought made him pedal even faster.

He wanted to get to the trail before it got too dark outside, or else he knew it would be difficult for him to find the path's hidden entrance. Luckily, he had been out this way so much lately that he was becoming very familiar with the terrain, and he seemed to find the trail with more ease each time he came looking. The road was very calm that evening, with only an occasional car—and its headlights—interrupting the quiet, and the darkness, of his ride.

Seeing the familiar convenience store to his right, Austin knew he was getting close. He pedaled up the road for another mile or so and then began to slow down. Squinting his eyes, he looked for the trail entrance as he crossed the road to the western side. There it was, just as he had left it. Austin hopped off his bike, and without hesitation, forced his way through the thick of the brush. After another rough battle with sharp thorns and pointy branches, he finally came out into the clearing of the dirt ail, scratched and slightly bruised.

Austin hopped back onto his bike and headed down the windy open trail. The path was even more treacherous in the dark, and he could hardly see anything more than a few feet ahead of him. And with the trail's steep decline, Austin was afraid of hitting a large rock or tree branch and flying over his handlebars, potentially ruining his covert operation altogether. He had thought about bringing a flashlight with him, but he knew that any light would just increase the chance of him being spotted, so he went extra slow, watching the trail right in front of him as carefully as possible.

Finally, Austin arrived at the edge of the cliff that overlooked the old RV campsite. The visibility was a little better here than it was on the trail, with the moon's faint reflection bouncing off the otherwise black ocean, and giving the area a touch of light. Austin looked down at the campsite. Looking even spookier in the dark, the old RV rested undisturbed in its usual spot. The dirt space next to it, where the Ford Escort normally parked, was empty.

Austin hopped off his bike and dropped his backpack onto the ground. He pressed a small button on the side of his watch, and the digital face lit up with a green tint, showing him that it was 7:42 p.m. Then he rolled his bike over to the brush at the side of the trail and pushed it deep enough into the bushes so that it wouldn't be seen from the dirt path. Sitting down at the edge of the cliff, he unzipped his backpack and pulled out the binoculars, a spiral notebook, and a pen. Then he waited.

It wasn't long before Austin heard the sound of a car coming down the trail behind him, and he looked at his watch again —8:02 p.m. Through his binoculars he watched as the green Ford made its way carefully down the steep and windy dirt path in the distance. Austin grabbed his items, moved to the side of the trail, and then hid behind a heavy patch of brush, waiting patiently as the car continued to make its way down the hill. When the car got close, he ducked behind the bushes and watched as it passed him by.

Knowing that the man who might be Bart the Burglar was so close to him sent chills down Austin's spine. As he hid in the dark, he hoped that somehow this would be the night that he would find the evidence he needed to prove his suspicions. He knew that time was running out and that he needed to act fast. The thought crossed his mind again that if he did find out that this was in fact Bart the Burglar, then the right thing to do would be to go straight to the police. But Austin couldn't get over the feeling that he had stumbled onto this trail, and had found this old RV, at this particular time, for a reason.

After he knew he was in the clear, Austin grabbed his belongings and hopped out from behind the bushes. He laid down on his stomach at the edge of the cliff and used the binoculars to watch as the car continued down to the old RV.

Arriving at the campsite, the car parked in its normal spot, the engine shut off, and the clearing returned to darkness. There was an eerie silence for a moment before the driver's door opened, and the rugged man stepped out. Austin watched the man carefully. Even in the dark, he could clearly see the exhaustion in the man's face. The man went straight to the back of the car, opened the rear door, reached deep into the back of the car, and struggled with something inside. Then, with some exertion, he pulled out a large duffel bag.

Continuing to watch through the binoculars as the man headed back to the RV, Austin saw that the man had to use both of his arms to carry the bag. Moving his sights down to the duffel bag, he saw something he hadn't seen during any of his previous stakeouts. The duffel bag was so full that it looked like it could almost burst.

Austin looked at the bag carefully and noticed that, although it had been zipped shut as best it could, there was a small opening at one end, where the zipper was unable to close completely. Looking closer, he saw that something was poking out from the inside of the bag. With every step the man took, the bag rattled, causing whatever was inside to shake loose and to poke further out of the bag's opening. Finally, the item jostled free and fell out of the bag, landing onto the dirt floor. The man stopped.

At first, in the darkness, Austin couldn't make out what the object on the ground was. But when the man carefully reached down to pick it up, the light of the moon hit the object just right, and for a brief moment, Austin got a clear picture of what had fallen out of the bag. As he had suspected, it was a bundled up stack of crisp one hundred dollar bills. Austin gasped, his blood pumping out of terror and excitement.

Once he had arrived at the RV, the man threw the heavy duffel bag through the creaky old door, and then entered inside the trailer himself, letting the door slam shut behind him.

The campsite was quiet once again, and Austin sat in the darkness, contemplating what he had just seen. He felt a flurry of mixed emotions flowing through his body. But now that he was certain of what he had suspected, he believed he was ready to reveal to his friends his plan of how they could save the Wendals.

Chapter 8

The parking lot of the local movie theater was packed full of cars, and large posters on the side of the theater wall advertised the top-grossing films—*Austin Powers: The Spy Who Shagged Me* and *Star Wars: Episode I – The Phantom Menace.* High above the movie posters, and right above the theater entrance, hung a large, glowing neon pink sign with the theater's name: The Movie Experience. This was the largest and busiest movie theater in Ocean View, and although the inside of the building was obviously packed with patrons, the outside of the theater was relatively quiet and empty.

The Wendals hung out next to Dylan's white Dodge Durango at the far end of the parking lot, about a hundred yards or so away from the theater entrance. This part of the giant lot had a lot fewer cars, and much more open space. The light bulb on the tall parking lot lamp nearest them had burnt out, making the area darker than the rest of the theater lot.

Steve rode around on his skateboard, doing tricks throughout the parking lot. First, he popped an ollie off of a long concrete curb, and then he made several attempts at a kick-flip, which he didn't land on the first two attempts but finally stuck on the third try. Feeling prideful at how smoothly he landed the trick, Steve smiled to himself.

Dylan, Austin, and Ryan sat along a cement curb near the car, laughing and joking with each other as they watched Steve skateboard. Next to Dylan was a bucket filled with water balloons, and on Austin's lap rested the yellow elastic water balloon launcher.

"Where is everybody?" Dylan asked as he looked at the

empty movie theater entrance.

"Well, we missed the end of the 5:30 showing," Ryan replied, checking his watch.

Dylan looked annoyed. "Yeah, thanks to Austin. Where'd you say you were again?" he asked accusingly.

"Research project." Austin was short in his reply.

"Yeah, yeah, I'm so sure." Dylan could tell when his brother was hiding something.

After what he had seen at the RV, there was really no reason for Austin to lie anymore. But he was waiting for the right moment to tell the whole story, and to fill the boys in on his dangerous plan. "Chill out, man, another movie will get out soon," Austin said.

Dylan rubbed his stomach. "Yeah, but I'm starving. We could be eating by now," he barked back.

Steve had ridden his skateboard back to the group and was now listening in on the conversation.

Ryan looked at his watch again. "Actually, the six o'clock should be getting out any minute now."

Steve got excited. "Well let's get ready for our attack!" he exclaimed.

Ryan picked up the bucket of water balloons and carried it to a spot in front of Dylan's car. Standing up, Austin tried to hand the water balloon launcher over to Steve, but Steve rejected it and pushed it back towards Austin. "Tonight's your night, man," he said with a smile.

Looking skeptical, Austin replied, "I'm no good from this distance."

"Well, you'll never improve if you don't practice," Steve laughed. "Besides, someone has to step up and be the new trigger man after I'm gone."

Austin looked at Steve resentfully and opened his mouth to give him a piece of his mind.

But Steve cut him off, laughing, "Don't worry about it. You'll do great." Steve grabbed one of the launcher handles and followed Austin over to where Ryan was standing. Taking the other handle from Steve, Ryan spread out to open up the launcher, and Dylan knelt beside the bucket and handed Austin the first balloon.

In the distance, the boys saw the doors to the movie theater open, and crowds of people flooded outside in complete commotion. Moviegoers laughed and smiled, and talked about the films they had seen as they headed towards their cars. Ryan and Steve braced themselves and held their handles high in the air while Austin nervously loaded the first balloon into the pouch.

"Now's your chance; hurry up," Dylan cried excitedly.

Feeling anxious, Austin pulled the balloon pouch back into firing position and stretched the elastic bands as he crouched low to the ground, giving the launch angle a good trajectory. Then, squinting his eyes, he focused on his target and made small adjustments to his aim. When he was ready, he let go of the water balloon pouch and the balloon shot high into the sky.

The Wendals watched excitedly as the balloon flew through the air and headed towards the theater. After what seemed like an eternity to Austin, the balloon finally splashed onto the ground, landing about thirty feet in front of the crowd, and missing the intended targets by a good distance.

Only a few movie patrons even noticed the balloon's splash, and they looked around slightly confused but barely even bothered. Austin was severely disappointed and more than a little embarrassed.

Dylan was even more disappointed. "Ah, man...this is why Steve always does the launching," he shouted.

Steve looked back at Dylan dismissively. "Just give him another balloon, quick."

Taking another water balloon from his brother, Austin loaded the launcher for a second shot. He looked at Steve and complained, "I can't do it. It's too far."

"Just take a deep breath and relax," Steve said with a patient smile. "You've got this."

Steve's calm demeanor helped Austin feel better instantly, and he took a deep breath and pulled back on the pouch for another attempt. Stretching the launcher bands a lot farther than he had the first time, he let go of the pouch and sent the balloon flying high into the air with much more force than his first shot. When the balloon finally landed, it crashed right into the middle of a large group of moviegoers and soaked everyone around it, sending screams throughout the crowd.

Steve looked back at Austin with a proud smile. Overjoyed with his shot, Austin confidently loaded another balloon into the pouch and quickly shot it into the sky. Then he launched two more in succession. Each one landed into the crowd of surprised bystanders and sent them scrambling. The theater entrance quickly became a chaotic scene as shouts of annoyance and anger filled the parking lot sky. A group of teenage girls took cover inside the building's front doors, and several theater employees hid behind a large cement column, not wanting to come out into the open. Others ran to their cars in a mad dash.

Austin launched another balloon, which flew faster and further than all the previous ones and crashed into the large neon pink sign high on the theater wall. One of the fluorescent bulbs shattered, darkening half of the sign and causing sparks to shower down all over the theater entrance. The shouting from the crowd intensified.

Looking on in awe, Ryan said to Austin, half sarcastically, "Nice going, man." And the boys stopped for a moment to watch the pandemonium at the entrance.

Soon, two middle-aged men in black security guard t-shirts and hats came running out of the entrance doors. Pausing just outside the entrance, they looked around frantically trying to spot the assailants.

"And, that's definitely our cue to leave!" Dylan shouted to the others as he took off running for the car.

"You don't have to tell me twice!" Ryan grabbed the launcher and followed quickly behind Dylan.

Austin turned to Steve. "Time to go!" he yelled.

But instead of retreating, Steve pretended not to hear his friends and grabbed two more water balloons out of the bucket. He charged towards the security guards and threw the first balloon as hard as he could in their direction. But even with Steve's strong arm, the balloon landed well short of the guards. Disappointed with himself, he wound up and threw the second balloon high into the air, this one getting much closer than the first, but still missing the two men. He reached into the bucket for a third attempt and saw that it was empty.

Now that they knew where the attack was coming from, the security guards started in a dead sprint towards the Wendals.

Dylan honked his car horn aggressively, and Austin looked back at the car and saw Ryan waving his arms wildly at them. Then he looked back at Steve, who had now lowered the back of his pants and was laughing hysterically as he shook his rear-end in the security guard's direction.

Austin started to panic. "Come on, man, you're going to get in trouble!" he shouted.

Steve stood up straight and looked back at Austin. "So what," he replied, completely unphased.

"Don't make me leave you fools behind," Dylan shouted angrily from the car.

The security guards were close enough now that Austin could see the angry expressions on their faces. Austin grabbed Steve by the arm and looked at him sharply. "Steve...let's go!"

Finally relenting, Steve grabbed the empty bucket, and both boys took off running back to the car. With the security guards hot on their tail, Austin and Steve hopped into the open rear door of the car, and before they could even get the door closed behind them, Dylan slammed his foot on the gas pedal. As the car drove away, Austin looked out the back window and could see the security guards keeled over with their hands on their knees, trying to catch their breath.

Dylan and Ryan laughed together in the front of the car. "What a rush!" Ryan exclaimed. He mimicked the look of terror on the moviegoers' faces as the balloons were crashing down on them, and Dylan thought his reenactment was hilarious.

"I have to admit, that was a great idea, Steve," Dylan said as his laughter calmed down.

"Agreed," Ryan said. "That might be one of the best spots we've ever water ballooned." He grabbed a large black leather CD case from the floor of the car and began searching through the CDs.

Seeing what Ryan was doing, Dylan said excitedly, "Throw on some good tunes. I've got the new Sisqo album in there."

"Sisqo?" Ryan asked in shock, making a loud gagging sound, and pretending like he was going to throw up. "Come on, man, you're better than that." He looked at Dylan, seriously embarrassed by his friend's choice in music. "You gotta listen to something a little edgier than Sisqo after you stick it to the man like we just did!" He pulled a black and gray CD out of the case. "How about some Rage Against the Machine?" he asked with a smile, and then shoved the CD into a slot in the car stereo, and turned the music way up. Loud electronic rock music played from the speakers, and Ryan and Dylan banged their heads back and forth.

The atmosphere in the back seat was in stark contrast to the jovial mood upfront, as Steve quietly stared out of his window, into the dark night.

Austin looked over at Steve, not understanding what was going on with his friend. "You wanna talk about it?" he asked, trying to be heard over the booming music.

Steve looked back at Austin, surprised at the question. "About what?"

Unaware of the conversation going on in the back seat, Ryan and Dylan continued goofing off in the front of the car.

"About why you're being so reckless," Austin responded.

Steve laughed. "Oh, come on. I was just having some fun. We all were."

Steve's attitude was severely bothering Austin. "You took it too far," Austin said. "You could have gotten caught...and maybe even arrested."

Steve stopped laughing and turned his face away from Austin. Looking back out the window, he spoke quietly. "I'm leaving here in a few days anyway, I might as well go out with a bang," he said.

Austin raised his voice, almost angry now. "Stop talking like that! We'll figure something out."

Finally realizing an argument was taking place in the back, Dylan and Ryan stopped their conversation, and Dylan quickly turned the music on the stereo down.

"Figure something out?" Steve laughed incredulously. "There's nothing for *us* to figure out. Wake up and smell the roses."

Austin shook his head in frustration. "I can't believe you'd give up on the Wendals that easy."

Now Steve's anger was starting to build. "You don't know what you're talking about. You live in your perfect little bubble, with your perfect little family, completely sheltered from the real world. You have no clue what it's like to be me," he said, almost shouting. "You can't solve my problems with a positive attitude and a wish on a shooting star."

Austin's anger left him, and instead, he felt hurt and disappointed. He lowered his head and silently looked at the back of the seat in front of him.

After a few deep breaths, Steve tried to calm down. He knew he should feel bad about what he had said, but he also felt strongly that it was the truth. Eventually, he put his hand on Austin's shoulder and spoke in a casual tone, "Let's not ruin the night. Can we just forget the whole thing for now?"

Austin nodded his head tentatively.

"Video games at my house?" Steve asked, clearly as his way of trying to patch things up.

Austin felt it was more like Steve's way of sweeping things under the rug, but replied with a solemn, "Sure."

Turning to Dylan, Steve shouted, "Head to my place. And turn the music back up."

Rock music boomed through the car speakers again, even louder than before, and it wasn't long before Steve, Dylan, and Ryan were singing along together. Not in the mood to sing, Austin sat in silence and stared out his window pensively.

Chapter 9

The walls of Steve's bedroom were chaotically covered in posters. Some were of his favorite punk bands—Blink-182, Face to Face, and No Use For a Name, just to name a few. And others were of popular skaters and surfers doing different high-performance tricks on their boards. The most random poster, however, was a movie poster for the 1997 film *Titanic* that was taped onto the closet door. Often, when Steve brought girls over to the house, he would show them the poster and then tell them the story of how he had been cast as Leonardo Dicaprio's body double for the film. It was a classic Steve line and made no sense at all —he would have been thirteen years old when the movie was being filmed—but unbelievably, and maybe partly because he had moved to Ocean View from LA, at least a few girls had fallen for the story.

The rest of Steve's room was even more chaotic than the walls. The floors were covered in dirty clothes and empty food wrappers, both his dresser and nightstand were piled up with large mounds of random clutter, and his Indiana Pacers bed sheets laid next to his bed, wadded up in a ball on the floor.

Looking through a stack of CD cases on Steve's dresser, Ryan finally decided on an album called *Pennybridge Pioneers* by the punk band Millencolin. He carefully took the CD out of its case and inserted it into a large stereo on top of the dresser, and when the music started blasting, he sat back on Steve's bed and browsed an issue of *Surfer Magazine*.

Meanwhile, Dylan and Steve were busy playing video games on a seventeen-inch projection TV that sat on a stand next to Steve's door. The Nintendo 64 was the Wendal's video game console of choice, and the boys were currently playing *Goldeneye,* their favorite first-person shooter game that was based on the most recent James Bond movie. Steve sat back in a giant blue bean bag chair in front of the TV, laughing confidently as he methodically hit buttons on his controller. Meanwhile, Dylan stood on his feet and aggressively struggled with the joystick on his controller, looking very irritated.

"You can't beat me at *the facility* with grenade launchers," Steve exclaimed, laughing hard as he played.

On the television screen, Steve's character shot a digitized grenade through a pixelated doorway, and the grenade exploded next to Dylan's character, killing him instantly.

Dylan was angry and almost threw his controller at the TV. "You're cheating!" he shouted. "Quit looking at my screen, you screen poacher."

"I'm not looking at your screen. I'm just better than you," Steve replied boastfully.

"Let's go again. Throwing knives only this time." Dylan was laughing now as he went back to the main menu to choose the new game options.

"Hey, I'm supposed to get the next game," Ryan shouted from the bed, lowering his magazine.

"I get one more turn...since Steve was screen poaching," Dylan shouted back. He chose a new game character, this time a short Asian man wearing a tuxedo and a top hat, and then laughed out loud. "You'll never beat me when I'm Oddjob."

Steve smiled. "Don't sing it...Bring it."

Out in the living room, Austin sat on the couch, writing into his notebook as he watched the local news. A woman with short brown hair and a blue blouse spoke in a heavy tone. "The bank robber, known as Bart the Burglar, is quickly making a big name for himself around Southern California," she reported, as the same black-and-white photo of the masked criminal from Austin's wanted poster popped up in the corner of the screen. "Another bank was robbed again this morning in Fullerton, and witnesses say it was once again a man wearing a Bart Simpson mask. Local police are ramping up efforts to catch the criminal, which some experts believe could send the thief into hiding, or even cause him to head over the border into Mexico."

Austin quickly made notes on his paper.

Brrring! The phone rang loudly behind him, startling him badly.

Austin laughed to himself as he thought about how jittery he had been lately, and then he went back to watching the news. *Brrring!* It rang again. He turned around and looked back at Steve's open bedroom door, and could see that Dylan and Steve were lost in their video game.

After the phone rang a third time, Austin finally put down his notebook and pen and headed into the kitchen. He took the black cordless phone off its charging station on the counter next to the fridge, pressed the *Talk* button, and held the phone to his ear. "Andretti residence," he said into the phone.

A middle-aged man on the other end of the phone spoke in a deep and professional voice, "Hello, I'm looking for Linda Andretti."

Lowering the phone to his side, Austin shouted towards the bedroom, "Steve!"

Soon, Steve came jogging out of his room and into the kitchen. "What's up?" he asked casually.

Austin shrugged his shoulders. "Someone's looking for your mom," he said as he handed the phone to Steve.

Hesitantly, Steve grabbed the phone and held it to his ear. "Hello," he said with some irritation, as if he knew the call would be bad news. After listening silently for a few moments, his irritation turned to anger. Austin was worried since he was unable to hear what was going on on the other end of the phone.

Finally, Steve responded aggressively, speaking into the phone, "If you want the car then come take it." He listened again for another moment and then shouted, "Just leave me and my mom alone." Then he pressed a button on the receiver that ended the call, and slammed the phone onto the counter, looking both distressed and embarrassed.

Figuring that the Andrettis were getting calls from aggressive bill collectors on the regular, Austin felt for his friend. He hated seeing him go through all of this and would have happily taken some of Steve's family's debts on himself if he could. But, at the moment, "Don't let them get you down," was the best bit of consolation he could offer.

Steve looked at his friend, vulnerably again, and nodded.

The front door opened and Steve and Austin turned to see Linda walking into the house. She was wearing the same waitress uniform that she had had on the last time the boys had seen her. Her hair was a mess, her outfit looked wrinkled and stained, and the look on her face said she was extra worn down and stressed-out. She threw her purse and a large stack of mail, which Austin assumed to be more bills, onto the couch and headed towards the kitchen.

"Hi, boys," she said in a failed attempt at being cheerful.

"Hi, Ms. Andretti," Austin replied with a smile.

Steve turned away from his mom, still very upset, and not willing to even look at her. He could have quickly gotten over the fact that she had gotten them into another horrible financial mess, but the decision to make him go live with his Dad was unforgivable in his mind. He was feeling abandoned by her—like he was something that she could just brush off when he was no longer convenient to have around. With their constant moving from town to town, he had always struggled to feel like he belonged anywhere, but now he was feeling like he didn't even belong in his own home, or with his own mother, and that was extra tough for him to deal with.

Linda could feel Steve's coldness. "What have you boys been up to tonight?" she asked, trying to ignore the awkwardness in the room. She opened the refrigerator door, stuck her head inside, and began to rummage around.

Realizing that Steve wasn't going to acknowledge his mom, Austin responded, "Oh, you know, just trying to stay out of trouble."

Linda pulled her head out of the fridge and gave Austin a skeptical look. "Yeah, I'm sure," she said with a smirk. "Hey, did you boys eat all the sandwich meat?" she asked, disappointedly.

Austin shrugged his shoulders. "Probably Dylan?"

Linda sighed, and then pulled a pitcher full of water out of the fridge. Then she grabbed a tall glass out of a cupboard next to the microwave and filled it all the way to the brim. "Well, I don't mean to be rude, but I'm going to call it a night. I had a rough day at work and I have an opener shift in the morning." Linda started to head out of the kitchen and towards her bedroom.

Feeling like he couldn't end the conversation with Linda on such an awkward note, Austin kept talking. "Whatever happened to that job at the bank that you interviewed for?" he blurted out. "Steve said they really liked you?"

Linda stopped and turned back around to face the boys.

"She didn't show up for the second interview," Steve chimed in, in a condescending tone, before his mom had a chance to respond.

Linda glared at her son. "They weren't going to give me the job anyway," she said defensively.

Worried now that he had started another fight, Austin piped back in, trying to diffuse the situation. "Ryan's dad is friends with the bank manager," he said enthusiastically. "He could ask his dad to put in a good word for you."

Linda shook her head. "It wouldn't matter. They don't hire people like me at the bank."

Austin started to respond, but Steve spoke over him. "You don't know that. You didn't even try. You never try."

Shocked at the way her son was talking to her in front of company, Linda raised her voice, "That's enough, Steven. I did try, and it didn't work out. And besides, I couldn't make it to the second interview because I had to work a double shift at the restaurant."

Steve wasn't backing down. "Who cares about the stupid restaurant?" he shouted back with disgust. "That place is the worst, and they treat you horribly." He was defending his mom at the same time as he was chastising her. Regardless of how he was feeling at the moment, he hated that his mom had been given such a tough lot in life.

Linda tried to calm down. "You can't talk down to me like that Steven," she said. But at the same time, she understood his anger and hated that he had to worry about all of her drama when he should be worrying about things like girls, and school, and friends, instead. "The restaurant isn't so bad, and it provides us with a living right now," she said softly.

Steve rolled his eyes. "Does it though?"

That was the last patronizing remark Linda could handle from her son. "I don't know what else to do," she said, now in tears. "I'm sorry that you got stuck with a mom like me, but you won't have to deal with that for much longer!" Linda turned and stormed off down the hall, crying hysterically as she went. After she disappeared into the bedroom, the door slammed shut loudly behind her.

Steve felt incredibly frustrated. Austin put his arm around his friend, and the two of them headed out of the living room and back into the bedroom.

The television was still on in the living room after Steve and Austin had left the room completely empty, and the woman with the short brown hair and the blue blouse was back on the screen for another report. The words *Breaking News* were captioned in bold type at the bottom of the screen, while the woman spoke, "With no progress from the police as to the whereabouts of Bart the Burglar, it was just announced moments ago that authorities are now offering a *fifty thousand dollar reward* for anyone who brings forward information that leads to the arrest of the criminal," she said smiling. The segment then cut to its next top story, which was captioned, "Local cats disappearing at an alarming rate."

As soon as Austin and Steve had entered the bedroom, Dylan

grabbed Steve from behind and put him in a headlock. Caught off guard, Steve playfully began to wrestle back, while Dylan hugged him from behind, lifted him into the air, and then slammed him backward onto the bed. Laughing hard, Steve sat up on the bed. Dylan quickly jumped next to him, and the boys stared at the TV.

The television had been changed to a WWF professional wrestling program, and on the screen, a large man with a shaved head and a goatee stood in the middle of the wrestling ring. He wore a black leather vest, and stone washed jean shorts. Yelling into a microphone, the man appealed to the raucous crowd, who cheered for him from the stands. "And that's the bottom line," the man shouted into the mic as the crowd went wild. Eating it up, Steve and Dylan finished the wrestler's catch-phrase right along with him. "Because Stone Cold said so!" they shouted in unison.

Now sitting on the large bean bag chair, Ryan laughed as he looked back at Dylan and Steve, and said, "And you guys think I'm a nerd."

Austin took the television remote from off the pile of junk on Steve's nightstand. He hesitated for a moment but then pressed the power button, turning the TV off. Then he braced himself for the backlash that would inevitably follow.

Dylan immediately grabbed a pillow and threw it hard at his brother. "What are you doing?" he shouted. "The main event is about to start!"

Looking upset, Ryan cried out, "Yeah, man, Stone Cold is about to whip The Rock's butt."

Austin stood his ground. "We need to talk," he said as he pulled a chair from the corner of Steve's room over to the bed, and then sat down.

"Oh come on, man, whatever it is, it can wait until after the match," Dylan protested. "Now give me the remote before I pile drive you."

Austin was resolute. "I'm calling for a Wendal meeting," he said. "So circle up."

Now Dylan looked even more annoyed. "Here we go again," he mumbled under his breath in exasperation.

Austin was known for calling Wendal meetings when he had something that he considered serious to discuss with the group, but by Dylan's estimation, nothing that Austin found to be serious was of any actual importance to him.

Ryan excitedly hopped to his feet and pulled the bean bag he had been sitting on closer to Steve's bed. Unlike Dylan, he loved it when Austin called Wendal meetings because for some childish reason they made him feel like he was a part of something important.

Steve found it funny how serious Austin got when he called for a Wendal meeting, and when he thought about it, he wasn't sure if anyone else, other than Austin, had ever called for a Wendal meeting before. Either way, he admired Austin's passion for all things Wendal, but still thought it would be okay to have some fun with the situation. Turning to face Austin, he said in a funny voice, "By our powers combined..." and he made a fist with his hand, and shoved it in the middle of the boys, mocking a popular Saturday morning cartoon.

Laughing, Dylan turned and joined in on the circle, and stuck his fist in the center of the group along with Steve's. "Earth!" he shouted jokingly.

Ryan was now laughing as well. "Wind!" he yelled as he shoved his hand in the middle of the group.

Not amused at all, Austin sat with his arms folded, waiting for the others to quit goofing around. Ryan saw Austin's displeasure and he quickly lowered his fist from the circle and sat up straight. Steve slowly stopped laughing as well and turned to listen to Austin.

Dylan was the last to come around but he eventually straightened up. "I've got the VCR setup to record the match at home anyway," he said with an assured smile. "So let's get this thing over with."

Austin took a deep breath. "So," he said, looking around the room at the others. Doubting he would receive a warm reception, at least initially, he struggled to know how to begin but went for it anyway. "I think I have a plan to help Steve."

In irritation, Dylan covered his face with his hands, and asked in a muffled voice, "This again?"

Steve was frustrated as well and looked up at the ceiling. "Dude, I thought we agreed to forget about this," he said. "There's nothing we can do, so just let it go already."

Dylan lowered his hands. "Yeah, how are we supposed to come up with that kind of money? Babysitting? Male modeling?" Dylan laughed hysterically to himself.

Keeping his composure, Ryan piped in, "Come on guys, I think we should at least hear him out," he said, and then he winked at Austin, happy to get his friend's back for a change.

After another sigh, Dylan replied, "Okay, fine. Let's hear it already. But this better be good, or I'm turning the wrestling match back on." He looked at Steve and shrugged his shoulders.

Steve looked off in the distance, taking a moment to think it over before responding. "Alright, we're listening," he said reluctantly. "But this is the last time we're talking about this, so make it count."

Not wanting to lose their attention, Austin got straight to the point. "I know exactly where we can get the money that Steve needs," he declared. "I know where Bart the Burglar is, and I know where he's hiding the stolen money."

Steve, Dylan, and Ryan stared at Austin in silence for a moment, and then all started laughing simultaneously.

"Come on, man," Ryan said through his laughter. "Now you're making me look like an idiot for sticking up for you." He was sure Austin was pulling their legs. "What's the real plan?"

Dylan was laughing the hardest. "Yeah, man, you're still following around that poor hermit guy at the bike jumps, or what? Get real!"

Austin waited patiently while the boys got it out of their systems.

Steve was the first to realize that Austin wasn't laughing. "Hold on, guys," he said to the others. "I think he might be serious—definitely delusional—but I think he's serious."

After their laughter calmed down, Dylan and Ryan looked at Austin, slightly confused.

Austin contemplated where to go next. There was so much ground to cover, but he knew that he needed to focus on the facts that would most prove his idea wasn't completely crazy. He continued, "It all started just a couple of weeks ago when I was out looking for the old bike jumps off PCH. I followed a trail that took me down the cliffs and dead-ended at a spot right above an amazing secluded beach."

"We've already heard this story," Dylan interrupted.

Austin gave his brother a bothered look, and then kept going. "On that spot, I found a very suspicious looking man, hiding out in an old run-down RV."

Steve shook his head. "These things always start out with you spying on someone," he said. "We've listened to your wild suspicions in the past, and none of them have ever turned out. Why should we believe this one now?"

"Like the time he thought our neighbor had murdered his wife and buried her in the backyard?" Dyan asked with a smile. "He watched their house with his binoculars every night for a week, spouting off crazy theories of how the guy did it." Dylan was laughing hard now. "We eventually found out that the wife was just out of town visiting her sick mother, and the large mound of dirt he saw in their backyard was from a sewer line that had to be dug up and repaired."

Steve joined back in. "Or the time he thought Mr. Lindsley was a big-time drug dealer and was selling crystal meth to his creative writing students?" he asked, laughing so hard that he could barely continue. "But it turned out that the 'meth' he had found in the teacher's desk drawer was just a batch of leftover rock candy that some of his students made in chemistry."

Ryan was now laughing again as well and couldn't help himself.. "Or when he thought the Irish Mafia was holding late-night meetings at the Blockbuster down the street," he chuckled, but then quickly felt bad and cut his story short as soon as he noticed Austin glaring back at him.

Austin was getting extremely frustrated. "Look, we still don't know that the mafia thing wasn't true," he said, speaking loudly to be heard over the laughter. "And I am way more sure of this one than I was of any of those other things."

"Oh yeah?" Dylan asked through his laughter. "And what makes you so sure this time?"

Austin raised his voice to a loud shout, "Well if you quiet down, I'll tell you!" This got the boys' attention again, and they stopped laughing and listened. After he was sure they were done, Austin went on. "First of all, the only solid tip that the police have on this guy is that he possibly drives a green Ford Escort." He paused for a moment to add to the suspense. "The guy hiding out at the RV drives an old green Ford Escort, and he parks it next to the RV at night."

Not buying into that piece of evidence, Dylan rebutted, "Lots of people drive green Ford Escorts. It's a very popular car. And the police say the burglar *possibly* drives that car?"

Austin put his hand up in the air, signaling for Dylan to quiet down. "That's just what started my suspicions," he said, lowering his hand. "So I continued to go back out there, to watch the hermit, and to try and gather more evidence."

"Hence, why you've been disappearing a lot lately, and showing up tardy to school," Ryan interjected.

Austin nodded his head and continued, "The guy takes off in the green car every single morning, as soon as the sun comes up, and doesn't come back until right after the sun goes down, every night - like clockwork." Dylan, Steve, and Ryan listened with interest now. "There was another robbery today, so I went by this evening. The man returned to the campsite at the same time as always; however, after he got out of his car tonight..." Austin paused and took a deep breath.

"What?" Ryan asked anxiously, and all three boys stared silently at Austin.

"After he got out of the car...he went into the back seat... and pulled out a giant sack...full of money," Austin finished.

Dylan didn't waste any time. "No way!" he shouted. "I don't believe it."

Steve took a moment to think. He wanted to give Austin the benefit of the doubt, but his friend's poor track record made this a tricky situation. "You sure you weren't seeing things?" he asked. "It was night time, right? So it was dark. And I'm sure you weren't very close to the guy."

"I had my binoculars, so I got a really good view," Austin replied confidently. "And the moon was giving off plenty of light."

"Okay, so even if you did see that, there could be lots of explanations for why the guy had a bag of money," Dylan retorted, with Steve and Ryan nodding in agreement.

Raising an eyebrow, Austin said confidently, "Then give me one good explanation."

The room went silent while Dylan, Steve, and Ryan thought hard. Dylan finally gave it a try, and said, "He could be an eccentric millionaire who's sick of people and wanted to get off the grid?" He shrugged his shoulders, lacking confidence in his answer even as he said it.

Ryan and Steve had nothing.

"I've done my due diligence, and it makes perfect sense," Austin said. "All of the banks he's robbed have been within a thirty-mile radius of Ocean View. And just think about it—this is a small town that never gets any public attention. And no one goes out to those secluded beach spots. The cops would never find him out there." Austin was getting even more excited as he made his case. "And we're close enough to the border here that he could make a clean break for Mexico when he's ready. It's the perfect place to hide out."

There was more silence as the boys considered everything that Austin had laid out, and at least Steve and Ryan seemed to be softening up.

"I mean, it's not a ridiculous idea...that this guy could be hiding out there," Ryan admitted. "He's gotta be hiding somewhere close by, right? So why not there?"

Feeling like he was gaining some ground, Austin smiled contently.

"So let's just pretend you're right about this guy for a minute," Ryan said. "What you're suggesting is that we steal his money?" he asked thoughtfully. "Because I can think of multiple problems with that. For starters, wouldn't that be insanely dangerous, robbing a robber?"

"Actually, we would be burglarizing, not robbing," Austin said. He knew that Ryan would bring up the danger issue, and was prepared to answer. "He would never even know we were there. Like I said, he keeps the same schedule every day, so we already know when he'll be away from his RV. And there's no way he takes all of that cash with him when he leaves, so he must be storing the money inside the old RV. We get into the RV while he's gone, we find the money quickly, and we get out. No danger at all." Austin smiled, feeling like he had nailed his response.

Without contesting, Ryan nodded his head slowly while Steve sat in silence, soaking it all in.

"And what about taking money that doesn't belong to us?" Dylan jumped in. "Doesn't that make us as bad as the robber?" he asked sincerely.

Now wondering the same thing, Steve and Ryan stared at Austin in silence, waiting for his answer.

Austin had thought about Dylan's point more than he had thought about anything else during his planning, and he knew that it was a very tough moral conundrum. Stealing went against everything he had been taught in his Christian upbringing, which made this a hard hurdle to overcome, but he had finally gotten to a place where he felt that what he was proposing could be justified. He looked at his friends earnestly. "If we don't take the money, it will just end up in Mexico with Bart the Burglar anyway. The bank would never recover a penny of it without us," he said. "And we would only take what we need to help pay off the Andrettis' debts. Can you think of a more righteous cause than that?"

Dylan looked down in contemplation. It was a fine line

they would be walking, but he thought that Austin's response was pretty valid.

"And if I'm right about this, we'll call the cops as soon as we get back into town, and they can go get the rest of the money," Austin said with conviction. "Everyone wins. The bank would get their money back, minus the small amount that we would take, that they would never even miss. The police would get their arrest, there would be one less criminal on the streets, and we would keep the Wendals together!"

Steve, Dylan, and Ryan exchanged glances.

Even Ryan, who was generally the most skeptical of the group, was starting to see some merit in the idea, and he suddenly smiled. "If Austin's right, and we pulled this off...we *would* become town heroes," he said with some excitement. "Chicks dig heroes."

Steve was finally ready to join in. "So, if we did go along with this," he said, still hesitant and contemplative. "Then what are you proposing?"

Austin felt a ray of hope now that Steve seemed to be budging. "The Wendals haven't been camping at the beach in a while," he said with a smirk. "We head out tomorrow morning with our camping gear, scope the place out for the night, go down to the RV and get the cash first thing in the morning, and we're home in time for dinner the next night. Nothing to it!"

Steve, Ryan, and Dylan all looked at each other again, each knowing that Austin was oversimplifying the danger and complexity of what he was proposing.

"Come on, guys," Austin cheered. "I'm talking about a campout at the beach. It will be fun." He looked at Steve, knowing that if he could win him over, then the other two would surely get on board. "If I'm right, then we find this money and save the Wendals. If I'm wrong, then we spend our last weekend together on one last Wendal adventure. It's a win either way." Austin looked at his friends desperately. "What could go wrong?" he asked emphatically.

"We could all end up dead," Ryan responded, clearly still

skeptical.

Shaking his head in frustration, Austin said, "You know I would never let anything bad happen to the Wendals."

Steve was thinking hard. He wasn't so worried about the danger of Austin's plan, but his objections came from his unwillingness to accept help from anyone when it came to his own personal issues. Growing up the way he did, he had never really been able to depend on anyone else for help, so his inclination was to face his problems all on his own. But as he realized how much this meant to Austin, he almost felt like he owed it to his best friend to go along. "If we do follow you on this," he finally said, "and it turns out that you're wrong, will you drop the whole thing and let me deal with this myself?"

Austin knew this was his last shot anyway, so he had nothing to lose. "Absolutely!" he exclaimed.

Steve looked at Ryan, and then at Dylan. "Alright," he said casually. "I mean, how do I say no to a campout at the beach, right?" He looked at Austin with a smile, and declared, "I'm in." Then he stuck his hand out into the middle of the group. Overjoyed, Austin quickly put his hand on top of Steve's.

Now that Steve was in, Dylan's defenses quickly dropped. "I guess I need to work on my tan this weekend anyway," he said, putting his hand in the circle.

Ryan was the last holdout, and he looked at the others nervously. This would take him completely outside of his comfort zone, but when he really thought about it, he realized that that was the case pretty much every time he hung out with the Wendals. Slowly, he reached his hand out and placed it on top of the others. "You guys will be the death of me," Ryan said, unsure whether he should laugh or cry.

Now that all of the Wendals were on board with his plan, Austin was completely content. But suddenly, out of nowhere, a spell of anxiety came over him, and he began to worry. *What if I am putting the Wendals in danger?* he wondered, knowing he wouldn't be able to live with himself if anything bad happened to his friends. But he quickly forced the thought out of his mind, determined that something needed to be done to keep the Wendals together, even if there was some risk involved.

"So, what happens if Austin's crazy plan doesn't turn out?" Dylan asked. "You just go live with your dad in Utah?"

"No way," Steve responded, standing up from the bed.

Dylan looked confused. "Well, what other option do you have?"

"I don't know," Steve said sternly. But Austin could tell that Steve had already spent some time thinking about it. "I can take care of myself if I need to," Steve said.

Dylan knew he had struck a sour chord, so he didn't press this issue any further.

Looking at his watch, Ryan started to panic. "It's almost my curfew," he shouted and then started to gather his stuff together. "Can I get a ride home, D-man?"

Dylan nodded and grabbed his own backpack, and the boys all headed out of Steve's room together. Before making their way outside to the car, Dylan and Ryan gave Steve the Wendal handshake, and then Steve plopped down on his living room couch in front of an episode of *The Fresh Prince of Bel-Air*.

Noticing the frustration on Steve's face, Austin sat down on the couch next to him. "Sorry about earlier with your Mom."

"I just don't get it. You'd think she would try a little harder to keep us together. Is it really that easy for her to get rid of me?" Steve asked, sounding vulnerable again.

Austin was feeling betrayed by Linda's decision as well but tried his best to see things from her point of view. "Maybe she really believes it's what's best for you?" he said. "She's in a pretty rough spot right now."

"It just seems like we're always in a rough spot," Steve said, agitated. "Did you know I moved nine times before starting the seventh grade?"

Of course Austin knew this about his best friend, but he acted surprised and upset. Steve's life was quite the contrast to his own, with the fact that Austin had been raised in the same house his entire life. And though his family wasn't wealthy, he had never had to worry about not having a roof over his head, or food on his table. His parents had always allowed him to just be a kid, which wasn't a luxury that Steve had been given. Trying to look on the bright side, Austin said, "Well, at least all that moving brought you here."

Steve caved in and smiled, and then put his arm around Austin. "Thanks for always being there for me, man."

The sound of Dylan's car horn blared into the house, interrupting the tender moment, and Ryan shouted from the car for Austin to hurry up.

Steve laughed. "Why don't you spend the night tonight?" he pleaded. "We could toilet paper Josie's house...just the two of us."

Austin could tell that Steve really didn't want to be alone at the moment, but he knew that he couldn't stay. "I'd love to," he said. "But I've gotta prep for the campout. We're heading out first thing in the morning." Austin smiled.

Steve nodded reluctantly, and the boys did the Wendal handshake and said their goodbyes.

After leaving Steve's house, Austin ran through the plan in his head one last time, which filled him with both excitement and anxiety, and he knew that he would be way too excited to sleep that night.

Chapter 10

It was a lovely morning for an adventure. Dylan and Austin had just arrived back at Steve's house and were laying their bikes on the front lawn when they saw Ryan pedaling his bike up the street towards them. Austin was wearing a tight-fitting white T-shirt, floral print board shorts, and black skater shoes. Dylan had on baggy athletic shorts and a black sleeveless shirt that said *Just Bring It* on the front. Both boys had small camping packs strapped to their backs.

Arriving out of breath and sweating heavily, Ryan laid his bike on the lawn next to the others. He was wearing a pair of baggy jeans and hiking boots and a straw beach hat with a wide brim that shielded his face and neck from the sun. On his back was a heavy-duty camping backpack that was twice the size of Austin's and Dylan's.

Appearing very anxious to be there, Ryan asked, "So did you tell your parents the story I worked up?"

Dylan replied with a condescending tone, "Yes, Ryan. We told them exactly what you said to tell them. Church youth camping trip...Meet at the Rushton's house...Coming home tomorrow night...Yadda yadda yadda."

Ryan looked relieved. "Okay, good," he said. "It's just that I don't want your mom calling my mom wondering where we are." Then Ryan seemed worried again. "Do you think Steve told his mom the story?"

Austin shook his head. "Don't worry about it, man," he said as he grabbed a hold of Ryan's backpack excitedly. "Just show us what you got in the bag already."

A large grin came over Ryan's face, and he pulled the

enormous bag off his shoulders and dropped it onto the grass in front of them. The bag was packed so completely full that goods started spilling out of it as soon as he opened the zipper. Ryan reached inside and pulled out a white plastic box with a red cross on the front. "I've got bandages and disinfectant and a bunch of other first-aid stuff in here in case anyone gets hurt," he said eagerly, as he held up the first aid kit. Then he pulled out a small ziplock bag full of tiny pink pills. "And plenty of Benadryl, in case anyone else has bad allergies like I do."

Smacking the pill bag out of Ryan's hand, Dylan shouted impatiently, "We don't want a list of everything you've got in there, you goober! Just show us the good stuff."

Austin chuckled.

Ryan looked embarrassed. "Alright, alright, take it easy," he said, quickly realizing exactly what the boys wanted to see. He dove back into the backpack, this time with both of his arms, and pulled out a large plastic bag. "This stuff is heavy, so you guys need to help me carry it down there." He put the bag on the lawn and opened it up for the boys to see inside. The bag was filled with fireworks of all different shapes and sizes, and Dylan and Austin's jaws dropped open as they grabbed at the fireworks and excitedly examined each one.

"I've got a bit of everything," Ryan said enthusiastically. "Bottle rockets, roman candles, M-80s. And even the big illegal ones."

Meticulously inspecting one of the larger fireworks, Dylan was surprised at how heavy it was. "These things look professional-grade," he said, sounding impressed.

Austin picked up a fiberglass tube that was a little over a foot long and had a square base attached to one end. "What's this?" he asked curiously.

Smiling proudly, Ryan grabbed the tube from Austin. "That's a mortar tube," he answered quickly. Then he pulled a red ball-shaped firework out of his bag that was about the size of a tennis ball. "These are the real deal. The same grade of fireworks you see at the professional shows." He stood the tube up on its base, on top of the grass, and then dropped the ball-shaped mortar firework into the tube. "You load it just like that, then you light the fuse and back away," he said. "And kaboom! You've got the grand finale." Ryan's face was beaming with pride.

Austin laughed approvingly. "You really came through, man," he said with a big smile on his face. "These will be fun to play with during our downtime out there."

The front door to Steve's house opened abruptly, startling the boys, and Linda walked out in a hurry. Ryan, Dylan, and Austin nervously began to shove the fireworks back into Ryan's backpack, hoping Linda wouldn't see what they had.

Dressed for her shift at the restaurant, Linda had the same look of stress on her face that the boys had been seeing a lot of lately, and as soon as she noticed the boys, she stopped at the top of the driveway. "What in the world are you taking those camping for?" she asked, looking confused. The boys froze with the last bit of fireworks still in their hands, and when Linda walked over to them, Austin immediately handed over what he was holding.

Linda looked the firework over carefully. "These look dangerous," she said, sounding worried. "Where did you get this stuff, anyway?"

With a sheepish tone, Ryan responded, "We got them over the summer on our family trip to Mexico." Thinking they were busted for sure, he figured that his best move was to be honest and to hope for mercy. "You're not going to tell my mom, are you?" he asked pleadingly. "If she finds out I snuck these out of the house I'll be dead meat." Ryan clasped his hands together in a show of penitence.

Linda looked over the fireworks one last time, and then looked back at Ryan. Feeling sorry for the pitiful expression on his face, her demeanor changed. "No...I'm not going to tell your mom," she said compassionately. "But you boys better be careful with these." She tossed the firework back to Austin, bringing smiles to the boys' faces, and then she looked at her watch. "I've gotta go. Have fun, and keep Steve out of trouble for me," she said as she hurried over to her white Dodge Neon.

Austin smirked at Linda's last comment, thinking about how he was the one potentially leading Steve into trouble this time around.

A few seconds later the boys heard the white Dodge's engine sputter several times before finally turning over. The car was old and had too many miles on the motor to be considered close to reliable, but a new vehicle purchase was obviously not in the cards for Linda at the time.

As soon as Linda's car disappeared around the street corner, Ryan began to laugh mischievously. "Good thing she didn't see these," he said as he pulled two small BB-guns out of his backpack and handed them over to Austin and Dylan. The boys looked at the guns excitedly and then began to aim them all around the yard, pretending like they were characters in one of their favorite first-person shooter video games.

Lowering the gun, Dylan noticed something on Ryan's waist. "What the heck is that?" he asked.

A small black canister with a yellow label was clipped to one of the belt loops on Ryan's pants, and Ryan smiled as he unclipped the canister from his belt and held it up for the boys to see. "Bear spray," he declared proudly. A confused look came over Dylan's face. "It's just like pepper spray but with a much longer range. Just in case we run into any wild animals out there," Ryan informed him.

Dylan burst into heavy laughter.

Unable to help himself, Austin started to chuckle as well. "There aren't any bears where we're camping," he said with a smile.

"Yeah, man, we're going to the beach. What do you think's gonna attack us?" Dylan asked, still laughing.

Ryan quickly clipped the canister back onto his pants. "You never know what we might need out there," he said defensively. "I've heard there are fierce raccoons the size of Rottweilers in the outskirts." Dylan had to hold onto his brother's shoulder just to keep himself from falling over from his laughter and Austin shook his head, embarrassed by both boys.

Steve's front door opened again and the boys turned around to see Steve finally making his way outside. He was wearing a tight-fitting white tank top undershirt and bright yellow board shorts and had a gray snapback baseball cap on his head—turned backward and slightly angled to the side. Around Steve's shoulders was a duffel bag–style backpack that was even bigger than Ryan's and that was a brilliant neon orange color that resembled the hue of a construction worker's safety vest. Holding a cordless phone to his ear, Steve had a slightly annoyed look on his face as he listened to the person on the other end.

After he dropped his giant duffel bag onto the lawn, Steve paced back and forth with the phone to his ear. "I don't know what else to say, Josie," he said into the phone. "I completely forgot about the lake, and I can't go now." He stopped and gave the Wendals a look as if to say that he was in real trouble, and, although they were unable to make out what she was saying, the boys could hear Josie yelling on the other end of the phone. Steve responded defensively, "We're just going to be down at the beach, below the lookout cliffs, past the convenience store."

Worried that it could ruin their whole weekend, as well as their mission, Austin didn't want anyone else to know where they were going—especially not Josie—and he waved his hands angrily at Steve, and silently mouthed the word *No!*

Shrugging his shoulders, Steve whispered *sorry* back to Austin. More yelling was heard from the other end of the phone until Steve finally cut Josie off. "Okay, okay, I have to go now. I'm sorry." He pressed a button on the phone, ending the call, and then immediately felt like a jerk. With all that was going on, he had genuinely forgotten about his commitment to spend the weekend with Josie and her family and wasn't trying to hurt her.

"Geez, man, that didn't sound good," Dylan said awkwardly.

"Yeah, she sounded pissed," Ryan interjected.

"Well, I don't blame her," Steve replied. "She was really excited about the lake."

Austin kept quiet. He didn't feel bad at all about ruining Josie's plans, and selfishly, he knew that if Josie never wanted to see Steve again, it would just mean more time for Steve to hang with the Wendals. He also knew that if their weekend plans didn't work out, nobody would be getting any time with Steve going forward anyway.

"Forget about it," Steve said as he saw the concern on Dylan and Ryan's faces. "I don't want to think about it right now."

Austin smiled. "Now that's the Wendal spirit," he cheered enthusiastically. "We've got more important things to be dealing with than girls."

Steve went into the garage and rolled his bicycle outside. Attached to the side of his bike was a small aluminum makeshift surfboard rack that had been altered to hold a skimboard instead of a surfboard, and Steve's light blue Victoria Skimboard was strapped snugly into the rack with a pair of bungee cords.

A skimboard was a smaller, finless version of a surfboard that was used to glide on top of the shallower water along the shore. Steve absolutely loved his skimboard, and wouldn't even think about heading to the beach without it. When he got back to the lawn, he grabbed his duffel bag and threw it over his shoulders.

Dylan looked surprised as he saw Steve's bag. "Holy cow, man, your bag's even bigger than Ryan's."

Shrugging his shoulders, Steve said, "You never know what we might need out there." And he hopped on his bike.

Ryan looked at Dylan, feeling vindicated. "See!" he exclaimed. "That's exactly what I just said."

After hopping on his bike, Austin paused to soak in the moment. He didn't know what the weekend would bring, but he realized that when it was all over there was a good chance that things would never be the same for the Wendals. He also knew that being worried about possibly losing Steve wouldn't help their cause, so he focused all his energy on the excitement of

93

one last adventure with his friends. "Everyone ready?" he asked the group.

Steve looked at Austin, and said, smiling, "We're following your lead."

And at that, Austin took off on his bike with the other boys right behind him.

Chapter 11

Steve lived on the southern end of Ocean View, so the boys had a long ride all the way across town to get to the cliffs at the rural northern outskirts. First, they made their way through a suburban jungle of tract home residential neighborhoods. Then they crossed through Ocean View's downtown area, where they passed by the pier and the small harbor. Since it was Saturday, the beaches were packed with surfers, volleyball players, and all sorts of other visitors.

As they rode past a group of bikini-clad highschool girls, Steve slowed down to say hello, and after a short conversation, he kindly offered to help the girls with the application of their tanning oil. The girls giggled excitedly, agreed to Steve's proposal, and then invited the four boys to join them at the beach. Steve, Dylan, and Ryan would have followed the girls without a second's hesitation if it weren't for Austin forcefully reminding them about the mission at hand and practically prying them away from their new friends. Especially devastated by the missed opportunity, Ryan looked back longingly as they pedaled away from the girls.

Next, the boys passed the local In-N-Out burger on Main Street, at the other end of the harbor. Against Austin's wishes, Dylan convinced the group that they would be able to ride faster if they got some food in their bellies. Steve and Ryan didn't need much convincing to stop, but to appease Austin's desire to not waste time, the boys agreed to go through the drive-thru instead of eating inside. When they pulled up to the food window on their bikes, the employee inside gave them a funny look but delivered their meals all the same. With one hand on their handlebars and the other hand clutching their Double Double cheeseburgers, the boys turned up PCH and headed towards their final destination.

Austin spent the rest of the journey trying to get the group to pick up their pace. Meanwhile, the other three boys goofed around and looked for any excuse to slow down, or to take a quick break from their arduous ride. Gradually, they made their way up the coast, and as they did, the city began to disappear around them, and their surroundings became more and more rural. Neighborhoods and industrial complexes gave way to thick brush and tall trees, and the road became less and less busy until there were hardly any cars passing by them at all.

All things considered, they were making decent time when Austin heard a sound that would give anxiety to any teenage boy who was doing something that he wasn't supposed to be doing, though this sound had an especially troublesome meaning for him.

Whee-yoo, whee-yoo, a police siren wailed from behind them.

"Oh shoot," Dylan lamented under his breath. Looking back and seeing a police car trailing closely behind them, with its red and blue lights strobing aggressively, he immediately felt the same panic that his brother was feeling.

All four boys simultaneously pulled their bikes over to the side of the road and waited nervously as the police car pulled up next to them. The front passenger side window of the car was rolled all the way down, and the Wendals smiled awkwardly at the officer inside. He was a clean-cut man in his early forties, with a strong build and thick black hair. His dark blue uniform was neatly pressed and the badge on his chest was polished and shiny. The officer lowered his sunglasses and stared at the boys.

"What are you guys doing out here?" the officer asked in a stern police voice.

Immediately going on the defensive, Austin replied, "I told you we were going camping this weekend, Dad."

Sergeant Kenney exchanged awkward glances with each one of the boys and then looked at his son skeptically. "Yeah, but your mom said you were going with the church youth group," he said without flinching, and the Wendals suddenly looked like children who had been caught with their hands in the cookie jar.

It didn't take Dylan long to crack under the pressure. "This was all Austin's idea," he said, not feeling an ounce of shame for throwing his brother under the bus.

Austin glared at Dylan in angry disbelief.

Ryan's response was almost just as bad. "Please don't call my mom," he exclaimed.

Austin shook his head, disappointed at his friend as well.

Sergeant Kenney looked back at Austin, waiting for an explanation.

Austin thought carefully about what he would say next. He didn't want to dig himself into a deeper hole, but he also knew that if he told his Dad the whole story, he would never allow them to continue with their campout. "Okay, so we told a little white lie," he finally responded, sounding apologetic. "It's just that... this is probably Steve's last weekend here with us, and we needed one last trip together before he's gone." Austin was speaking the truth, just not the whole truth. "I couldn't tell Mom because I knew that she wouldn't understand," he said, looking distressed.

Austin's plea seemed to soften up his father, and Sergeant Kenney looked at Steve. "I'm sorry to hear about everything going on, Steve," he said compassionately.

"I really appreciate that, Mr. Kenney," Steve replied.

"I heard that you're probably going to Utah for a while?"

"That's what my mom wants anyway," Steve said with a hint of disdain.

"Well, we will definitely miss you," Sergeant Kenney responded. He looked back over at Austin. "Where exactly are you guys planning on camping?"

"Just a few miles past the convenience store, down by the

water," Austin answered, feeling a spark of hope.

Sergeant Kenney looked confused. "There's no public access out there," he said. "No one is supposed to be out on those cliffs."

Austin made sure his tone was as respectful as possible. "There's a bike trail that leads down to the beach, I've been out there several times," he said. "It's not a tough ride if you know your way."

Sergeant Kenney sat thinking for a moment before he responded. "Well I guess there's no one else out there for you guys to bother," he finally replied. "Okay...I won't tell your mom if you promise me you will *stay out of trouble*."

Cheering enthusiastically, the four boys nodded their heads in agreement. Austin felt an extreme amount of relief and he promised himself he would find a way to repay his dad after they got back home.

"You stay in that spot at all times though. That way I know exactly where you are, in case anything happens," Sergeant Kenney said with a smile. "But if I get a single call about any issues going on out there, you guys will be in serious trouble. You understand?" he asked, again with his stern police officer voice.

"Yes, sir!" Ryan shouted submissively.

Smiling, Steve responded, "I'll make sure to keep them all in line."

"Thanks, Dad, you're the best," Dylan nodded gratefully to his father.

The boys sat back on their bikes, getting ready to move out.

"By the way," Sergeant Kenney said, and the boys stopped and looked back at him from where they were on their bikes. "I got a call about a water balloon attack at the movie theater last night. You guys wouldn't know anything about that, would you?"

Looking around at each other awkwardly, the boys all shrugged their shoulders.

Sergeant Kenney cracked a smile. "Alright, you boys get on your way."

The Wendals all smiled back in relief, knowing that they were only being let off the hook because Sergeant Kenney felt bad about Steve's current situation, and they were very grateful for it.

"And if you do get into any trouble out there, call me directly at the station, and I'll come to get you myself," Sergeant Kenney said. "I'd rather not have your parents find out that I let you out there all alone." For a moment he looked like he was questioning his decision, but then continued, "There's a pay phone at the convenience store right off the highway."

"Of course, sir," Ryan blurted out, looking very serious. "My mom would be the last person I'd call if I got into any kind of trouble." He wasn't joking in the smallest bit, so he was confused when everyone else laughed at his comment.

After thanking Sergeant Kenney again, Steve hopped on his bike and started pedaling back up the main road. Dylan and Ryan also gave their thanks, and then followed right behind Steve, while Austin stayed behind.

About to put his car into drive, Sergeant Kenney realized that Austin was still standing by his window, something clearly still on his mind. "What's wrong?" he asked.

Austin stared up the road at his friends. "It's Steve," he said, not hiding his deep concern. "They're really in trouble this time, and I'm worried if they don't get this figured out, he's going to do something stupid."

"Steve's a big boy, son," his Dad replied. "And Linda is doing her best. She means well, but..." He paused for a moment and then smiled awkwardly, rethinking what he was going to say. "Well, I'm sure everything will work out for them."

"Isn't there anything you can do to help them out?" Austin pleaded. "Maybe you can get the collectors to leave them alone for a little while? Give them some more time?"

Sergeant Kenney could see the pain in his son's eyes and he wished that there was something he could do. "Unfortunately, it doesn't work that way," he said sympathetically. "You know if I could do anything at all, I definitely would."

"It just seems so unfair," Austin's shoulders slumped in disappointment.

"I know. Life isn't always fair though. Steve's a good kid, and he'll land on his feet," Sergeant Kenney responded, and then smiled at his son. "I'm proud of you for being there for him," he said. "Not everyone's lucky enough to have a friend like you."

Smiling back, Austin said, "Thanks, Dad."

"Now go have some fun. And remember to call me if anything goes wrong." Sergeant Kenney waved goodbye to Austin as he put the car in drive. He did a quick U-turn on the empty highway, kicking up dust as he did, and then headed back towards town.

Austin hopped on his bike and quickly chased after his friends.

Chapter 12

It didn't surprise Austin that Ryan was the one who complained the most as the boys pushed their way through the sharp stabbing bushes at the entrance of the dirt path. He had warned everyone that this would be the most painful part of the journey down to the beach, but he knew he would still hear plenty of gripes. Dylan complained a good amount as well, and since he had the widest frame of any of the Wendals, he was actually the one who had the hardest time making it through the heaviest parts of the brush. The sharp twigs and large branches scratched and cut at the boys' exposed limbs with each step they took.

Because he was wearing a tank top, Steve received quite a few deep gashes to his naked shoulders and arms. Getting his bike through the brush was also an extra challenge, because of the skimboard that was attached to its side, but Steve never complained.

Just as Ryan was yelling up from the back, asking again how much further they had to go, Austin broke through the last bit of brush and arrived at the open trail. Steve was right behind him, scraped all over, but still in good spirits. Then Dylan popped out next, looking annoyed, but also trying his best to act tough. And lastly, Ryan stumbled out of the brush, falling to the dirt floor in total anguish. After dusting themselves off and evaluating their cuts and scrapes, the boys checked out their new surroundings.

Austin pointed down the open trail. "The path is clear of brush from here on out but it's a really steep ride. So be careful," he advised.

Not paying any attention to his friend's warning, Steve

hopped on his bike and took off down the trail quickly and carelessly. Dylan looked at Austin laughing and then got on his bike and followed right behind Steve. As he mounted his bike, Ryan noticed the sharp rocks and twisty turns of the trail, and after a bit of hesitation, he started down the path moving slowly and carefully. Austin wanted to make sure his friend made it down the hill in one piece, so he decided he would stick close to Ryan.

When Austin and Ryan finally arrived at the cliff that overlooked the beach, Steve and Dylan were already there, standing in front of their bikes and staring down at the scenery below. Excited to show off his discovery, Austin dropped his bike to the ground and joined his friends at the edge of the cliff.

"Well, what do you think?" Austin asked, beaming with pride as he motioned towards the landscape all around them. The ocean water in the distance ahead of them was a deeper shade of blue than the boys had ever seen before, and they watched as perfectly shaped waves rolled towards the sandy shores of a gorgeous private beach cove at the bottom of the cliffs.

Steve admired the distant beach in awe. "It looks incredible down there," he whispered.

"I can't believe we didn't know this was here," Dylan said excitedly.

Noticing that there was no sign of civilization anywhere nearby, Ryan had a completely different take on their surroundings. He looked to the north and to the south, and then back up the cliffs behind them, and saw nothing but brush-covered wilderness and jagged cliff edges in every direction. Excitement wasn't at all what he was feeling. "You were right about it being secluded," he said tensely. "What happens if one of us gets hurt?"

Steve put his arm around Ryan. "Is that really all you can think about at a time like this?" he asked with a smirk.

Dylan was the first to notice the clearing just below them and the old RV that was parked all alone at the campsite. It looked strangely out of place to him, and he stared for a moment before he asked, "I'm assuming that's what we're here for?"

The boys collectively looked down at the crummy old RV. Looking even more ancient and rusty in the brightness of the noonday sun, the trailer creaked and screeched softly as the wind gently rocked it.

"Yep, that's it," Austin replied.

Ryan felt panicked when he saw the trailer. "Should we be standing here then? What if someone sees us?" he asked in a whisper.

"I told you, he's never here during the day," Austin replied as he pointed to the empty dirt spot next to the RV, where the boys saw tire tracks, but no car. "As long as the car's not there, we're good."

Ryan nodded his head, still not totally convinced.

The wind picked back up, and with it came a loud crash that made the boys jump. Ryan lept so hard that he nearly tripped backward over his bike.

Seeing how startled his friends were, Austin chuckled. "That gets me every time," he said, still laughing. Dylan looked at him questioningly, and Austin said, "It's just a loose latch on the RV; don't worry about it."

Then, a completely different noise came from down at the campsite, and the boys turned and stared back at the RV in silence.

"What was that?" Ryan whispered nervously.

"What was what?" asked Austin, hearing the noise but trying to downplay it, not wanting Ryan to get spooked.

"The noise," Ryan whispered aggressively. "After the crashing sound, there was another noise." His voice was shaky.

"You must be hearing things," Austin replied. But he wondered what the noise was as well.

"No, I heard it too," Dylan confirmed. "It was like a rattling sound. Almost like a metal chain or something. It definitely came from inside the RV."

"Yeah, I heard it," Steve said. "Maybe something fell over inside…from the gust of wind?" He didn't seem too concerned about it.

"Yeah, the wind makes all sorts of weird noises out here. Don't let it get to you," Austin assured his friends. "I promise you the hermit's not in there."

The boys went back to silently staring at the old RV, wanting to be sure. When nothing else was heard, Ryan felt a little better but still spoke in a paranoid whisper, "Either way, let's camp as far away from this place as possible."

"We can make camp on that cliff," Steve said, pointing to an area that was further down the coast and a lot higher up the hill. "We should have a good view of the RV from up there." The boys all turned to look at the spot Steve was talking about, which was a good distance away and was separated from their current location by more thick vegetation, wide canyons, and jagged cliff edges. No clear path to get to Steve's spot was visible.

"That looks perfect," Austin said enthusiastically. "He definitely won't be able to see us all the way up there."

Dylan and Ryan stared up the cliffs skeptically. "But how do we get there?" Ryan asked.

"We'll make a path," Steve replied confidently.

Dylan wasn't looking forward to starting another intense hike. "Why don't we just go look for the money right now?" he asked impatiently. "You said it yourself— the guy's not down there."

Being very stubborn about the timing of his plans, Austin was quick to respond. "No! We need to strategize first," he said assertively. "Now that you guys are here and can see what we're dealing with, I'll need your help finalizing our attack strategy."

"What's there to strategize about?" Dylan shot back. "We're just looking for big bags of money, right? Sounds pretty simple to me."

But before Dylan could finish his protest, Steve stepped in. "I don't want to haul this gear around any longer than we have to," he said. "I say we get to our spot and set up camp before we do anything else."

Ryan shook his head in enthusiastic agreement. "Yeah,

let's make camp now," he said anxiously. "I'm going to need some time to talk myself into this whole thing again." He stared down at the old RV. "Now that I've seen it in person, it's really giving me the creeps."

The boys glanced down at the campsite one more time. The wind had picked up a little and the RV was starting to make strange creaking noises again. Even in the daylight, there was something about the secluded campsite that made the hair stand up on the back of their necks.

He wouldn't admit to it, but even Dylan was becoming more unsettled about their plan as he looked at the RV below. "Okay," he conceded, his eyes still locked on the trailer. "Let's get to our camp."

Chapter 13

Linda Andretti was clearly disgusted as she cleaned leftover food and dirty dishes from off the messy diner table. Although she was used to cleaning up after other people by now, the filth that these last customers had left behind was extra repulsive. Ketchup had been smeared across the majority of the table's surface; cut up hot dogs had been smashed into the seat cushion of the booth; chewed up bits of hamburger patty were scattered everywhere; and an entire children's cup of milk had been spilled into a large puddle underneath the table. Linda didn't know how much more she could take. It was more than just the messes though. She was also sick and tired of dealing with demanding customers, ungrateful bosses, overdramatic co-workers, and poor tips.

On top of it all, Linda worried that the restaurant was at risk of going out of business soon. The outdated diner was in serious need of a makeover, but Management refused to spend money on improvements. Because of this, they were losing customers to many of the newer restaurants that were popping up all over town. Linda tried to be grateful just to have any job at all, but the fact that she had to deal with all of the restaurant's issues day-in and day-out, and still couldn't make ends meet, was slowly driving her into madness.

As she continued cleaning, she thought about her blown opportunity at the bank. Going for an interview there had been an uncharacteristically bold move for Linda, and surprisingly enough, she had felt like she had really hit it off with the bank manager. However, it hadn't taken long before her insecurities crept back in, and she convinced herself that there was no point in going back for the second interview and that she would be better off saving herself from the disappointment and embarrassment of trying and failing. It was a vicious cycle of self-sabotage that she couldn't seem to break free from.

After clearing most of the dirty dishes and leftover food from off the table and into the dish tub, Linda noticed the check holder hiding under a wet napkin at the back of the booth. She picked it up, dumped the loose coins that had been left behind into her hand, and added up the change in her head—seventy-five cents—another horrible tip. She took a deep breath and exhaled in frustration.

Another waitress, about the same age as Linda but with short, jet black hair and thick white-framed eyeglasses, stopped by the table and glanced at the change in Linda's hand. "Ouch," she said sympathetically. "And they were here for a long time, weren't they?"

"Yep," Linda said stoically. "Took up my best table for almost two hours." She opened up the pocket on the front of her apron and dumped the coins inside. "But I guess I shouldn't have expected anything more."

"I'm so sorry," the waitress responded.

"What can you do?" Linda said, trying to fake a smile. "Hopefully my day can only get better from here?"

"I wouldn't speak too soon," the waitress said grimly. "It looks like our favorite derelict just sat in your section." Looking disgusted, she pointed to a booth in the back corner of the restaurant.

A disheveled man wearing a dark blue baseball cap that covered his messy brown hair sat alone in the booth, silently reading the newspaper. His jean pants and plain white t-shirt looked like they hadn't been washed in weeks.

Grinning when she saw him, Linda said defensively, "Give the guy a break."

"Oh, come on. He's been eating here every day for how long now? And he can't even put on some clean clothes?" the waitress chided. "Maybe take a shower?"

It had been about two weeks that the man had been coming into the restaurant around the same time every day, always requesting to sit in the back corner of the diner. The other waitresses had made a big deal about not wanting to serve him, mostly because of his dirty appearance and musty smell, but also because they had found him to be very unfriendly.

Rumors were floating around the restaurant about where the man came from and what he was doing in town, but Linda didn't pay them any attention. She was as curious as anyone about his backstory, but because of her own recent life challenges she was slow to judge others who looked to be less fortunate than herself. She felt bad for the guy, and whenever she waited on him, she tried to be as friendly as possible and to respect his privacy. As long as she did this, the two of them seemed to get along just fine.

"You know, they're calling him the Cat Man," the waitress said with a gossipy grin. Linda gave her a skeptical look, but the waitress continued anyway. "A couple of weeks back, Whitney was out sweeping the front sidewalk when she saw him pull up in his run-down car. He went straight to the back of the car and opened the trunk, and Whitney's sure she saw a black trash bag with a dead cat inside."

Linda laughed out loud. "And you believe that?" she asked, and then put her hand on the waitress's shoulder. "Listen, I've learned that you can't take half of the stuff you hear in this place seriously." She looked over at the disheveled man who sat patiently at her table. "He's quiet, he pays in cash, and he always leaves a good tip," she said. "He can come sit in my booth any time he wants, even if he does smell a little."

Smiling back at Linda, the waitress jeered playfully, "I think someone has a crush."

Linda laughed again. Then a look of annoyance came over her face as she signaled towards a different booth. "Now these guys over here are a different story," she said.

The waitress looked at the booth in question, where three clean-cut men in their early forties sat and ate their meals.

Dressed in collared shirts, dark slacks, and expensive dress shoes, the men laughed loudly as they discussed business and politics.

"I don't know, they're kinda cute," the waitress said. "And they look like they've got thick wallets." A smile came over her face and she raised her eyebrows up and down at Linda. "You could sure use a man with some money right about now, couldn't you?"

Looking repulsed, Linda contested, "No, thanks. They're a bunch of arrogant jerks. And if the tall one keeps hitting on me, I swear I'm gonna scream."

"I don't mind arrogant jerks," the waitress said grinning. Then, noticing some new customers arriving at one of her booths, she quickly said goodbye to Linda and headed over to her table.

Linda grabbed the heavy tub of dirty dishes and carried it to the back of the restaurant. Once there, she dropped the tub in a large sink and began to hose off the dishes one by one. Then she placed them into a large industrial dishwasher.

A shrill voice shouted from somewhere behind her. "Linda! Can you come in here for a minute?"

Linda immediately felt annoyed, as she was convinced that it was never a good thing when management wanted to see her. After putting the last bit of her dishes into the sink, she rinsed her grimy hands the best she could, and dried them on the front of her apron. Then she took a deep breath and headed slowly down a long hallway that was lined on both sides with condiment boxes and canned goods. At the end of the hall, there was an open door with a small plaque on it that read, "Manager's Office." Linda walked through the door.

An overweight, balding man in a mustard colored dress shirt and a *Jerry Garcia* tie sat at his desk on a swivel chair that looked much too small for his round body. He didn't acknowledge Linda at first but was busy punching numbers into a large calculator and writing hastily on a sheet of paper in a large three-ring binder. Linda waited patiently. Finally, when the man was satisfied with his work, he put his pen down and looked at Linda.

Skipping any type of pleasantries, the man went straight into business. "I've got to give your Thursday night shift to Nicole," he said in his same shrill voice, and then stared at Linda without giving any further explanation.

At first, Linda was shocked by his bluntness, but then she quickly became angry when she realized what he had said. "What?" she asked, surprised. "Why?"

"Nicole's starting classes at the community college on Tuesday nights, so she needs to pick up a different shift," he said, unapologetically. "And frankly, Nicole has been showing a lot of promise here, and I think she is ready for a busier shift."

Linda stared into the manager's beady little eyes, trying to hold back her fury. Resisting the urge to scream, she responded to him with as much patience as she could muster. "I've been here twice as long as her, and you already took my Sunday night shift," she said. "And I really need the money right now."

The manager thought for a minute and seemed to soften up a little. "Look—it's already done. I can give you her Tuesday night shift if you want it, but that's the best I can do for you," he said with the tiniest hint of empathy.

"Tuesdays are the worst shift of the week," Linda whined. "No one makes any money on Tuesday night."

The manager went back to writing in his notebook. "I'll give the Tuesday shift to Becky then. If you don't want it," he responded nonchalantly.

"No, no, no," Linda shot back in defeat. "I'll take Tuesday night," she said reluctantly, realizing it was a battle she couldn't win. Management at the restaurant treated most of their employees like they were a dime a dozen and could be replaced in a moment's notice. There were only a select few waitresses that were given special treatment, and Linda was not one of them. "Can I at least have the closing shift on Tuesday night?" Linda pleaded.

The manager looked back at her with an arrogant smile. "Come on, Linda," he said with a condescending chuckle. "You know you haven't proven yourself to be closer material."

Once again, Linda had to bite her tongue to refrain from giving him a piece of her mind. She wanted so badly to throw her apron in his face and storm out of the restaurant, never to return again. But she thought about the mortgage she was behind on, and the past due bills that were piling up on her kitchen counter, and the car that needed replacing, and those thoughts kept her from doing anything she might regret. Instead, she gave her manager a phony smile and then turned around and headed back out to her tables.

Chapter 14

After leaving the old RV, the Wendals had traveled further down the coast and back up the cliffs, traversing around deep gullies and climbing up intense inclines. The trip was rough, and the boys were forced to cut their own path through the brush, but eventually they had arrived at the designated area and had found a nice flat clearing on the top of a large cliff. They were completely exhausted, but they felt good about the spot they had chosen and were excited to make camp.

With a spectacular view of the surrounding landscape, their elevated campsite was the perfect place to spy on the old RV. They were close enough to see the hermit's clearing with the help of Austin's binoculars, but far enough away that the man would hopefully never even realize they were there. So far things were going very much according to Austin's plan.

Rummaging through his backpack, Austin carefully organized the gear that he had brought with him. He picked up a large bag of water balloons and smiled to himself as he looked at them.

Steve and Dylan were on the far end of the campsite, away from the cliff edge, setting up their spacious eight-man tent. Looking for the perfect area to place the tent, they argued about where the flattest spot of ground was until Dylan finally won the argument, and they secured the tent into the dirt with a hammer and some stakes.

Ryan gathered large rocks from all over the clearing to be used for the fire pit he was building in the middle of their campsite. Noticing a perfectly sized rock underneath some thick bushes, he got down on his hands and knees and slowly reached under the brush. To his surprise and horror, the bushes started shaking violently right in front of him. Ryan jumped backward, letting out a shriek of fear, and falling straight onto his back. Stopping what they were doing, the other boys looked over to see what all the commotion was about. Ryan nervously scooted backward on his butt, trying to flee from the creature in the bushes. Suddenly, a small grey squirrel hopped out of the brush and harmlessly scurried back up the side of the cliff and away from their camp.

Dylan burst into hysterical laughter. "You should have used your bear mace!" he shouted from across the camp. "There are wild animals in these parts!"

Ryan's face turned a deep shade of red.

Fighting off the urge to laugh himself, Austin rushed over to his friend and helped him to his feet. "Well, at least no one else was around to see that?" Austin offered, smiling and shrugging his shoulders.

Dusting himself off, Ryan responded, "Thanks, Austin," and Dylan and Steve went back to their business. Then Ryan noticed the pack of water balloons in Austin's hand. "What do you have there?" he asked.

In a discouraged tone, Austin replied, "I brought a pack of water balloons, but I didn't think about how we would fill them up."

A big smile came over Ryan's face. "Come with me, young Padawan," he said confidently, and he led Austin to where his bag was lying on the ground. After unzipping the bag, he pulled out a plastic water bottle with a squeeze top and then reached out his hand and said, "Give me a balloon." Austin handed Ryan one of the balloons from the plastic bag, and Ryan secured the water balloon to the small opening on the top of the water bottle, turned the bottle upside down, and squeezed. The balloon quickly filled with water, and, once it was the right size, Ryan pulled the balloon off and tied the end shut.

Austin was amazed. "You're so flippin' smart, Ry!" he shouted excitedly as he grabbed the balloon and hefted it up and down in his hand. "Why didn't I think of that?" Austin looked over at Dylan, who was kneeling down by the tent, digging into his own backpack. After winding up like he was throwing a pitch in the world series, Austin chucked the balloon hard at his brother, and the balloon crashed onto the top of Dylan's backpack, splashing water everywhere.

Dylan stood up in anger and saw Austin and Ryan laughing. "You tools!" he shouted. "You just soaked all my protein bars!"

Continuing to laugh, Austin mocked, "Oh no, now you can't eat every seven minutes... whatever will you do?"

Dylan took a few angry steps in Austin's direction before Steve stepped in front of him with his hand out, signaling for him to back down. Steve turned to Austin and Ryan. "Camp looks good," he shouted. "So what's the game plan now?"

"It's a beautiful day," Austin replied. "I figured we'd head down to the beach for the rest of the afternoon."

Pausing for a moment before he spoke, Steve said, "Well, I've been thinking. We got here plenty early, and we set up camp so quickly. And seeing that we have tons of daylight left... I think we'd all agree we might as well go check out this RV right now." He looked at Ryan and Dylan, hoping for their approval.

Austin shook his head in disagreement. "My plan was to have some fun first and enjoy our time together," he argued. "Then we were going to spend the evening scoping the place out and coming up with an attack strategy."

"Dylan was right. What strategy do we need?" Steve asked assuredly. "We go to the RV, we look around, and we find out whether or not this money is hiding out there. Isn't that exactly how you described it to us? You said it would be easy, right?"

Dylan looked at his brother and shrugged his shoulders. "I agree with Steve. You did promise it would be straightforward," he said. "So we might as well get it over with now."

Now everyone looked at Ryan. Clearly not ready for the pressure of making the decision, Ryan thought about it, and then looked concerned. "What if someone's there right now?

I'm telling you, I heard something inside that RV," he said.

"I guess we just have to trust Austin's intel," Steve replied, looking at Austin for confirmation.

"The hermit's definitely not in that RV right now," Austin sounded confident. "I'm absolutely sure of it." He hesitated for a moment and then decided it wasn't worth an argument. "I guess we can do it now if that's what everyone prefers." Austin looked around at his friends. "All Wendals in favor of going right now, raise your hand."

Dylan and Steve's hands shot up quickly. Ryan hesitated, still nervous about going anywhere near the RV at all. But with Steve and Dylan staring daggers at him, he gave in to the pressure and slowly raised his hand.

Austin looked slightly disappointed but knew there was nothing he could do. "Alright, guys, majority rules," he said with a little reluctance. "Let's get going then."

The sun was at its highest point in the sky—meaning it was the hottest time of day—when the Wendals made their descent towards the old RV. Without their bikes and their camping gear on their backs, they were able to move more quickly and fit through the brush more easily. But because of the scorching heat and the fact that they were already tired from the last journey up the hill, the boys struggled with this trek more than the last one.

At one point, while crossing a very narrow pathway high on top of a steep rock, Ryan lost his footing and would have fallen fifteen feet straight onto some jagged boulders, if Dylan hadn't caught him by the shirt, saving him from serious injury.

Austin continued to push the boys forward, until finally, they breached through a last patch of brush and found themselves on top of a very small cliff, just a stone's throw away from the old RV.

Speaking through heavy, exhausted breaths, Ryan cried, "I'm never letting you convince me to go on an adventure, ever again."

Austin, Dylan, and Steve were all feeling pretty exhausted as well. "Let's take a breather and scope the place out a little," Austin said. All four boys nodded in agreement and then laid down on their stomachs at the edge of the small cliff, overlooking the RV.

Dylan stared at the rundown trailer. "It's even creepier from up close," he remarked.

"Agreed," Ryan said. "That thing must be forty years old. How do you think this guy got it down here?"

"I bet you it's been here since before we were born," Austin responded, also seeing it up close for the first time. "My guess is that our robber found it abandoned out here and decided to make it his hideout spot."

"Why haven't the police found it yet?" Steve wondered out loud.

"They would never even think to come out here unless they had a tip," Austin said confidently. "It's too far off the radar. I'm sure that's why he chose it. It's the perfect hiding spot."

"Well if he was so smart, he wouldn't keep his money in the same spot where he sleeps," Ryan interjected. "He'd be much better off hiding it somewhere else, just in case the police found him here."

Dylan looked at Ryan, annoyed. "Well if we run into him down there, please make sure to give him that recommendation," he said sarcastically.

Ryan knew that Dylan was joking, but the very mention of possibly coming face to face with a fugitive criminal out here sent his mind back into panic mode, and his face went pale.

Austin noticed his friend's frightened look. "We're not going to run into anyone down there," he tried to assure him.

"But what if you're wrong?" Ryan blurted out. "What if he drives back down the hill early and catches us snooping around in his RV?"

"He won't come back until sundown; he never does," Austin asserted. He looked up the cliff, in the direction the car would come from if it did make an early descent, and he thought for a moment. "But if you're still worried, then why don't you take lookout? You can stand guard on that cliff up there, and if you see him coming down the trail you can yell down to us." Austin pointed to a spot higher up the cliff where Ryan would have a good view.

Looking up at the cliff, Ryan gulped nervously. "Go up there alone?" he asked.

"Well you don't have to," Austin replied. "You can come into the RV with us."

Ryan looked back at the creepy old RV and thought about all the horrors that could be waiting inside. "You're right. I'll take lookout," he said resolutely, and then he got up and started climbing up the hill carefully.

Steve stood up next. "Everything looks clear to me. Let's do this," he exclaimed as he started to make his way down the last bit of hill, and Dylan and Austin followed close behind him. The three boys dropped down onto the flat clearing where the trailer was parked, and they headed towards the RV.

A strong gust of wind blew loudly through the campsite towards the boys, and a horrific stench filled the air. All three of the boys covered their mouths and plugged their noses simultaneously.

Steve looked like he was going to be sick. "What in the world is that smell?" he lamented, barely being heard over the loud wind.

Austin's eyes were watering and he could barely speak. "Maybe it's coming from the RV's waste tank?"

"It doesn't smell like poop," Dylan cried, still plugging his nose and waving his hand rapidly in front of his face. "Whatever it is, it's worse than Ryan's belly button!"

The wind slowly calmed down, making the campsite quiet again, and the horrible smell receded just enough for the boys to be able to bear it. Still feeling a little sick, Steve signaled for the others to keep moving, and then he trudged forward in the lead. Austin and Dylan followed behind him, the lingering residue of the putrid smell continuing to burn in their nostrils.

The three boys approached the back side of the RV cautiously, and even though they planned on no one being inside, they still moved as quietly as possible, just in case Austin was wrong.

Then Dylan stopped dead in his tracks, and asked in a startled whisper, "Did you hear that?"

Steve and Austin came to a quick stop as well, and stood in complete silence, listening intently. For a moment there was nothing. Then they all heard it again, and they looked at each other, confirming that it wasn't just their imaginations. At first, it was a soft sound, and they were unable to make out what it was, knowing only that it came from inside the RV. But growing louder and louder, the sound became unmistakable, and they eventually recognized it as the clanking of a metal chain. Not knowing what to do, the boys stood silently and stared at the old RV.

Suddenly, the near silence of the campsite was shattered by the loudest sneeze that the three boys had ever heard. The sound of the sneeze seemed to echo off the sides of the cliffs and reverberate throughout the entire canyon. All three boys cringed as they looked behind them to see Ryan, standing at his lookout spot in the distance, wiping his nose on the sleeve of his shirt. Noticing that his friends were staring at him from afar, he cupped his hands around his mouth and yelled, "Sorry, guys. Just my allergies!"

His yell seemed even louder than the sneeze, and the boys at the RV cringed, even more, knowing now that whatever was inside the RV would now surely know that they were there. Austin, Steve, and Dylan frantically and silently put their fingers up to their mouths, giving Ryan the universal sign for *Shhhh!*

Immediately feeling panicked again, and not knowing what his friends were going on about, Ryan assumed the worst and he quickly covered his mouth with both of his hands and went still.

The three boys turned back around in silence and faced the old RV. The sound of the clanking chains had stopped, but another sound had taken its place: a deep, growling sound that was becoming more intense. Hearing this sound, the boys quickly went from being confused to being completely terrified. Then the sound of the rattling chain started back up again, but this time at an accelerated pace. The boys were too scared to move, and everything seemed to happen absurdly fast. They heard the creaky RV door open on the other side of the trailer, and then slam shut abruptly. Then, from around the corner of the RV, a large and angry dog came charging straight at them.

Before any of the boys could react, the dog was already right in front of them. It pounced at Dylan with surprising quickness and knocked him straight onto his back with a powerful force. Growling fiercely, the massive animal mounted itself on top of Dylan, attempting to chomp down on any part of his body that it could sink its teeth into. Adrenaline filled Dylan's body and he immediately began to punch and kick at the dog, fighting for his life with everything he had. He landed a strong kick to the animal's head, and the dog reeled backward, yelping in pain. Stunned only momentarily, the creature recovered fast and clenched down onto Dylan's shoe with its powerful jaws, sinking its teeth deep into the rubber sole.

Austin and Steve raced forward, coming to Dylan's aid. They grabbed their friend by each arm and tried to pull him away from the dog with all of their might. But the dog was relentless and, refusing to let go, it growled deeply through its clenched jaws. Dylan kicked and kicked until he eventually landed another shot to the front of the dog's nose. Finally, the dog released its grip and retreated backward just long enough for Austin and Steve to pull Dylan away from the angry animal.

Not wasting any time, the dog quickly shook off Dylan's kick and charged at the boys again. This time it directed its vicious attack at Austin, and it snarled loudly as it shot towards him. Stumbling backward in fear, Austin lost his footing and fell hard onto his butt. He crossed his arms in front of him in an attempt to shield his body from the impending attack, and he clenched his eyes shut in frightened anticipation. Like a graceful lion going in for the kill, the dog leaped off the ground and flew through the air towards Austin, but then suddenly came to a jolted stop in the middle of the air, and fell hard onto the ground just in front of the boys.

Luckily for Austin, the thick metal chain that was keeping the dog bound to the old RV had been extended to its maximum length, and the boys had stumbled back just far enough to be slightly outside of the dog's reach. Austin exhaled in grateful relief.

Growling and shaking violently, the irate animal fought with all its strength to break free of the restricting chain, but to no avail. Steve and Dylan, grateful for their narrow escape, helped Austin to his feet, and all three boys dusted themselves off and checked their bodies for wounds. Other than a few minor bruises and scratches, they each seemed relatively unscathed.

Ryan had come running down the cliffside as quickly as he could and was now reunited with his friends. "Are you guys okay?" he asked frantically. He was both sorry that he hadn't been there to help and at the same time grateful that he had missed out on the intense scuffle.

With his pride being hurt more than anything else, Dylan was very angry. "Never been better!" he shouted sarcastically. "I love being almost mauled to death!"

A smile came over Ryan's face. "I bet my bear spray doesn't look so stupid to you now, does it?" he laughed, feeling vindicated. His comment enraged Dylan even more.

Looking puzzled, Steve turned to Austin. "You're telling me," he said in a bothered tone. "That in all of your stake-outs of this place, you never once noticed a guard dog?" Dylan and Ryan looked at Austin, with the same question on their minds.

Austin was completely stunned. It was a very fair question and he wasn't sure how he could have missed something so important. "No. I never saw the dog once," he said, baffled at his mistake. "I guess it never had a reason to come out of the RV when I was here? I mean, I only came for short stints first thing in the morning and late at night..." he thought back to his spying sessions at the campsite but couldn't recall a single clue that would have given away the fact that there was a dog living in the RV.

"You told us you had this all figured out," Steve said, disappointed and slightly angry. "We trusted you."

"Yeah, some detective you are," Dylan said scornfully. He looked over at the snarling dog, picked up a small rock from off the ground, and then wound his arm up aggressively and threw the rock at the animal as hard as he could. The rock just barely overshot the dog and crashed into the dirt behind it. Dylan quickly reached down to pick up another rock.

"Wait a minute here!" Ryan exclaimed, grabbing Dylan by the arm before he could take another shot. "The dog's just trying to protect his home. Look at the poor thing."

All four of the boys looked at the animal, which, now that they could see it clearly, appeared to be an abnormally large pit bull terrier. The dog had finally given up on trying to free itself from the metal chain and now laid on its stomach, unflinchingly staring at the boys and growling a deep throaty growl.

But despite its intimidating snarl, the boys now noticed how pathetic the dog looked. It was extremely tall and incredibly long, but also looked greatly malnourished and woefully mangy. Its ribs were severely protruding through the flesh of its skinny torso, and its eyes looked deeply sunken into its skull. Its coat of fur was patchy and balding, and the hair that did remain looked dull and brittle. The dog even appeared to be missing a couple of its teeth. All in all, it was a very pitiful sight, and the boys' fear of the dog began to fade, and a touch of sympathy for the creature set it.

"Do you think he ever gets fed?" Steve asked, concerned.

"I don't know, but he doesn't look healthy," Ryan responded, sympathetically. "And I'm sure it gets lonely being out here by himself all day." Ryan knew what it was like to feel discarded and mistreated, and because of that, it was easy for him to feel a kinship to any creature that was on the fringe of society.

Dylan's rage had diminished for the most part, and he let

the rock in his hand fall to the ground. "I ain't planning on being his next meal though," he said resolutely. "Let's get out of here."

Austin quickly shot back defensively, "We can't leave yet."

Steve pointed to the dog. "You wanna try and get in there now?" he asked Austin incredulously.

Looking nervous again, Ryan said, "Yeah, man, I haven't even had my rabies shots."

Austin looked at his friends, who seemed defeated and exhausted. Then he looked back at the dog, who was still guarding the RV and appeared ready to attack if the boys went in for a second try. "Okay, okay," he relented. "We can come back again tomorrow. That will give us some time to think about what we do with the dog."

"We're just going to leave him here alone?" Ryan asked. "Maybe we figure out how to unchain him without getting our arms bit off?" he asked hopefully.

"We can't do that," Steve replied. "When the guy comes home tonight he'd know that someone had been here."

"Yeah, we can't take the risk," Austin agreed quickly, putting his hand on Ryan's shoulder. "He's obviously survived out here for quite a while. I'm sure he'll be alright," he reassured his friend.

Ryan tried to understand and nodded his head.

Dylan rubbed his stomach. "More important topic—what are we doing for dinner?" he asked. "All this excitement has really worked up my appetite."

After thinking for a moment, Austin decided, "We can grab our bikes back at camp and then head up to the main road for some food."

"I'm not riding up that hill again," Dylan objected. "Just bring me back a hot dog and a slice of pizza from the liquor store. I'll take a nap back at camp instead."

Chapter 15

Linda was feeling defeated as she folded white linen napkins by herself in the back of the dining room of the restaurant. She wondered how she had let herself become so trapped in her current situation and how she had made such a mess of everything. She thought again about how badly she wanted to quit her job at the restaurant, but she knew she just didn't presently have the inner strength, nor the financial means to do such a thing.

The waitress with the short black hair approached Linda, looking concerned. "Is he really taking away your Thursday night shift?" she asked angrily.

"Yep," Linda responded, not looking up from her napkins. "He's giving the shift to Nicole."

The waitress became even more upset. "Well, what a coincidence," she said loudly. "Shauna saw that slimeball hanging out with Nicole at the promenade Saturday night. Supposedly they were getting pretty cozy together." She looked around the restaurant to make sure that no one else was listening. "I guess that's the only way to get a good shift around here."

Not surprised at all, Linda said, "If that's the case, then you can count me out. I'd rather be jobless."

The waitress continued to get worked up. "He can't do that to you. You should..."

"Hold that thought," Linda cut her friend off, sounding annoyed. "It's this guy again." One of the customers from the table of arrogant businessmen—the tallest one of the group—was waving urgently across the dining room of the restaurant, trying to get Linda's attention, while the two other men at the table laughed. "Must be *really* important," Linda said sarcastically. She finished folding the last napkin she was working on and then headed out towards the table.

As Linda got closer, the tall businessman, who was obviously the leader of the group, signaled for his two friends to quiet down, and the two men promptly stopped laughing. Linda tried her best to put her frustration away and to continue to do her job in a professional manner. "What can I do for you gentlemen?" she asked with the friendliest voice she could offer.

Empty plates lay on the table from a large meal and each man had a coffee mug in front of him. The tall man looked Linda up and down with a smile and then spoke with a flirtatious voice. "I was just wondering if you could pour me some more coffee, honey," the man said, and his two friends began to giggle like adolescents.

Linda gave the men an awkward smile and then grabbed the coffee pot from the warming station behind her. When she turned back around to them, it was obvious that the tall man had moved his coffee mug further back away from Linda, forcing her to lean over the table to fill the mug.

The man smiled deviously and nodded in approval, staring at Linda as she leaned over the table and poured the coffee. "That's it, sweetie, keep it coming," he said in a way that gave Linda the creeps. The two other men continued their immature giggling.

Linda finished pouring the coffee. "Enjoy," she said briskly, hoping to leave the table as quickly as possible.

"Now hold it right there," the man said laughing. "Don't go running away on us just yet."

With a pit in her stomach, Linda took a deep breath. She tried to stay calm but was beginning to feel very uncomfortable. "What else can I do for you?" she asked, her smile now long gone.

The tall man smiled at her. "Well, we were having a debate over here about your age," he said, and then turned and looked at his friends, who were smiling sheepishly. "My pals here think you're in your forties, but I say you can't be a day over thirty-five. So who's right?" The three men all stared at Linda, waiting for her response.

It was starting to show on Linda's face that she was done playing nice. "That's really none of your business," she replied sternly.

All three of the men laughed together, and the tall man slapped the table with the palm of his hand as he howled in delight. "You see, Bill," he said to his friend, once he had stopped laughing. "I told you that it wasn't polite to ask a woman about her age." His friend continued to laugh. Linda wished to be anywhere else but there at that moment, and she turned to leave the table. "Wait a minute," the tall man shouted with more laughter. Linda reluctantly stopped and turned back towards the men, feeling trapped. The tall man stopped laughing and calmed his voice down. "I'm sorry," he said, sounding sincere. "That isn't really important anyway. The bottom line is, you look very good for your age." He gave Linda the same devious smile as before. "There *is* something I need for real though."

Linda felt a sharp pang of anxiety as she waited for his next request.

No longer laughing, the man now looked slightly concerned. "You see, the problem is…" he said. "I lost my phone number. So I was wondering if I could have yours?" He looked back at his friends and all three of the men burst into laughter again.

Linda felt embarrassed and angry as the men laughed at her expense. She wanted to give the tall man a real piece of her mind but resisted the urge. At the same time, she refused to encourage their behavior. "Sorry, but I don't go out with customers," she responded coldly, clutching tightly to the coffee pot still in her hands.

The tall man's two friends laughed even harder at Linda's rejection of their friend. No longer amused, the tall man looked shocked and embarrassed. "Well that's no way to earn a good tip," he said to Linda in a haughty tone.

Linda bit her tongue again, refraining from saying one of the many responses that were floating around in her mind. "That's okay," she finally said bluntly. "I don't need your money."

The tall man grew red in the face while his friends continued to laugh at him.

Surprised at herself for the way she was holding her ground, Linda felt a tinge of pride, and she gave the men a disdainful smile and then quickly turned and tried to leave. But to her horror, she was unable to walk away. Something was physically keeping her from leaving. Looking down, Linda realized that the tall man had grabbed onto her apron, and was holding her tightly in her place.

"Wait just a second, sugar," the man said in a voice that sent chills up Linda's spine. "I didn't say we were done here."

Feeling like the room was spinning all around her, Linda yanked at her apron, hoping that the man would let her go—but he didn't. With the situation escalating so quickly, she suddenly felt numb and didn't know what to do. Then something came over her, and without realizing what she was doing, Linda lifted her left foot and stomped down as hard as she could on top of the tall man's shiny dress shoe that was poking out from underneath the table.

The man let go of her apron and quickly covered his mouth with both of his hands in an attempt to muffle his shriek of pain. The man's two friends stopped their laughter and looked at their friend, completely shocked by what had just happened. Then they turned and stared angrily at Linda.

Thoughts swirled through Linda's mind at a million miles an hour and she was filled with intense anxiety, almost paralyzing her. She didn't know if she should apologize to the tall man, or if she should tell him how much he deserved what he got. Instead, she turned and walked away from the table as quickly as she could, holding back tears as she went.

Linda had almost made it back to the kitchen when she noticed that the disheveled customer in the back corner was trying to get her attention. Stopping in front of the man's table, she tried to keep her emotions in check. "What do you need?!" she blurted out harshly, clearly on the verge of a complete breakdown.

The man stared up at her in total confusion, and then looked at the coffee pot that Linda was now hugging tightly to her chest. "I just needed some more of that coffee," the man said softly.

Feeling even more embarrassed, Linda gasped and released her tight grip on the pot. "Of course. I'm so sorry," she muttered, trying not to make a scene. Leaning over the table anxiously, she started to pour the coffee into the mug in front of the man. But she was so flustered by what had happened at the other table that her hands shook uncontrollably as she poured. Then, right before the mug was full, her trembling got the best of her, and she clumsily knocked the mug of hot coffee over, spilling the coffee all over the table. The coffee flooded onto the man's lap, and the man yelped in pain and surprise and quickly jumped out of his seat.

Linda was mortified. She turned and grabbed a towel from the cleaning station behind her, and then rushed to clean the man off. Not wanting her help, the man grabbed the towel out of her hand and started to clean himself.

"I'm so sorry. I can't believe I did that," Linda cried nervously. She was still trembling and looked like she was close to crying. "I'll get this cleaned up right away, and then I'll get my manager. Your meal will be on us." She spoke rapidly. "And I'll pay for your dry cleaning, I just need to get your information."

Remaining surprisingly calm, the man stopped wiping his pants, took a deep breath, and looked around the dining room, seeing that the majority of the restaurant's customers were nosily staring back at him. The restaurant had become deathly silent, and the three businessmen watched the scene from their booth with smiles on their faces. Suddenly looking nervous, the disheveled man pulled his baseball cap lower over his dirty face. "No," he said quietly to Linda. "No managers. Just the check."

Linda was confused. "No, we can't charge you for this meal," she said. "It'll just take a second to get the manager. Just let me clean up real quick." Linda went quickly to the back of the restaurant, frantically searched around for cleaning supplies, and then grabbed a wet rag and some more large towels.

But by the time she got back to the table, the man was gone, and a feeling of panic rushed over her. With her heart pounding in her chest, she looked all around the dining room, but couldn't see the man anywhere. Then she noticed a thick wad of cash, left on a dry spot in the middle of the table. She grabbed the folded-up stack of money—the bills were crisp and brand new—and she counted it carefully. The man had left enough to cover the entire bill, plus give Linda a very generous tip.

Confused at what had just happened, Linda exhaled slowly. She looked back at the table the businessmen had been sitting at and saw that they were gone as well. She didn't expect to find a tip left behind at their table. The waitress with the jet black hair rushed over to console her, and Linda buried her head in her friend's shoulder and cried.

Chapter 16

Back at the convenience store, Austin filled a giant styrofoam cup with Dr. Pepper from the fountain soda machine. He had already grabbed a personal pre-cooked pepperoni pizza from the hot food rack, as well as a large bag of Doritos Cool Ranch chips, and a box of Twinkies. Now he just needed something to wash it all down. The boys had worked up quite an appetite on their strenuous ride back up the cliffs and were grateful to have such an array of processed food in front of them—and no parents to stop them from eating all the junk their stomachs could handle.

Steve had already paid for his food and was scarfing down a hot dog while he browsed the store's small magazine rack, and Ryan was outside, across the parking lot, making his mandatory check-in call to his mom from the pay phone. Figuring Ryan would be on the phone for a while, Austin joined Steve at the magazine rack after he had paid for his meal.

Looking over Steve's shoulder, Austin shoved a slice of pizza into his mouth. He saw that Steve was reading an article about his favorite basketball player, Reggie Miller, in *Slam Magazine*. "Why you reading about that old man?" Austin asked with his mouth full.

Steve jeered back in defense, "Doesn't matter how old he is. He's still going to destroy the Lakers this season."

Austin laughed out loud sarcastically. "No chance! Kobe is getting better and better every year," he argued. "He's going to be the best there ever was. Just wait and see."

"Come on man, get real," Steve responded. "Reggie drops threes all over Kobe every time they play each other. Kobe can't handle him."

The boys continued to argue playfully.

Ryan stood outside at the pay phone, his backpack strapped on his shoulders, and his bike on the ground next to him. Looking bothered, he held the phone's black handset up to his ear and listened to his mother ramble. It embarrassed him that he was the only one of the Wendals who had to check in with his mom while on a one-night camping trip.

Ryan's mom had always been overprotective, but he had really hoped she would've relaxed a little by the time he had gotten to high school. Things had seemed to only be getting worse though. He loved his Mom, but felt like it was time for him to start being a little more independent and for her to start trusting him more. He wished he could get her to see that she couldn't protect him from the outside world forever.

Ready to add time to his call if he needed to, Ryan rubbed two dimes together in his right hand as he spoke to his Mom. He could see Steve and Austin through the convenience store window laughing and filling their bellies with junk, and he wished to be inside the store with them.

Ryan heard the laughter of several young people arriving from behind him, and he saw their shadows approaching quickly. He figured it was someone needing to use the phone, which gave him more reason to end his call as soon as possible. "Yes, I've been reapplying my sunscreen every two hours," Ryan said into the phone, looking even more annoyed as his mom continued to badger him with questions. "Yes, I've got the bear spray just in case, but I haven't had to use it." He anxiously listened again. "No, I won't stay up too late tonight. Listen, I really have to go now mom, someone else needs to use the phone. I love you. Goodbye." And he hung up the phone before his mom could get another word in.

The shadows behind him grew larger, and Ryan could feel someone getting oddly close behind him. He turned around to see who was encroaching on his space, and when he saw who it was, his heart instantly went cold in his chest.

"Mommy, I promise I'm wearing clean underwear," Tyler mocked in a childish voice. He and his two goon friends laughed hysterically together, positioned with their bikes just feet in front of Ryan, cutting him off from any potential path of escape.

Terror filled Ryan's body as he stared at the boys. From his point of view, with the sun low at the bullies' backs, the three boys looked to him like dark shadowy creatures from some terrifying underworld.

"Mommy, I'm scared of the dark!" one of the bully friends cried in an even more over-the-top mock voice, and the three boys laughed even harder.

Fear robbing him of his ability to move or speak, Ryan stared back at the bullies in silence and dropped the two dimes he had been holding into the dirt below him. His young life seemed to quickly flash before his eyes as he wondered how it was possible that he was now standing face to face with one of his worst nightmares.

Moving in closer to their prey, the bullies stopped laughing.

"What are you doing out here all alone?" Tyler asked with a ruthless smile.

One of Tyler's bully friends cackled, "I'm glad we decided to come riding out here today. I guess it's fate that we found him here."

"Yeah, without his Wendal buddies to protect him," the other goon said as he shook his head grimly.

Ryan suddenly remembered his friends, and he looked back at the convenience store. Through the large front window of the shop, he saw Steve and Austin still arguing heatedly. But with their backs turned to the situation, they had no clue what was happening outside. Ryan tried to call for them, but his voice still didn't seem to be working. He looked back at the bullies, and the three goons laughed like a pack of hyenas, excited about capturing their next meal.

"I warned you what would happen if I ever caught any of you Wendals outside of school," Tyler said, salivating at the mouth. He lowered his bike to the ground, and his two bully friends followed his lead.

"Yeah, you were definitely warned," one of the bullies said with another evil laugh, and the three boys continued to move closer to Ryan.

Watching the boys close in on him, Ryan somehow mustered up enough courage to finally speak. "What do you want from me?" he asked with a shaky voice.

The three bullies looked at each other and then burst into laughter again. When Tyler's laughter finally calmed down, he thought for a moment before answering. "Well, I wasn't planning on this little interaction today, but I guess now that you're here, it would be a great time to send a message to the Wendals," he said somberly.

"I can give them a message for you," Ryan stammered out. "What do you want me to tell them?"

The three bullies laughed even harder. "This is not the kind of message that involves words," Tyler replied as he grabbed Ryan by the strap of his backpack and pulled him in close. Ryan could feel Tyler's sour breath on his face, but even more disconcerting than his breath was the savage look that he saw in Tyler's eyes.

"Get down on your knees and beg for mercy," Tyler said, snarling. "And I might let you live when this is all over." His tone left Ryan with little doubt of his sincerity.

Attempting to fight off the fear and panic he was feeling, Ryan quickly ran through his options in his mind. He looked back at his friends through the store window and thought about calling out to them again. But knowing that Tyler would cover his mouth, or begin the pummeling before anyone even heard him scream, he decided it would be useless. For a moment, Ryan thought about doing what Tyler asked, and begging for mercy.

But then, he thought about all the times he had given into bullying, and he remembered the deep shame he felt every time he did. Then he remembered what Steve had said to him about standing up for himself. And somehow, he found the will to stand his ground, and instead of begging for mercy, he stared at Tyler dead in the eyes.

Surprised by Ryan's noncompliance, Tyler said, "And I thought you were the smart one." His two bully friends moved in even closer, anticipating the inevitable beating, and a wicked smile came over Tyler's face. "That's okay. I wasn't really going to show you mercy anyway."

Still holding onto Ryan with his left arm, Tyler pulled his right arm back, balling his hand into a tight fist, and getting ready for the first of what would surely be many punches.

Ryan closed his eyes and braced himself for the hit. But at the same time, his instincts kicked in, and he impulsively reached down towards his waist and grabbed onto the small metal bear spray can that was hooked onto his pants. Without fully realizing what he was doing, he pulled the can from off his belt loop, aimed it towards Tyler's face, and unleashed the liquid spray on his attackers.

The moment the spray hit Tyler in the face, he was done for. He instantly released his grip on Ryan and let out a loud shriek of horrific pain. Stumbling backward, his hands shot up to his face, and he frantically grabbed at his eyes, trying to both protect himself from further damage and to quell the burning sensation he was feeling deep in his sockets.

Tyler's two bully friends were momentarily stunned as they watched what was happening to their leader. But in a matter of seconds, the boys collected themselves and simultaneously lunged towards Ryan. But Ryan was ready for them, and he hastily refocused his aim and unleashed a steady stream of spray into each set of their naked eyes. The bullies immediately reeled back in terrible pain, wailing loudly at the top of their lungs. Hopped up on adrenaline, Ryan stood tall and continued to aggressively discharge the spray all over the teenage bullies.

Inside the convenience store, Steve and Austin's argument was interrupted suddenly by a loud wailing sound coming from outside. The boys quickly turned and looked out the window, and saw a chaotic and confusing scene going on between Ryan and the three bullies. Unsure what was happening, Steve dropped his magazine and immediately sprinted towards the store's front door.

Austin stayed back for a moment and watched the spectacle through the window. A smile came over his face as he realized that Ryan seemed to be the surprising victor of the odd skirmish. Then an idea came to his mind and he speedily headed to another aisle and grabbed a boxed disposable camera from off of the shelf. As he headed out of the convenience store, he waved the camera in the air, and shouted to the confused employee at the register, "I'll come back to pay for this, I promise!"

Outside, Steve ran towards his friend, who was still excitedly spraying the bear mace all over the downed bullies. All three of the goons were on their knees and curled forward in a crouching position, protecting their faces from the stinging liquid, and crying for Ryan to stop his attack.

Steve came to an abrupt stop in the middle of the parking lot, as his eyes suddenly felt the burning sensation from the spray's residue that now filled the surrounding air. Reeling backward defensively, he covered his face with his arm. It was obvious to him that the bullies were no longer a threat to anyone. "Ryan!" Steve shouted, smiling in awe of what his friend had done. "I think you can call it a day, buddy." Still in an adrenaline-induced trance, Ryan didn't seem to hear his friend and continued to unload the spray until the canister eventually ran out of liquid.

With the small camera box in his hands, Austin ran out of the convenience store excitedly but came to a surprised stop as his eyes began to water from the polluted air as well. Ryan was coming to his senses, and he looked back at his two friends. Then he looked at the bullies, still lying on the ground. Finally aware of what he had done, he threw the empty bear spray can to the floor, his eyes bloodshot and swollen from the assault.

Running to Ryan's side, Austin and Steve made their best

guesses as to what had happened, based on the mess they were seeing. Austin was overjoyed, and shouted enthusiastically, "You did it, Ry! You conquered your demons!"

Steve was just as excited. He gave Ryan a huge hug and lifted him up into the air. "That's what I'm talking about, Wendal!" he cheered. "I knew you had it in you!" The three boys coughed and rubbed their eyes as they laughed and celebrated Ryan's victory.

Now that the attack was over, the three bullies slowly stumbled to their feet, dazed and still in pain. "My eyes...my eyes!" one bully shouted, still rubbing his face aggressively. "I can't see!" Tyler shouted in agony, holding his arms out in front of him like a blind man. The skin around the boy's eyes was red and puffy, and lines of tears ran down their cheeks.

Austin and Steve burst into laughter as they watched the miserably pathetic looking bullies, and Steve began to taunt them, dancing around in celebration. "Wendals for life!" he shouted in Tyler's ear, and then kicked him playfully on the rear end.

Joining in on Steve's taunting, Austin shouted, "Don't mess with the Wendals!" Then he boastfully rubbed one of the bullies on the head, messing up his hair. Ryan looked on, and a smile finally came over his face as he began to feel the importance of what he had just done.

Excitedly ripping open the cardboard box in his hands, Austin pulled out the small plastic yellow and black disposable camera. He quickly wound a dial on the back of the camera and then started to take shot after shot of the bullies in their unflattering state. As he took a closeup shot of Tyler, the camera's flash burst across the bully's tear-filled face.

Tyler's mood worsened, and he became vengefully angry, "I'm going to kill you," he howled. "All of you!"

"No you're not," Austin shouted back with a devious grin. "In fact, you're never going to mess with Ryan, or any of the Wendals, ever again. Because if you do, then the entire school is going to see these photos of you three tough guys crying for your mommies." Austin waved the camera in front of Tyler's face.

Lunging forward aggressively, Tyler attempted to blindly grab at Austin's camera. But with little effort, Austin moved sideways and easily dodged Tyler's attack. Tyler tripped on some uneven pavement and fell forward, landing hard on his face.

The Wendals laughed hysterically again and then watched as the bullies got to their feet slowly and gathered their bikes. Once the three goons had finally situated themselves onto their bikes, they took off clumsily back down the road, in an embarrassing retreat.

Steve grabbed Ryan by the shoulders. "Do you realize what you just did?" he asked Ryan excitedly. "These guys will never mess with you again!"

Ryan looked back at Steve, and feeling more proud than he had ever felt in his young life, he rubbed his eyes and smiled from ear to ear.

Chapter 17

Linda diligently cleaned another one of the restaurant's dining tables as she quietly contemplated the events of the day. After the coffee mishap from earlier, she had almost had a complete mental breakdown in the back of the restaurant, crying by herself in the employee restroom for a solid seven minutes or so. It took every ounce of strength she had left in her, but Linda pulled herself up by the apron and resolved to finish her shift with the most positive attitude possible. Her attitude adjustment seemed to be paying off, and her day had taken a strong turn for the better. The latest customers she had served were some of the friendliest and cleanest of the entire day, and Linda was starting to feel like things at the restaurant weren't quite as bad as she had been feeling.

Linda scooted herself down the freshly cleaned booth, found the tip tray at the end of the table, and saw there was a twenty-dollar bill left on top. A smile came to her face as she looked at the money.

Linda's waitress friend approached the table. "Well, it looks like your day's ending on a high note," she said warmly.

"Yes, it is," Linda replied thankfully. "I actually ended up having one of my better days—as far as tips go, at least."

"You see? I told you things would work out. They always do," the waitress said with a smile. "Don't worry about earlier. I'm sure it isn't as bad as you think." She winked at Linda and then headed off to visit one of her own tables.

Linda finished cleaning and then grabbed the tub of dirty dishes from off the table, and headed to the back of the restaurant. She usually thought rinsing customer's dirty dishes was one of the most disgusting parts of her job, but oddly enough, she had a smile on her face as she washed each of the plates and utensils, and placed them in the large industrial dishwasher.

"Linda!" the manager called from his office in the back. "Can you come and see me when you're done?"

Linda finished the last of her dishes and headed into the manager's office. The same manager from earlier sat at his desk, counting a large wad of cash, and writing numbers into a thick notebook. When he noticed Linda, he held his hand up in the air in her direction. Linda folded her arms and leaned against the inside of the office door frame, waiting patiently while the manager continued to write into his notebook. Once he had finished his work, he put his pen down and looked up at Linda.

Linda eagerly spoke first, with a smile on her face. "I filled all the napkin holders and decided I would clean them out as well. They were disgusting," she said with a sour look. "Also, I mopped the bathroom floors. It looked like it had been a while since the busboys had done that, so maybe we should talk to them about that." It was obvious in Linda's tone that she was trying to impress her manager with her report. "Also, Brooke isn't feeling well, so I'm happy to stay late for her if you want to let her go home early. I'll even clean her booths so she won't have to worry about that. Just let me know what you think."

The manager gave Linda an awkward smile. "Um, Linda, that's great. But listen," he said, and then took a long pause. Linda didn't feel good about the look on his face. "I have to let you go," he said sharply.

Stunned, Linda's smile quickly disappeared and her pulse quickened. It took her a moment to respond, but when she did, her words came out fast and muddled. "I don't understand. Why?" she said anxiously. "Because of earlier? I told you what happened. It was an accident. And you said that since he paid his bill it wouldn't be an issue. Did he call back and complain?" she asked agitatedly.

The manager was calm and apathetic. "Actually, we haven't heard from him at all," he said. "But another one of your customers called to complain."

Linda was now more confused. "Who?" she shouted, unable to control her frustration. But a split second after she asked, she realized she knew which customer it was that had complained.

"An executive that works next door," the manager responded. "He said that first you were extremely rude to him and embarrassed him in front of his co-workers."

Linda felt her blood starting to boil.

"Then he said he witnessed you get into an argument with the customer at the other table," the manager continued. "And he claims that you threw the coffee at the customer on purpose."

Linda shook her head in complete shock. "I can't believe it," she said, trying her best to not scream. "First, those creeps harass me, and then they lie about me just to get me in trouble. That is not the way things happened."

"Well, the two gentlemen that were with him confirmed his story," the manager said.

"And you believe his friends?" Linda asked in frustration. "Of course they're going to lie right along with him."

"Well, it's all I have to go with in this scenario," he responded, shrugging his shoulders.

Linda couldn't believe how crazy and unfair the whole situation seemed. "What about the guy I spilled coffee on? He can tell you it was an accident."

"And how am I supposed to get a hold of him, Linda?" the manager said in a more annoyed voice.

"I'm sure he'll be in tomorrow. Just wait and ask him then," Linda cried.

"I doubt he'll be in tomorrow after what you did today," the manager said accusingly.

"I told you. It was an accident!" Linda shouted. She was at a complete loss.

The manager was taken aback by Linda's strong reaction, but he kept his composure. "There's nothing I can do, Linda," he said in an overly calm tone. "It's your word against theirs, and we have to go with the customer in this situation. Even if I did believe you, it's not my decision to make. The complaint was made to the regional manager, so it's out of my hands." He looked at Linda with a patronizing smile. "I would fight for you if I could."

"Yeah, I'm sure you would," Linda said sarcastically, and she yanked her apron from around her waist and tossed it in the manager's face. Then she stormed out of the office.

Chapter 18

The Wendals casually made their way along another rocky path descending down the side of the cliffs. The trail here was much more open, and a lot less rugged than the previous trails they had taken. Austin carried beach towels and a volleyball in his arms; Ryan had a bottle of sunscreen and a large water jug in his hands, and his backpack on his shoulders; and Steve held onto his fiberglass skimboard. All four boys were wearing their board shorts and they laughed and joked with each other as they walked.

Dylan tossed a football high into the air and then caught his own throw. " I can't believe I missed out on all the action," he said disappointedly. "I wish I could have been there to crack some bully skulls."

"Nah, it was better this way," Steve said, looking at Ryan with pride. "Ryan had his back against the wall and he finally faced his fears. I always knew he had it in him."

Dylan dropped the football, grabbed onto Ryan, and playfully put him into a headlock. "My little buddy is becoming a man," he joked as he wrestled with Ryan. Ryan laughed as he fought back, and Dylan eventually let him go. "I guess I just wish I would have been there to witness it, then," Dylan said.

Ryan smiled, feeling better than he had felt in a long time. "It wasn't even the end result that made me feel so good," he said. "It was just the fact that I stood up to those jerks, face to face, for once in my life. Even if I would have gotten a beating for it, I'd still be happy right now."

"That's pretty profound, buddy," Austin said, laughing. "We're all proud of you, Ry."

"I'm done being a pushover," Ryan said confidently, feeling a level of excitement for life that he wasn't quite used to. "Things are going to be different when we get back to school on Monday, that's for sure."

"Yeah," Steve said in a somber voice. "Things sure are going to be different on Monday." He looked away from the Wendals and off into the distance.

In all of the excitement of the afternoon the boys had almost forgotten about the issues with Steve and the reason they were out camping in the wilderness in the first place. Ryan's victory had given them a much-needed break from their current concerns, but Ryan instantly felt bad for his unintentionally insensitive comment. "Sorry, man, I wasn't thinking about that," Ryan said to the group.

Austin and Dylan both looked at Steve sympathetically.

"No worries," Steve said, shaking it off. "I know what you meant, and I'm stoked for you."

"Well it's been a good trip so far," Dylan said, but then thought back to earlier in the day and he frowned. "Except for me almost getting eaten by a rabid dog." He became annoyed all over again as he relived the attack in his mind.

"Oh, that reminds me," Ryan shot back. "I had a brilliant idea while I was on the phone with my Mom, right before Tyler showed up. About what we can do with that dog." He was beaming with enthusiasm, and the other Wendals gave him their attention. "My mom was reminding me to take my allergy pills because my sinuses get really bad when I'm camping. So then I remembered how we used to give our German Shepherd Benadryl whenever we went on long car rides because it would make him real drowsy and calm. And sometimes it would just put him to sleep altogether."

Austin instantly realized where Ryan was going with his line of thinking and knew he was on to something good.

Steve nodded as if he also understood what Ryan was saying, but inquired, "How do we get the dog to take the allergy pills though?"

The answer came to Austin quickly, and his eyes went wide. "Dylan's protein bars!" he shouted excitedly. Dylan shot Austin a look of disapproval, but Austin ignored his brother and continued. "We stick the pills in the peanut butter protein bar. Dogs love peanut butter."

"Wait a minute," Dylan responded unhappily. "I'm low on bars as it is. Why can't we just blast the dang dog with Ryan's bear mace? It worked on Tyler, didn't it?"

Ryan looked shocked. "I'm not spraying that poor animal. It hasn't done anything to us."

"Hasn't done anything to us?" Dylan shot back.

"Come on, D-man, we would only need one or two bars. You'll survive without them," Austin pleaded with his brother. "I'll buy you a whole new pack when we get home."

Dylan gave up the argument and went silent.

"I think that just might work. It's at least worth a try," Steve said approvingly. "Great idea, Ry!"

Ryan felt proud of himself again as they continued walking.

The boys pushed through one final stretch of thick brush on the trail and popped out onto the top of a small cliff just a few feet above a sandy beach. Austin stopped on top of the cliff and looked out at the beach. "Well, boys," Austin said gleefully. "We've arrived."

The other Wendals settled themselves onto the cliff next to Austin and stared out at their newly arrived destination in awe. The view was breathtaking, and for a moment the boys didn't believe that what they were seeing was real. The private beach cove looked like the type of place that only existed on posters that hung on the walls of a travel agency, or like the scenery they saw while watching their favorite surfing videos. They never would have guessed that something like it existed such a short distance from their home.

The beach was white, and clean, and looked as if no human being had ever stepped foot on its powdery sand. The water was crystal clear, with a perfect mixture of deep blues and emerald greens. The waves were large and smooth and rolled towards the shore in perfectly shaped glassy barrels. And the best part of it all was that they had the entire cove completely to themselves.

Steve sucked in a deep breath of the fresh, salty air, and then exhaled slowly. "I've died and gone to heaven," he said softly.

"Wendal heaven," Austin corrected him with a grin.

Dylan ripped his shirt off and tossed it down the cliff and onto the sandy beach below, and then basked in the pleasure of the warm sun hitting his bare chest. "Well, Austin, at least you got this part of your plan right," he said, extremely pleased.

Looking back at his friends, Steve shouted, "Last one in the water has to lick Ryan's belly button," Then he hopped down the last section of the rocky cliff and slid to the beach below, running fast with his skimboard still tucked under his arm.

Dylan and Austin looked at each other for a split second, and then both boys bolted down the cliff right behind Steve, grabbing and pushing at each other as they went. Ryan stayed behind on the cliff and liberally applied sunscreen to every part of his exposed body before joining the rest of the group.

The defining attribute of the Wendals was their ability to have fun. However, it had been some time since the four boys had had as much fun together as they had that day. In the cool ocean water, they splashed and wrestled, and laughed and joked, feeling completely and utterly carefree. The boys bodysurfed wave after wave, catching some of the best rides they had ever caught on some of the best waves of their lives. They took turns skimboarding along the shore and out into the break, and Steve performed high-flying aerial flips as he exploded off each wave.

Once the boys were done in the water, Ryan took a large pack of bottle rockets from his backpack along with four small *Bic* lighters. Each Wendal eagerly grabbed a handful of rockets and a lighter and then ran off in their own direction, preparing for war—and the battle began.

Steve shot first, holding the tip of the rocket's stick with the thumb and index finger of one hand, and lighting the fuse with the other hand. He aimed the projectile at Dylan like a pistol. There was a small explosion that sent sparks flying back at Steve's chest, and then the rocket flew off in Dylan's direction. "Chew on this!" he yelled excitedly as he watched his rocket fly towards his friend.

Dylan fearfully covered his face and crouched down in a defensive position. The rocket flew high over his head and landed somewhere in the sand behind him. He sighed in relief and stood back up straight, now feeling cocky. "Ha! Nice try, you dweeb!" he yelled playfully back at Steve. Then another rocket came flying at him from a different direction and exploded on the sand just inches from his left foot. Dylan jumped backward and let out a pathetic yelp of terror. Turning to his right, he saw Ryan laughing hysterically at his sneak attack.

Ryan then noticed Austin aiming two rockets simultaneously in his direction. He let out a startled scream that was even worse than Dylan's and then quickly started sprinting away from Austin. The two rockets fired at the same time, and both shot past Ryan, narrowly missing him on each side.

The boys tirelessly continued their skirmish until the last bottle rocket had been launched.

"I have more back at camp if we wanna do this again later," Ryan said enthusiastically as the boys gathered back together by the edge of the water's tide.

Breathing heavily, and laughing and joking about the fun they had just had, all four of the Wendals sat on the beach next to each other and laid on their backs in the sand. The sun was setting and it was quickly getting darker in the cove. The waves had calmed down and were now crashing softly onto the sandy shore, their rhythmic sound providing a soothing ambiance for the boys.

"What a day," Ryan said as he laid back, staring at the sun setting in the pink sky.

"Amen to that," Dylan replied. "I guess every now and then it pays to hang out with you goobers."

"Actually, *we* let *you* hang out with *us*," Austin said with a smile. Then he sat in silence with the others, enjoying the peaceful evening.

Quietly staring off into the sunset, Steve tried his best to push away the thoughts that were creeping into his mind about the pending foreclosure. He would have preferred to just enjoy the beautiful moment he was having with his friends, but he couldn't stop wondering about his uncertain future. He wondered what Utah might be like if he did decide to go with his mom's plan and move in with his Dad. He wondered if he could make himself a new home in a new town once again. He wondered if he could possibly find new friends that meant as much to him as the Wendals. *No way,* Steve decided at that moment. *I won't go live with my Dad,* he thought. *If I'm going to be forced to make a new path in life once again, then I'm going to do it on my terms.*

In his mind, Steve was becoming more serious again about the idea of running away. *If I can't depend anymore on the people that mean the most to me, then I don't need anyone. I'll do it on my own.* But he wasn't sure if he could. For a young man that everyone viewed as so incredibly confident, he was feeling extremely insecure, and he really had no clue what he would do when the time came for him to decide. But he didn't have to decide tonight. Tonight he was with his friends, and for the moment everything was right.

"Promise me something when I'm gone," Steve finally broke the silence. "Promise me that you guys will keep the Wendals together, without me...Promise me you won't let girls, or parents, or Tyler, or anyone break up what you have."

"You mean, what *we* have," Ryan said insistently. "You'll still be a Wendal, even if you move to Utah."

"Yeah, man, you'd still come to visit us, right?" Dylan asked, concerned.

"Who knows where I'll end up," Steve responded somberly. "Things just don't look so good for me right now."

"What are you talking about?" Ryan asked, confused. "Utah can't be that bad, can it? We'll still talk on the phone and see each other whenever we can."

"I don't know. I guess I just have a lot to figure out," Steve replied.

Austin could tell that his friend was keeping something from them, but he didn't know what, and as he looked at Steve, he wished he could read his thoughts. "Don't lose hope yet. Anything can happen," Austin said. "We're still together—here and now. Just wait until tomorrow before you give up on us. Wendals can do anything when we do it together." Austin smiled, feeling good about his pep talk.

Dylan started to laugh. "Dude, your cheese level is so high just now."

Nodding in agreement, Steve and Ryan began to chuckle.

Austin smacked Dylan on the shoulder. "I'm serious though," he said, and then looked at Steve. "Do you remember when we first met you?" he asked his friend.

Steve scrunched his face and put his hand to his chin as if he was thinking hard.

"Oh come on," cried Austin.

Steve smiled. "Of course I do, I'm just giving you a hard time, man," he replied. "How could I forget? It was at a Tuesday night youth group at our church."

Austin laughed. "I thought you were such a tool when you first came up to us. I mean, the new kid in town challenging us to a game of basketball on his first day?" Dylan and Ryan laughed as well, thinking about that night.

"You were so cocky," Dylan joked. "You walked straight up to our group with no hesitation, and said..." He sat up straight, puffed out his chest, and made a ridiculous-looking tough guy facial expression. "Do you guys even know how to ball?" he said, mimicking Steve's laid back overconfident voice.

All four boys laughed even harder.

Thinking about another memory got Ryan excited. "The

next time we saw you at youth group, you swore to us that you could make an explosive out of nothing but your shoelace, a calculator, and some chewed up bubble gum," he said laughing. "We all waited anxiously in the bathroom of the church as you 'activated' the device and threw it into the toilet." Ryan shook his head. "I was pretty disappointed when nothing happened."

"Yeah, nothing happened except for a clogged and over-flowing toilet," Austin added, and the boys all laughed together again.

Steve smiled deviously, laughing even harder. "You guys were total suckers. You would have believed anything I told you."

"Well, you were the cool new kid from LA," Ryan said through his laughter.

"We thought you were all sophisticated and stuff," Dylan joked.

Chiming in, Austin asked, "You guys remember our first Wendal sleepover at Steve's house?"

"Ha!" Dylan laughed loudly. "Four dudes staying up all night, daring each other to do ridiculously stupid stuff," he said. "That memory is burned into my brain."

"Well that's because you had to spray an entire can of whip cream down your pants," Ryan said, laughing hard.

Dylan cringed. "Well you had to run on the treadmill buck naked, with nothing but a cowboy hat to cover yourself, so..." he rebutted.

"And Austin had to lay down with his mouth wide open while my dog licked inside his pie hole for sixty seconds," Steve reminded them, and the boys all laughed even harder.

"And then we all went running down Steve's street in nothing but our underwear," Austin commented.

Dylan shook his head and responded, "We were so imma-ture."

"Has anything changed?" Steve asked, chuckling.

Ryan nodded while he laughed. "I can't believe you guys convinced me to do that stuff. No way I would have done that with anyone else."

"That's what makes the Wendals special," Austin responded. "We're better together than we ever would be apart. Steve, you chose the name Wendals for our group that night." He looked at each one of his friends admiringly. "And we committed that we would always be there for each other, no matter what."

The mood became somber, and the boys sat in quiet reflection. The waves continued to roll peacefully onto the shore, and the sun was almost fully set behind the horizon.

After a few moments of silence, Steve spoke. "I'm sorry if I haven't been myself lately, with everything going on," he said quietly.

Austin continued to stare off into the ocean. "Don't even worry about it, man."

"We know you've had a lot on your mind," Ryan replied.

"I guess we could forgive you," Dylan said sarcastically. "As long as I can have your Playstation when you're gone." He put his arm around Steve and the two boys laughed together.

Austin laid back down onto the sand, staring up at the stars that were just beginning to appear in the sky, and he silently prayed that everything would go as planned in the morning.

Chapter 19

Steve threw another large, dried-out tree branch onto the already blazing campfire. The boys' campsite would have been pitch black if it weren't for the light from the fire's orange and yellow flames. Dylan sat on a log next to the fire, snacking on a bag of Doritos Nacho Cheese chips. Ryan rested on a large rock next to Dylan and held his hands up to the fire, trying his best to stay warm. And Austin sat on a tiny collapsible camping stool, using the light of the fire to read through the notebook that he used to keep the information he collected on Bart the Burglar. After Steve was content with his work on the fire, he sat down on top of his skimboard that was lying on the ground next to the fire pit.

Turning the Dorito bag upside down over his open mouth, Dylan let the last bit of chip crumbs spill onto his tongue, and then he looked at the empty bag disappointedly. "We gonna make another food run up to the convenience store for breakfast in the morning?" he asked as he crunched on his chips.

"We totally should. We found a shortcut on our way back from the store today. It cuts the travel time to the main road in half," Ryan said excitedly.

Steve laughed. "You mean *I* found the shortcut," he said with a smile. "I don't know what you guys would do without me."

Austin looked up from his notebook and chuckled. "It's a great time saver for sure, and a much easier trail in general. I wish I would have known about it sooner," he said. "But we don't have time to go up the hill in the morning. We've got to get an early start with all we have to do."

Dylan frowned and threw the empty chip bag into the fire.

"Tomorrow's the big day," Steve interjected. "Why don't you give us some more details on this Bart the Burglar guy so we have a better picture of what we're dealing with." Ryan and Dylan stopped what they were doing and looked up at Austin in anticipation.

After thinking for a moment, Austin grabbed a folded-up piece of paper out of the notebook and then closed the book and put it onto the ground next to him. "Okay," he said, trying to decide what to tell them. "Well, he's robbed six banks in two weeks and totaled over three million in stolen money." He paused briefly again before continuing. "Investigators really have no solid leads as to where he's hiding. In fact, they don't really know much about the guy at all, except that he wears the same Bart Simpson mask to every robbery."

Austin unfolded the piece of paper that he had taken from the notebook, which was the Bart the Burglar wanted poster that he had printed at the school library. He passed the paper to Dylan next to him.

Taking the paper, Dylan said in awe, "Six banks and three million dollars. Gosh, I thought only the guys in the movies got away with that kind of stuff." He stared down at the printout.

Austin continued, "The last bank he robbed was in Corona, about thirty minutes northeast of Ocean View, and all of his robberies have been within thirty minutes of here. In Southern California, that means a lot of populated territory for the police to search." The boys nodded in agreement. "He can't do this forever though. He'd eventually make a mistake and get caught. That's why criminal experts think there's a small window to catch him, because when he feels like he has enough cash, he'll most likely cross the border into Mexico, and he'll be gone for good."

"Three million seems like plenty of money to live a comfortable life, especially in Mexico," Ryan interrupted. "What if this guy already left town?" He took the printout from Dylan and started to look it over.

"Yeah, good point, Ry," Steve said, and then he asked Austin, "What if you're wrong? What if everything you think you saw was just your imagination, and this guy in the RV is nothing more than a homeless dude that wants to be left alone?"

The fire's light flickered across Austin's face. His doubts still nagged at him from the back of his mind, but he knew he couldn't show his friends any sign of uncertainty. "There are just too many clues for it to be a coincidence," he said. "The car, the duffel bag full of money..."

"And if you're still wrong?" Dylan asked, cutting his brother off.

Austin looked his brother in the eyes. "Then I guess we'll find out tomorrow," he replied.

Steve took the printout from Ryan, and he chuckled as he looked at the picture of the thief. "That goofy mask," he said. "He doesn't look very dangerous with that thing on. I bet you his gun isn't even loaded."

Ryan cleared his throat loudly and looked at Austin, who was staring stoically into the fire.

Austin saw the stern look Ryan was giving him, but he hesitated for a moment before speaking. "About that," he said, and then paused nervously.

Dylan looked up, surprised. "About what? Let's hear it."

"Well, during his last robbery..." Austin started, looking at Ryan, who was nodding for him to continue.

Steve looked at Ryan, and then at Austin. "Come on, man, what's going on here?"

"Yeah, spit it out already," Dylan cried.

Finally building up enough courage to say it, Austin responded, "During his last robbery, he shot three people. And one of them died."

"What?!" Dylan shouted, with a look of shock on his face. "You never told us that!"

Steve looked down at the bottom of the wanted poster and saw that it read "Armed and dangerous" in bold print, and an uneasy feeling came over him.

"Why wouldn't you tell us that from the start?" Dylan asked, clearly upset. "That's not the kind of detail you leave out."

Austin looked guilty. "Well, I guess I figured it was implied when you knew that the guy was a bank robber," he said defensively.

"A lot of people rob banks and never actually hurt anybody," Dylan argued. "This takes things to another level. Now you're talking about stealing money from a killer." He was slowly becoming more and more irate. "Forget this. You can count me out."

"It doesn't change anything!" Austin shouted back. "He won't be anywhere near the RV while we're there, so what difference does it make?"

"What difference does it make?" Dylan laughed sarcastically. "Because if your scheme doesn't go as planned, we could have a murderer show up at the RV, while we're raiding his home and stealing his cash." Dylan looked at Ryan and Steve, hoping they would back him up.

Steve continued to look down at the wanted poster. "Maybe Dylan's right," he said. "I've been thinking about this all day. I really don't want to put you guys in danger." He paused for a moment, and then looked up at Austin. "It's not too late to call the whole thing off. I don't want any of you guys getting hurt on my account."

"So we just let you get sent off to Utah without a fight?" Ryan asked.

Steve couldn't hold it in any longer. "I'm not going to Utah," he said sternly.

Dylan was confused. "What do you mean?"

"There's no way I'm going to go live with my jerk of a dad," Steve responded angrily. "And I'm done moving back and forth from town to town, running from my problems. I'd be better off just taking care of myself from now on."

Even though Austin knew Steve to be impulsive and unpredictable, this new revelation still shocked him. Ryan and Dylan couldn't believe what they were hearing either, although when the boys started to think about it, they began to realize that the clues to what Steve was planning on doing had been right there in front of them all along.

"Now I get why you packed so much in that giant backpack," Dylan said, sounding like it was all starting to click for him. "It's your backup plan."

"You can't do that," Ryan said, suddenly alarmed. "Where would you go?"

"I don't know, but I'd figure it out," Steve said, sounding only half sure.

The boys went quiet for a moment, and all that was heard was the sound of the campfire crackling and the crickets chirping all around them.

Feeling more determined about his plan than ever before, Austin said, "We can't let you do that. That's why we have to go down to the RV tomorrow. It's the only way we keep the Wendals together."

"I'm not worth risking your lives over," Steve shot back in frustration.

"Then what is worth risking our lives for?" Austin pleaded. "If not for your friends?" He turned his gaze to Ryan.

With the fire illuminating his face, Ryan looked confident. "Austin's right," he said with a determined look. "I'm still in."

Staring deep into the fire's flames, Dylan took a moment and contemplated everything. When he finally spoke it was in a solemn tone. "Okay," he said. "I'll do it for Steve."

Austin looked at Steve, knowing it all depended on him now. If Steve wasn't committed to saving the Wendals, then everything they were doing here was pointless.

Steve took his time, thinking long and hard about the situation. After a while, he finally nodded in approval. "But if this doesn't work out," he said, looking very serious. "Then I deal with things my way."

"Okay," Austin agreed, knowing that he really didn't have any other choice. He felt a tinge of anxiety as he realized that the stakes were now higher than they had ever been.

"Guys..." Ryan interrupted, looking up at the top of the cliff. "Is that him?".

The boys shot their gazes up to where Ryan was looking. High up the hill and back towards the main highway, they saw headlights slowly descending down the cliffs.

"Put the fire out!" Austin shouted to the group nervously, and Dylan and Ryan jumped up instantly and started to kick at the fiery logs with their feet. Steve folded up the wanted poster and put it in his back pocket and then started rapidly throwing dirt on the flames. After some work, the fire was extinguished, and all that was left in the pit were orange glowing embers.

Austin rushed to grab the binoculars from his backpack, and then ran to the far end of the campsite and laid down on his stomach, at the edge of the cliff that overlooked the RV. He watched as the car made its way carefully down the trail in the dark, and the other Wendals soon laid down on the cliff next to him.

Finally arriving at its destination, the car parked in its spot near the old RV, the engine went silent, and the headlights went black. The boys waited anxiously for someone to get out of the car.

"What's he doing?" Steve asked impatiently.

Through the binoculars, Austin could see a dark, shadowy figure sitting in the driver's seat of the car, not moving at all. "I don't know. He's just sitting there, I think," Austin said. "It's hard to tell in the dark."

"Can he see us?" Ryan asked uneasily.

"I don't think so. We're too far, and it's too dark," Austin responded, trying to sound sure. He couldn't tell whether or not the man was looking in their direction, but even Austin was starting to get nervous at the thought.

"Maybe he noticed the fire before we got it out," Dylan said, worried.

The boys continued to watch, growing more and more uneasy until finally the driver's side door of the car opened. The dark figure slowly stepped out of the car, shut the door behind him, headed towards the old RV, and then disappeared from their view. Lowering his binoculars, Austin turned to see that Ryan's face was pale white, and he put his hand on his shoulder comfortingly.

Steve exhaled in relief. "Well, at least we know that Austin wasn't wrong about someone living in that beat-up trailer," he said. "That already makes him more right than he was with the whole Blockbuster mafia thing."

Staring at the campsite below, Dylan responded gravely, "I don't know whether that should surprise me, or terrify me."

Austin stood up slowly and dusted himself off, wondering why he was feeling so nervous about seeing the robber at that moment. "We've got a busy day tomorrow," he said, taking a deep breath. "Why don't we call it a night."

Chapter 20

Immediately after she walked into her house, Linda threw her belongings onto the kitchen counter, and then sank down into the living room couch and began to cry. This was the second time that day that she had found herself crying uncontrollably into her own hands. But now that she was in the privacy of her own home, she could cry as loudly as she needed, and for as long as she wanted.

Though she had been through similar circumstances before—out of work and behind on the bills—for some reason, this time around, it all felt different. Things felt heavier, more threatening, and she worried that this was the straw that might finally break the camel's back and cause her whole world to come crashing down on top of her.

As she cried, she thought about Steve. And she realized that even though she had pretty much always stressed about bills, and work, and providing for her small family, she had at least always had her son by her side. Now, on top of everything else, she had the fear of facing her challenges completely and utterly alone, and this was something she didn't know if she could live with.

Linda had been convinced that sending Steve away to live with his dad was in his best interest, but she was now questioning that decision. She loved Steve very much, and would never intentionally do anything to hurt him, but she realized that lately she had been so overwhelmed with her challenges as a provider that she was unintentionally neglecting her other roles as a mother. Her only hope was that someday Steve would recognize all of the sacrifices she had made for him, and forgive her for her failings. But she was beginning to fear that if she did this—if she sent Steve away now—that she may end up losing her son for good.

After she had gotten out all of her tears, Linda made her way into the kitchen for a drink of water. As she poured herself a glass, she noticed that the light was blinking on the answering machine on top of the counter. She went to the machine and pressed the button next to the light.

"You have three new messages," said the robotic answering machine voice. Linda hit another button on top of the machine and the messages started to play.

The first voice was unfamiliar to Linda. "Hello, my name is Tom Shinedling and I'm calling from the CAC collection agency about your..." Linda angrily hit another button on the machine and the message was cut off and deleted. She was not in the mood to deal with another relentless creditor hounding her for money that she clearly didn't have.

The next message began playing and was a voice that was very familiar to Linda—Steve's dad. "It's me," the voice said. "We need to talk details about picking Steve up on Sunday. I'm not sure what you've done to the kid, but I've left several messages for him, and he won't return any of my calls. I'm getting very frustrated. Call me ASAP," the voice spoke in a very bothered tone. Just another person Linda didn't want to talk to at the moment. She tapped another button, deleting the message, and moving on to the next one.

The next voice sounded a lot friendlier than the previous two. "Hi, Linda, it's Paul Hartman," it said. "Ryan let me know that you were interviewing for a position at the bank. The manager over there is a good buddy of mine. I don't know if I'm too late, but I'm going to send him over a recommendation letter. I hope this helps you out. Give me a call if you need anything else. I'm happy to help." The message ended.

Linda let out a long sigh of frustration. "That would have been a huge help two weeks ago, Paul," she said quietly to herself. A part of her wondered if she should give the bank a second try, but her internal voice of doubt began nagging at her again. *Why would the bank hire me when I couldn't even keep a job at a low-class diner?* she thought. Then she pressed the delete button again.

Linda took a sip of water and then headed toward her bedroom with the glass in her hand. She was anxious to crawl into her bed, turn on a mindless television program, and put the horrible day behind her. But as she headed down the hallway, she heard rock music coming from Steve's bedroom. Backtracking a little, she opened Steve's bedroom door and looked around the room. The room was a complete mess, but, as Linda suspected, no one was inside. She saw that Steve had forgotten to turn his radio off before he had left the house that morning, which was standard practice for her son.

After making her way across the room to the stereo that sat on top of Steve's dresser, Linda turned the radio off. The top of Steve's dresser was even more of a mess than the rest of the room, if that was even possible. Papers, magazines, CD cases, and photos laid scattered and piled, in no discernible scheme, all around the stereo. Linda told herself that she would reprimand Steve when she saw him again, but then she quickly softened up, realizing how hypocritical it would be to chastise him about his messes when her own life was in such disarray.

She looked at the pile of junk on the dresser and then casually fished through it all. Her hand stopped on an old 4x6 photograph, and she pulled it out of the pile and looked at it. The photo was of Steve and the Wendals, dressed in matching black tuxedos and dark blue vests and neckties. Linda fondly remembered how the photo had been taken at her house, right before the boys headed to their school's homecoming dance—the first school dance they had been to together.

Linda put the photograph down and then continued to rummage through the messy pile until she eventually grabbed a crumpled-up award certificate with a black border and a red ribbon printed in the bottom corner. In bold print on the front of the certificate, the top line read, "Ocean View High

School Talent Show." Then below that, a second typed line read, "First Place Award: For Professional Wrestling Performance." In smaller print at the bottom of the award were the first and last names of all four Wendals. Linda turned the award over and saw that stapled to the back of the certificate was another photo of the Wendals, each one dressed as their favorite professional wrestler and posing in goofy wrestler stances. She laughed out loud as she looked at the photograph, and it pained her to remember how she had missed the school performance that night because of a late shift at the restaurant. She had only seen the recorded version from a videotape that Ryan's dad had shot with his Sony Camcorder.

Dropping the award certificate, Linda then picked up a stapled-together packet of papers with a cover that read, "Group Science Project, by Austin Kenney and Steven Andretti." On the top right corner, the teacher had written in thick red ink, "A+, Great work." Linda remembered Steve coming home from school that day, waving the science packet in the air, and excitedly bragging about the first A+ he had ever gotten on a science project.

Then Linda saw another familiar photo lying in the pile, and she picked it up and examined it. This picture was of the four Wendals again, but this time the boys were wearing matching white fedora hats, along with black domino masks that covered the upper half of their faces. They had no other clothing on their bodies except for small black brief-cut speedo swim picked trunks and long red capes that were tied around their necks and drooped over their shoulders and backs. Painted on each one of the boy's naked chests was a large black W that stood for Wendal. Linda remembered this night as well. The boys had dressed up in these outfits for a friend's Halloween party, and then had declared it the official costume of the Wendals.

Linda laughed as she thought about that night and about all the other goofy mischief that her son had gotten into with the Wendals. Then, she stopped laughing and a single tear came from her eye and streaked down her cheek. Closing her eyes, she affectionately held the photograph tightly against her chest.

Brrring! The phone rang from outside the room. Linda wiped the tear from her face and then headed out of the room and into the kitchen, taking the photograph of the Wendals with her. Once she got to the kitchen counter, she took a deep breath, grabbed the black cordless phone from its dock, and then pressed the *Talk* button as she raised the phone to her ear.

"Hello," she said hesitantly.

The voice that came through the other end was angry and aggressive. "Linda! I've been trying to reach both you and Steve nonstop," Steve's Dad shouted. "What's the deal?"

Linda was startled by the rude tone. "I'm sorry," she said defensively. "There's been a lot going on over here."

"Well I'm supposed to be driving all the way out there this weekend and I've had no communication from you two," he chirped angrily. "I don't really care what kind of mess you've made over there. I have my own issues I'm dealing with. Are you forgetting that I'm the one going out of my way to help you out here?!"

Linda didn't respond immediately. She was extremely frustrated and was now feeling very confused, and she looked again at the picture of Steve and the Wendals in her hand.

"Hello?" the voice yelled. "Are you there, Linda?"

"Yes, sorry, I'm here," she replied. "Listen, I've been thinking..." Linda knew that what she was about to say would not be received well at all, but she felt sure of her new decision—at least for the moment. "Don't worry about coming down here to get Steve," she finally said.

"What? What do you mean?" Steve's Dad was confused.

"We'll figure things out," Linda spoke boldly. "We don't need your help. Steve's better off staying here with me."

"No way. You can't change your mind like that, Linda..."

Linda cut him off abruptly, "I have to go now," she said. "We're all good here. Thanks for being willing to help out." She anxiously hit the *End* button on the phone, trembling nervously, and then took a deep breath and allowed herself a moment to calm down. Then she quickly flipped through a black notebook on the counter that she used to keep important phone numbers. Once she found what she was looking for under the *H* section of the alphabetical list, she picked the phone back up and dialed the number from the book. She held the phone to her ear and waited as it rang.

Finally, a voice came from the other end. "This is Paul," it said in a friendly tone.

"Hey, Paul," Linda responded through the phone, still slightly anxious. "I got your message, and I wanted to talk to you about the bank."

Chapter 21

Outside of the boys' tent, the campfire embers had lost their heat and were faded into an ashy black color, and other than the faint light of the waxing crescent moon, and the twinkling stars scattered across the sky, the night was pitch black. The boys had long fallen asleep in the comfort of their large canvas shelter, leaving the deserted campsite perfectly quiet.

Then, something stirred in the bushes, breaking the peaceful midnight silence. A shadowy figure loomed in the darkness and crept into the previously undisturbed clearing.

Inside the tent, Ryan's eyes opened slowly. He was still in the early stages of sleep when he thought he heard a noise coming from the outside of the tent. Ryan tended to be slightly paranoid as he was dozing off, so he initially assumed that he was imagining the sound, but he opened his eyes to investigate nonetheless. After waiting patiently for a moment, he heard more rustling sounds coming from outside, and, half asleep, he rolled over in his bag and stared at the tent wall behind him. To his horror, he saw, through a shadow cast onto the tent's facade, a large dark figure lurking around the outside of the tent. He trembled as he wondered if his eyes were playing tricks on him, knowing how easy it was to be fooled by shadows in the night.

Ryan continued to watch with trepidation. The figure appeared to continue its creeping movements straight into the middle of their campsite, and the rustling noises got louder as it did so. Then he heard the unmistakable sound of a zipper being opened slowly, and he froze in complete fear. Knowing for certain that something was outside of their tent, he found himself unable to do anything other than to lay still and listen. He decided that something, or someone, was going through the belongings they had left lying around their camp outside.

Finally convincing himself to wake someone else up, Ryan quietly nudged Austin on the shoulder, until his friend's eyes shot open. Austin looked up at Ryan, startled and befuddled. Putting his finger up to his mouth, Ryan signaled for his friend to stay quiet. "Do you hear that?" he whispered as quietly as possible.

Austin could see the look of panic on Ryan's face as his friend pointed at the shadowy projection cast on the tent wall. A pang of fear shot up his spine as well as he started to realize what was terrorizing his pal. Both boys sat in silence, watching the shadow's movements, and listening to the sounds as the figure shifted and stirred outside. After a short time, the boys watched the shadowy figure move away from their tent, and head back towards where it had come from. Eventually, the shadow disappeared from their view altogether, and the boys could hear something pushing through the brush, heading in the opposite direction of their campsite, until everything went quiet again.

"What was that?" Austin asked in an alarmed whisper.

"It was him!" Ryan said loudly now. "He must have seen our campfire last night and come to run us off his turf!"

Dylan and Steve were now waking abruptly from Ryan's loud talking. Both boys sat up and took a minute to become aware of the panic that was going on around them. "What's going on?" Steve asked groggily.

"Someone was at our campsite, going through our stuff," Ryan reported hysterically. "I told you guys not to leave your backpacks outside, but no one ever listens to me." Ryan found his large backpack laying on the ground nearby, and he pulled it in close to him. "And I think it's pretty obvious who it was out there..."

Much more alert now, Steve quickly covered Ryan's mouth and signaled for him to be quiet. Then he pointed towards the front of the tent.

All four boys went completely still and listened carefully as they stared at the wall of the tent. At first they heard nothing, but seconds later, the rustling noises came back. They were soft initially but then grew louder as whatever was causing the noise seemed to get closer to the tent. Then they saw them—not one large shadow this time, but several smaller, shadowy figures, sneaking around the middle of their campsite. Afraid for their lives, and bewildered by what was going on outside of their tent, the boys continued to wait and listen. They were dreadfully aware of just how vulnerable they were in that moment, out in the middle of nowhere, in an area that was too secluded for anyone to hear them cry for help.

Then they heard a new, much less subtle, noise that sounded like something being dragged on the ground, through the coarse dirt and rock of their campsite floor. Whatever was dragging the item seemed to be struggling with its weight. The boys exchanged confused glances. Moments later, the noises stopped, the shadows disappeared, and everything was calm again outside.

Always the calmest under pressure, Steve reached for Ryan's backpack, and Ryan handed it over without argument. After silently unzipping the bag, Steve pulled out the two BB guns that Ryan had brought with him and handed one to Dylan. Dylan was caught off guard at first, but then took the gun, nodding to his friend in agreement. Steve then began to unzip the tent door as carefully and as quietly as possible, and once the door was open, he and Dylan slipped out of the tent and into the dark night.

Austin looked at Ryan to see if he would be willing to go outside with the others, and after thinking about the situation for a moment, Ryan gave his friend a semi-confident nod of approval. Austin quickly grabbed a small flashlight from Ryan's bag and shoved it into his pocket, and the two boys followed their friends, stealthily making their way outside of the tent.

In the darkness, everything seemed calm and quiet outside of the tent, as if no wrongdoing had taken place. The boys quietly made their way around the campsite, looking for any sign of intrusion. Dylan and Steve gripped their BB guns tightly and pointed them like soldiers in whatever direction they headed. Not ready to use his flashlight for fear of drawing unwanted attention back to their campsite, Austin searched around in the dark. The boys moved slowly and carefully, not yet realizing what was missing.

Dylan was the first to finally notice that something was out of place. "My backpack!" he shouted in an angry whisper. "Where is my backpack?" He lowered the BB gun to his side and began to search all around the ground, straining to see in the dark.

"What?" Steve forcefully whispered across the campsite, barely even able to see Dylan. He was still aiming his gun, and ready to shoot if needed.

"I left my backpack right by the firepit," Dylan responded. "And it's not there anymore."

"Are you sure you left it there?" Ryan joined in.

"Positive," Dylan sounded annoyed. "I left it right in front of where I was sitting."

Curious, Austin carefully made his way over to Dylan, and his brother showed him where the backpack should have been. Austin kneeled down, low to the ground, and squinted his eyes, looking all around the dirt below. His vision took a moment to adjust in the dark, but once it did, he noticed something in the spot that Dylan had pointed out. Starting at that spot, and moving through the dirt towards the bushes, there was one long track mark, about the width of Dylan's missing bag. Austin thought the mark looked like the kind that would be left behind by dragging a backpack along the ground.

While Dylan continued to search the current area, Austin got down on his hands and knees, and carefully followed the drag marks away from the firepit and out towards the surrounding brush. Sharp rocks and pointy sticks jabbed at Austin's hands and knees as he crawled, and eventually, the track hit a dead end at some dense bushes on the far side of the camp. Still on his knees, Austin searched all over the ground in front of the bush but didn't see any sign of Dylan's bag. Then, he dropped down flat on his belly and reached his arms under the bushes, right where the tracks dead-ended, searching blindly. Deep under the bush, his hands finally landed on the canvas material of what could only be his brother's backpack, and Austin grabbed onto the bag and began to pull at it. But the bag moved only several inches before it got caught on something underneath the brush. He yanked hard on the backpack, but it wouldn't budge.

Austin lowered his head to the ground and tried to see underneath the brush, but it was much too dark for him to make out what was restraining the bag. Reaching into his pocket, he pulled out Ryan's small flashlight, aimed the light under the bushes, and flicked on the switch, shooting a bright beam of light in the direction of the backpack. Now he could finally see the bag clearly, but to his surprise, above the bag, and deep under the brush, he saw two glowing eyes staring back at him.

Even more chilling than the glowing eyes, was that just below them Austin saw a set of sharp, pointy teeth, clenching down fiercely onto the top of the backpack. Austin reeled backward in terror, dropping the flashlight, and falling back onto his butt. A loud growl came from the dark bushes, and, in the black of the night, the creature leaped out of the brush and landed on top of Austin.

Shrieking in horror, Austin frantically fought against his attacker, as the creature growled and hissed and clawed at his face and body. The other Wendals quickly rushed over to help their friend, not completely sure what was going on. When they got close enough to get a good view of the fight, they realized that Austin's attacker was a large and fierce raccoon.

Dylan and Steve exchanged glances, and then simultaneously aimed their BB guns at the skirmish, and immediately began shooting into the dark. With loud *bangs* and *pops*, they unloaded BB after BB—each shot being followed by either a squeal from the angry raccoon or a howl of pain from Austin. After about a half dozen shots from each boy, the raccoon finally relented its attack and retreated back into the safety of the dark bushes. The scuffle was over, and all that could be heard in the otherwise quiet night was the sound of Austin moaning, as he rolled around on the ground in pain. Ryan ran to his friend's aid.

Dylan and Steve lowered their guns and looked at each other again. The thought of what they had just witnessed was too much for them to handle, and they both started to laugh uncontrollably. Eventually gaining control of themselves, they headed over to check on Austin.

With Ryan's help, Austin got to his feet and slowly calmed down. For the most part, he was relatively unharmed, other than the huge shot to his pride. He did, however, wonder about his friend's motives with the BB guns. "What the heck was that?" he shouted in annoyance.

Steve continued to laugh. "Well, how else were we supposed to get the thing off of you?"

Dylan got defensive. "Yeah, bro!" he said. "We just saved your life. That little baby raccoon was tearing you apart!"

"Baby raccoon?" Austin shot back. "You didn't see how big that thing was? It was the size of a small bear."

Dylan laughed even harder. "Maybe to a puny little dude like you."

Austin lunged forward and grabbed onto Dylan's BB gun, but Dylan quickly wrestled it away from him. Steve laughed as he watched the brothers tussle with each other. Then, noticing something on Austin's face, Dylan stopped wrestling. "Wait a minute, bro," he said, looking at Austin's forehead. "That little son of a gun cut you."

Austin put his hand up to his head and felt the wet warmth of fresh blood pooling up just below his hairline. "That stupid animal!" Austin shouted in shock and anger. He brought his hand down to his eye level and could see that his fingers were soaked in blood.

"I told you, man, you totally lost the fight." Dylan began to laugh again.

Ryan got excited. "Didn't I warn you guys about the raccoons?" he interjected, feeling vindicated once again. "I've got a first aid kit in my backpack. I can patch you up back at the tent." Then he turned to Dylan. "But first, you better come check this out, D-man." He held Dylan's backpack up in the air.

A look of panic came over Dylan's face as he frantically pushed Austin out of the way to get to where Ryan was, and then grabbed the backpack out of Ryan's hands. The bag was still zipped shut, but there was a large hole at the bottom of the bag, where the raccoon had chewed right through the canvas, and most of the contents from inside were gone. "Where's all my stuff?" Dylan shouted.

Ryan picked up a protein bar from off the ground and pointed his flashlight beam at it. The bar had a large and jagged chunk torn out of the side, about the same size as a raccoon's mouth. Then he pointed the light at the bottom of the bushes where random food contents and other items from Dylan's bag were scattered all over the ground. "Some of the food looks alright, but I think he tore up quite a bit of it," Ryan said.

Gasping in anger, Dylan dropped to the ground in front of the bushes and started to collect as much of his belongings as he could salvage.

"Serves you right," Austin said under his breath, still annoyed by the BB gun attack.

Steve approached the group, holding his own backpack in his hands. "Someone went through my bag too," he said, alarmed.

"Stinking raccoons!" Dylan shouted from his spot on the ground, still trying to gather his items.

"I don't think so," Steve replied. "A raccoon can't unzip a backpack, can it?" He was still contemplating the question in his own mind as he asked it.

A curious look came over Austin's face. "What are you saying?" he asked.

"My bag was completely unzipped on the ground over there, and my wallet was lying in the dirt next to it," Steve said, pointing to the spot where he found his bag. "And my school ID is missing." He was clearly very confused about the last part.

Ryan started to get worked up again. "Do you think it was him? The RV guy?"

"Hold on a minute," Dylan said, standing up and shoving the last bit of his items back into his pack. "It's pretty clear that it was a raccoon that was rummaging through our camp. I've got the bite marks on my food, and Austin has the scratch on his forehead to prove it." He shrugged his shoulders. "Case closed, don't you think?"

"How could a raccoon take my ID card out of a pocket in my wallet and leave everything else where it was?" Steve said, more as an argument than as a question.

"You sure you had your ID in there?" Austin asked.

"Yeah, pretty dang sure," Steve responded.

"Okay, then let's just pretend that the RV dude was up here. Why in the world would he even want your school ID?" Dylan asked skeptically.

Ryan chimed in very quickly. "Maybe he came up to our campsite to try and figure out what we're doing out here, so he went through our stuff? Maybe he's onto us?"

"Stop being ridiculous," Dylan exclaimed to Ryan, and then he looked at Steve again. "I bet you left your bag open on accident, and your ID fell out because a raccoon was messing around with your wallet. I'm sure it's around here on the ground somewhere," Dylan said as he reached over and grabbed the flashlight out of Ryan's hand. He flicked the light on and started flashing its beam all over the ground by where Steve had found his bag.

"Turn it off!" Ryan whisper-shouted at Dylan, now sounding anxious again. He nervously pointed down the side of the cliff towards the old RV. "He's awake!"

All four of the boys froze where they were, and Dylan covered the flashlight beam with his hand, while he frantically searched for the off switch. Now that their campsite was quiet again, the boys could hear the sound of a dog barking in the distance below them.

Following Steve's lead, the four boys made their way slowly and silently to the edge of the cliff to get a better view of what was happening. Once they could see the hermit's campsite in the distance, they saw that the light was on in the old RV and that the mangy dog stood outside, howling into the night. It was too dark, and they were too far away to be certain, but it looked like the dog was barking up the cliff in their direction.

"Get down," Austin whispered to the group, and the four boys dropped down on their stomachs, trying not to be seen. "We must have woken him up."

"Is the dog barking at us?" Steve asked.

"I'm not sure. I can't tell without my binoculars," Austin responded. "Can someone grab them for me?"

Ryan left the group as quietly as possible and then returned moments later with Austin's binoculars in hand. But before he could give them to Austin, Dylan quickly grabbed the binoculars out of his hands and used them to look down at the campsite below.

"What's going on down there?" Steve whispered.

"I'm not sure. I see the dog, but I don't know where the guy is," Dylan responded, as he scanned the campsite through the magnified lenses. "Oh wait, I found him."

"Well, what's he doing?" Steve asked impatiently.

"I can't tell," Dylan replied. "It looks like he's just standing there." He continued to stare through the binoculars and then tilted his view downward. "Ah gross!" he suddenly lamented and then threw the binoculars to the ground. "The guy's taking a leak!"

The other Wendals burst into quiet laughter. "Did you see anything?" Steve asked as he laughed.

Ryan was laughing intensely as well. "Seriously, though... Do you think you could use what you saw to identify him in a police lineup?" Ryan asked, and then fell backward from laughing so hard.

Austin chuckled for a moment but then got serious again and waved at Ryan anxiously. "Keep it down already," he said, and then he grabbed his binoculars from off the ground and used his shirt to clean the fresh dirt off of the lenses.

Peering through the binoculars, Austin watched the hermit at the campsite below. The man finished his business and zipped up his pants, while the mangy dog barked uncontrollably by his side. With the magnified vision, even in the dark of the night, Austin could tell that the dog was definitely barking back up in their direction. This gave him an extremely unsettled feeling, as he worried the dog would give away their position. As the man sloppily stumbled over towards the dog, almost tripping on his own feet, Austin could see a dark-colored glass bottle in his hand.

"He's drunk," Austin said to the others.

Steve looked relieved. "So maybe he doesn't know we're here then?"

"Let me see," Ryan said as he grabbed the binoculars out of Austin's hands.

Ryan looked through the binoculars and watched the man stumble over to the mangy dog. And as the dog continued to bark, Ryan could see that the man was becoming annoyed by it and began to yell angrily at the dog, waving his hands in the air wildly.

Faintly hearing the yelling in the distance, Steve asked, "What's going on now?"

What Ryan saw next made him gasp. The man pulled a handgun from the back of his pants and pointed it at the dog, yelling viciously for the animal to stop its barking.

"He's got a gun," Ryan exclaimed nervously, keeping his sights focused on the situation below, and praying that the man wouldn't resort to pulling the trigger.

But instead of pulling the trigger when the dog didn't stop barking, the man turned the pistol around and started to hit the dog violently with the handle of the gun. Ryan shrieked in terror and lurched backward, lowering the binoculars to his side. The boys could hear the dog yelping after every painful hit.

Ryan shook his head, with a feeling of deep sorrow in his chest. "Poor dog," he cried sympathetically.

Steve took the binoculars from Ryan and looked through the sights. He could see that the man had finally stopped his bitter attack, and the dog lay quietly on the ground with its head buried in its paws. Then the man walked around to the opposite side of the trailer, disappearing from the boys' view. Moments later, the light inside the trailer went dark.

Steve lowered the binoculars. "He's gone," he said.

Sitting up on the edge of the cliff, the boys thought about everything that had just transpired. Steve was the first to speak up. "He's got a gun," he said grimly. "One more thing that confirms Austin's story."

The three other boys slowly nodded their heads in silent acknowledgment.

Ryan was feeling more and more anxious. "What if that was him at our campsite?" he asked again. "What if he knows we're here? What if he knows what we're trying to do?"

After what had just happened, Dylan was starting to feel almost as worried as Ryan was about the whole situation.

"No way," Austin rebutted defensively. "Even if he did come snooping around up here, all he would see is that we're just a bunch of kids, camping out at the beach. It wouldn't change anything." But he sounded like he was trying to convince *himself* just as much as he was trying to convince the others. "Besides, I'm sure it was just the raccoons."

The boys stared back down at the dark RV.

"I sure hope you're right," Steve said bleakly.

Chapter 22

The bright light of the morning sun shining through the thin tent wall, mixed with the anxious anticipation of another trek down to the old RV, had caused the boys to be up and about at the crack of dawn the next morning. The mood around camp was a somber one. Dylan finished a set of push-ups on a smooth plot of ground just behind the tent, and then guzzled a chocolate protein shake from a small cardboard carton. Ryan rolled his sleeping bag up tightly and forcefully stuffed it back into its canvas sack. And Steve sat by the empty fire pit, quietly eating a cold hot dog that he had saved from the night before. The three boys looked tired and worn out, none of them having slept well after they had been woken up by the night's campsite intruders.

Feeling much more alert and energetic than the others, Austin lay on his belly at the edge of the cliff and watched the old RV campsite below through his binoculars. A large white bandage was taped to his forehead, with a splotch of dark red blood seeping through at the spot where he had been cut. After his late-night close encounter, he had spent the rest of the night dreaming of rogue raccoons jumping out of random bushes and clawing him half to death, which had kept him from a good night's sleep. However, the excitement of the morning's mission was invigorating and motivating to him.

Slightly behind schedule, the hermit eventually exited the old RV, looking even more tired and worn out than the Wendals, and Austin attributed this to the man's late-night drinking binge. The man headed straight to the parked Ford Escort, got into the driver's seat, and took a moment to get adjusted and comfortable in the car. Then, suddenly, the man appeared to glance up the cliff and look directly at Austin. Austin quickly ducked back behind the cliff and out of the man's sight. Startled, he wondered if the man had seen him, or if it was just his mind playing tricks on him again. With all the excitement of the past couple of days, it was getting harder for him to tell what was real and what was just his imagination.

Anxiously keeping his head ducked low, Austin eventually heard the sound of a car engine starting up. After a couple of deep breaths, he slowly peered back over the cliff edge to see that the Ford Escort was beginning its ascent back up the mountain and toward the main road. He continued to watch the car until he was quite sure that it was all the way up the cliff and completely out of sight.

"He's gone," Austin shouted back to the group. The other boys stopped what they were doing and looked at Austin, not speaking for a few moments.

Steve eventually shoved the last bit of hot dog into his mouth. "Okay," he replied, nodding his head resolutely. "What are we waiting for then?"

Standing up from the ground where he had been doing another set of pushups, Dylan said, "I guess there's no time like the present." Then he looked over at Ryan, making sure he was still on board.

"I'm ready," Ryan said, lacing up his shoes. "It's now or never."

The boys finished up their last bit of morning prep and then began their long hike down the mountain. Now that they knew the trail well, they were able to avoid the dead ends and mistakes of the previous day's hikes, and their descent down the rock face of the cliff was quite a bit easier this time around. With the heaviness of what they were doing hanging over them, they hiked in almost complete silence, focusing their minds on the mission at hand.

Steve was the first to hop down the final few boulders and arrive at the clearing where the RV was stationed, with the others not far behind him. It was extremely quiet at the campsite, other than the sound of the wind rushing through the surrounding brush, and the RV creaking and rattling with each strong gust. Approaching the trailer cautiously and attentively, the boys looked around their perimeter for signs of any unanticipated surprises. At a minimum, they knew the mangy dog would be waiting for them, and that was enough to keep them anxiously on their toes.

The boys positioned themselves at the back of the RV, at a spot that, if they had remembered correctly, would put them just out of reach of the hungry animal's grasp. Austin ran through the plan in his head one last time, and when he finally felt good and ready, he turned to the boys and gave them a confident thumbs up.

Looking at Dylan, Steve spoke in a whisper that was barely audible, "Okay, give me the bars." His hand was out, ready to receive the peanut butter–flavored bait.

Dylan hesitated. "Can't you try it without the bars first?" he whispered, figuring he'd give it one final shot. Now that the raccoons had destroyed most of his food, he was especially on edge about sacrificing his snacks. "These are my last ones."

Austin gave his brother an angry glare but kept his voice low. "We talked about this already."

"Yeah, man, don't be a tool," Steve whispered sternly. "Just hand them over."

Reluctantly, Dylan stuck his hand in his back pocket and retrieved two peanut butter protein bars in plastic packaging.

With a nod of approval, Steve grabbed the bars from Dylan and then turned to Ryan. "The pills," he whispered, sticking his other hand out in Ryan's direction.

Ryan reached into his pocket and carefully pulled out a small box of Benadryl. After opening the box, he slipped out a small plastic bubble wrapper containing the pink pills and carefully forced the pills out of the plastic bubble and into the palm of his hand. Then he stuck his other hand out towards Steve. "I'll do it," he whispered.

Steve looked surprised, and asked, "You sure?" still whispering. Ryan nodded back confidently.

A smile came over Austin's face as he watched Ryan take the bars from Steve. Ryan shoved one of the protein bars into his back pocket and then opened the wrapper of the other one. Once the bar was uncovered, he stuck his pinky finger into the end of the bar and created two small holes, just deep enough to hide the pills. Then he shoved a pink pill into each one of the holes, and smashed the end of the bar back together, burying the pills, and preventing them from falling back out of the bar. After he finished, he looked at Steve and gave him the thumbs-up sign.

"Alright then, we're doing this," Steve whispered to the group.

Steve, Dylan, and Austin each took a few small steps backward, leaving Ryan all by himself, closest to the RV, and the four Wendals braced themselves for what came next. Pinching his lips together with his thumb and index finger, Steve let out a deafeningly loud, two-syllable whistle, that pierced through the silence of the cove, and echoed off the rocky cliffs that surrounded them. The sound of the whistle, along with the knowledge of what would follow it, sent a shiver down Austin's spine.

After the sound had faded away, the clearing went quiet again—but only for a moment. The next sound that was heard was a familiar deep growl that came from inside the RV and progressively got louder. Next, there was a loud commotion from within the RV, and immediately after the commotion, the boys heard the door of the RV burst open and slam against the trailer's exterior wall. A split second later the mangy dog came charging around the corner of the RV like a bolt of lightning, pumping its short but powerful legs as hard and as fast as it could. The dog snarled angrily, bearing its intimidatingly large teeth, and heading straight for the Wendals. The look in its eyes told the boys that it had been anxiously anticipating their return.

Austin silently prayed that the dog was still securely fastened to its metal chain.

Being the first in the line of the dog's attack, Ryan felt so nervous that he almost turned around and fled for safety. But surprising even himself, he did not turn and run away, but stood strong, keeping his faith in their plan. With his eyes clenched shut and every muscle in his body tightened, he waited for the dog to arrive.

Thankfully, his faith was substantiated, and the ferocious creature came to a sudden halt right in front of him, as the length of the chain ran out. The dog yelped and wailed again as if it had forgotten how it had already lived through a similarly irritating experience just the day before.

Ryan opened his eyes and smiled as soon as he realized he was safe, while the other boys let out loud sighs of grateful relief. Hopping around angrily, and spinning in small circles, the dog snapped its jaw viciously in the air, hoping it would find something to bite on to. Ryan imagined the dog's sharp teeth chomping down into the flesh of his leg, and he quivered at the thought. Hoping the dog would eventually calm down some, he decided he would give it a moment before he made his next move.

Steve stepped forward, sensing his friend's hesitation. "Let me do it," he suggested. But Ryan quickly signaled for him to back off.

Just as Ryan expected, the dog's furious barking eventually calmed down and turned into a much more gentle whimpering. Finally, exhausted and defeated, the dog laid down on its belly, rested its head in its paws, and let out nothing more than a pathetically passive soft growl. Ryan saw his opportunity and took a small step forward. When the dog didn't react to his movement, he continued to inch his way closer. He moved slowly and cautiously, and once he was within arms reach of the animal, he squatted down low to the ground.

The animal suddenly didn't look so vicious to Ryan. "Hey boy," he said with a friendly tone, looking the dog directly in the eyes. "We're not going to hurt you." He slowly raised the protein bar into the dog's line of sight. "I've got a snack for you buddy."

Seeing the bar, the dog quickly perked up and stood back

up on all four paws. Its tail began to wag slowly in anticipation of a meal.

"You want a bite?" Ryan asked with a smile.

The dog hesitated at first, as if it thought Ryan might be playing a cruel joke. Then it slowly became excited, and finally lunged forward, chomping down in the air, in a failed attempt to snatch the bar from Ryan's hand. When the dog realized the bar was still out of reach, it became angry again and let out a hungry howl. Ryan nervously took a small step backward.

The other Wendals watched on with anxiety for their friend. "Just give him the bar," Dylan said loudly, not sure what Ryan was waiting for.

Ryan paid his friends no attention but focused on what he was doing. He stepped forward again and held the bar up in the air, just out of the dog's reach. The dog pulled on its chain, attempting to gain a few more inches of freedom.

"Calm down," Ryan said, trying to sound as friendly, yet as authoritative as possible. "Just calm down." To the other boys' surprise, the dog responded to the command and stopped struggling against its chain. Instead, with its tongue hanging loosely out of its mouth, it stood calmly and stared unflinchingly at the peanut butter bar.

Ryan continued to hold the bar slightly higher than the dog's eye level, and commanded, "Sit boy, sit down."

The dog let out an excited whimper, but seeing that Ryan meant business, it slowly lowered its rear end to the ground and sat calmly in the dirt again.

"Good boy," Ryan cheered in an affirmative tone.

Then Ryan lowered the unwrapped protein bar all the way to the ground and said, "Now lie down."

The dog hesitated, panting with excited hunger, but then rested its entire body calmly on the ground with its eyes still fixed on the treat.

"Good boy," Ryan exclaimed with a smile. Now that he was content with the dog's newfound obedience, he carefully scooted closer to the much more tame creature. He thought about how bad of a mistake his next move could turn out to be, but he decided to go with it anyway. With the Benadryl-filled bar in the palm of his open hand, he slowly moved his hand right up to the dog's nose.

The mangy dog sniffed the bar cautiously once, and then twice, making sure it liked what was being offered.

"Go ahead, boy," Ryan encouraged.

And at that, the dog grabbed onto the bar with its front teeth, jumped up, and carried it to a nice shady spot at the back of the old RV. Then it laid down onto the dirt floor and gnawed savagely on its new treasure. The starved animal devoured the bar in a matter of seconds, eagerly licking up even the tiniest of crumbs from off the dirt.

Ryan felt good inside as he watched the dog eat the bar, almost forgetting that their end goal was to drug the poor animal into unconsciousness. He turned back to look at the other Wendals and saw how relieved they were that the dog had taken the bait.

Austin gave Ryan an approving smile. "Now we wait," he said.

Chapter 23

The boys had been sitting in the hot sun for thirty minutes or so, waiting anxiously, and watching the mangy pit bull drift off slowly into oblivion next to the old RV. Austin was perspiring heavily and wasn't sure if it was more because of the humidity in the air or his own nerves. With how close they were to finding out if he was right about the man in the RV, he could hardly stand the thought of their weekend ending in disappointment and failure.

Slowly becoming more impatient and irritable as he sat in the sun, Dylan was thinking about his hunger, and about how he had been forced to give one of his precious protein bars to the dog that had almost killed him. Steve's mind drifted off to thoughts of his canceled weekend plans with Josie, where he could have been wakeboarding, tubing, and relaxing by a lake, and he was starting to wonder whether he made the right decision by coming on Austin's wild adventure.

Watching the mangy dog as it laid in the shade, resisting the urge to sleep, Ryan was feeling more and more sorry for the obviously abused animal. "He's not so bad," he said quietly.

Dylan became even more annoyed. "Easy for you to say," he replied callously. "He didn't try to eat you."

"Aren't you the one who starts to get angry when you've gone two hours without a meal?" Ryan shot back. "I would think you, of all people, could sympathize with a starving animal."

Dylan thought about what Ryan said for a moment.

"Ryan's right. It's not the dog's fault," Steve agreed. "You don't understand because you've always had a comfortable life."

Dylan didn't know whether to consider Steve's comment a compliment or an insult, so he kept quiet.

"I think he's finally out," Austin interrupted, signaling towards the animal. The dog's head was buried in its lap, and its breathing looked like it had slowed down substantially.

"Are you sure he's asleep?" Dylan asked hesitantly.

"If the drugs haven't worked by now, then they're not going to," Ryan said.

Steve looked at Dylan. "Feel free to go poke him if you want to be sure," he said sarcastically.

After rolling his eyes, Dylan stood up and moved in closer to the dog, trying to get a better look at the situation. "I think you're probably right," he said. "I won't poke him, but I'm gonna make sure he can't come after us if he does wake up." Dylan got even closer to the dog, and then reached down and quietly picked up the metal chain, about ten feet or so from where it was attached to the dog's collar. He quietly dragged the loose chain over to the front of the RV and carefully wrapped it around a rusty metal rod on the hitch of the trailer. Then he pulled on the chain to make sure it was secure. "That should keep him back here," Dylan said confidently.

Steve looked at Austin. "There's only one way in, right?" he asked. Austin nodded.

Steve, Ryan, and Austin hopped up to their feet and took one final glance at the sleeping dog. Then all four boys headed around to the other side of the RV, where the entrance was waiting for them.

Stopping in front of the old RV, the boys took a moment to inspect things from the outside before going any further. The front of the trailer looked even more run down and shabby than the back. The glass of one of the front windows had been shattered, and the window was boarded up from the inside. The white, yellow, and orange exterior paint job was faded and cracking. The metal trim that ran around the border of the front wall, as well as each door and window, was rusty and corroded, and the front door looked like it was barely hanging on to the frame by its decrepit hinges. The boys saw the thick metal dog chain snaking its way around the trailer and into the bottom of the RV door.

The wind picked up again, and the small compartment door on the side of the trailer slammed back against the RV with a thunderous crash. All four of the boys were startled, but Dylan, being closest to the side of the RV where the crash came from, jumped the most by far.

Being the first to realize where the familiar sound had come from, Austin chuckled at his brother. "Not so tough today, huh?" he mocked. Steve and Ryan snickered as well, while Dylan gave them all dirty looks.

The wind continued to rush through the campsite, bringing back the same odor that the boys had smelled the day before. Hitting all four of their nostrils at the same time, they all immediately cringed as soon as they got a whiff of the stench.

"It's back!" Dylan shouted in disgust as he plugged his nose and covered his mouth.

Steve gasped and buried his face into the inside bend of his arm. "I've never smelled anything like it," he cried. "What in the world is it?"

Ryan and Austin pulled their shirt collars up over their noses and mouths. "Is it coming from inside the RV?" Austin asked, his eyes watering.

The wind slowly calmed back down, and the smell of the air became bearable once again. After thinking hard for a moment, a look of panic came over Ryan's face, and he uncovered his mouth and looked at his friends. "I think I know what that smell is," he said grimly, as the horrid stench started to jog a recent memory of his. The other boys focused on Ryan, curious as to how he could recognize such a smell. Then Ryan became even more worked up as he said, "That's the smell of a dead body!"

Steve and Dylan looked at each other, their worries about the situation starting to grow immensely, and Ryan continued with serious trepidation, "I know that smell because that's exactly what it smelled like when we dissected cats in AP Anatomy. It's the smell of decomposing flesh! What if he's got a dead person in there?" He pointed to the RV, and the boys stared in silence, pondering what Ryan was saying.

Austin looked incredulous and replied, "Don't be ridiculous, a lot of things could be making that smell."

"I don't know, Ryan might be right," Steve said. "I mean, I don't know what a corpse smells like, but if I had to guess, that would be it."

Dylan slowly nodded in agreement, still staring at the RV. "Yeah, man, whatever is making that smell, I don't want to go near it."

Austin worried that his friends were getting cold feet and were close to backing out. He carefully thought about the situation. "Okay," he finally said. "Well, if you think there is a dead body in there, then all the more reason to go inside and take a look." The other boys looked at him as if he had lost his mind, but Austin continued, "I mean, who else is gonna find the body all the way out here and report it to the police? Seems to me like it's our civic duty to go investigate."

Ryan thought about what Austin was saying and agreed that he didn't want to live with the guilt of ignoring something like that. "I guess that makes sense," he said tentatively. "But if there is a body in there, we leave and immediately call the cops, right?"

"Yeah, of course," Austin agreed.

Ryan and Dylan both looked at Steve for confirmation, and Steve slowly nodded his head in approval. Then Steve started walking towards the RV slowly and motioned for the others to follow behind him. When the boys arrived at the entrance of the old RV, they stopped and stared at the decaying door, which was slightly ajar.

"Looks like the door doesn't even close all the way. Not very secure for a guy hiding millions of dollars," Steve said skeptically.

Austin defended his position, "I'm sure he figured no one would ever even find his hideout, so what's the need for a lock on the door?"

Steve cautiously reached forward and grabbed the broken metal door handle. The door opened with a rusty creaking sound, and Steve was the first to step inside the RV and look around.

The inside of the RV was a complete disaster like nothing Steve had ever seen before. Empty food wrappers and boxes, old milk cartons and water bottles, and any other variety of trash covered the floor. The tiny kitchen sink against the side wall was filled with disgustingly dirty dishes, that were all covered in hard-crusted food remains, and grimy towels and stained clothes were piled on top of the dining table at the front of the RV.

Steve thought about how his bedroom back home didn't look so bad compared to what he was seeing here. Kicking trash out of the way, he moved forward towards the front of the RV, making room for the other boys. Dylan, Austin, and Ryan squeezed into the tight main quarters and looked around the room in disgust as well.

The boys saw that most of the wood cabinets lining the walls were missing their doors and were crammed with junk of all kinds. The stove next to the sink looked like it had survived several small gas fire outbursts and was charred black all around the burners. Any part of the stove that was not charred was covered in old melted and dried food stains. The wood siding on the walls was dirty and falling apart, and all of the window blinds and shades were torn to shreds or missing altogether.

"Who lives like this?" Ryan exclaimed in shock.

"Well, he doesn't have a mom cleaning up after all his messes...like some people do," Steve replied.

Ryan wasn't offended by Steve's comment in the least, and as he looked around at the mess, he felt grateful for how spotless his mother kept everything at his own house.

Austin waved his hand in front of his nose, and said, "It definitely smells disgusting in here."

"Yeah, but it smells like the inside of a dumpster," Steve

responded as he picked up a milk carton with chunky curdled milk inside, and then dropped it back down in repulsion. "It's definitely not the same smell from outside."

"I don't see any dead bodies," Austin said, trying to be optimistic.

"Well, I don't see any money either," Dylan responded quickly.

Austin kicked over a pile of ripped-up dirty blankets on the floor. "He could be hiding the money anywhere under this garbage. Let's get searching."

"At least he'll never even know anyone went through his stuff," Ryan said, only half in jest.

Splitting up, the boys began their search. Ryan and Steve headed to the front of the RV where the dining area was. Starting with the cabinets and drawers, Steve pulled the junky contents out of each compartment and then put it all back when he found nothing of value inside. Ryan took the torn seat cushions off of the benches and searched all around the seating area. He looked under the dining table and saw that the end of the dog's chain was tied off to the thick pole that held the table up and was bolted to the RV floor. Under the table, he also saw a pile of stained yellow blankets, and as he got closer to them he smelled a strong urine odor. Ryan shook his head in frustration. "Can't even give him a clean place to sleep," he said to himself, feeling even more sorry for the dog's situation.

Meanwhile, the brothers were at the opposite side of the RV, where Austin headed into the small bedroom area and Dylan into the bathroom. The bedroom wasn't any cleaner than the rest of the trailer. The sleeping mattress was stained yellow with long tears down the middle where the interior padding was coming out. Sheets and blankets were piled sloppily at the foot of the bed and looked like they hadn't been washed in thirty years, and more food boxes and dirty dishes were scattered all over the floor. Austin began to search around the room, looking in every spot where a large sack of money could possibly be hidden.

As soon as he opened the door and peeked inside, Dylan was absolutely horrified at the sight of the bathroom, and the stench he smelled rivaled any odor that they had sniffed outside of the RV. The tiny bathroom with only a toilet, sink, and compact shower reminded him of some of the porta potty outhouses he had been forced to use during Boy Scout camping trips, that had been long overdue for janitorial attention. Dylan gave a quick glance around the room, and concluding that there was nowhere to hide money inside such a tiny and disgusting place, he shut the door and started searching back in the main room.

The four boys looked in every nook and cranny of the interior of the RV. They pulled off and replaced any piece of furniture that was easily removable, and they intensely examined all walls and floors for any possible hidden compartments. The interior space was not large, and it didn't take them long to check every reasonable hiding spot they could think of. Eventually ending their search, Dylan, Ryan, and Steve huddled back in the main room, dejected and discouraged.

Not ready to give up yet, Austin began looking through the cabinets a second time.

"Nothing," Steve said, loud enough to make sure Austin heard him. He was clearly irritated.

Austin heard his friend but didn't stop his search. "There's gotta be something we're missing," he said. "A hidden compartment or trap door."

"You said it was a large bag of money," Steve shot back. "It couldn't be that hard to find if it was in here."

Austin yanked open another cabinet and threw the contents that were inside out onto the floor. "It's here. I know it is."

Sensing Austin's panic level rising, and knowing how important this was to his brother, Dylan tried to de-escalate the situation. "It's okay, bro," he said, softly grabbing Austin by the arm and pulling him away from the cabinets. "There's no money in this RV. Time to let it go."

Ryan felt horrible for his friend, "It was a good try, man," he consoled.

Austin looked distressed and confused for a split second before an idea came over him. "We didn't look *under* the trailer," he said enthusiastically, and then he bolted outside of the RV door. Steve gave the other boys a bothered look, and then the three Wendals followed after Austin.

Outside of the RV, Austin quickly laid down in the dirt on his back and slid underneath the trailer's undercarriage.

Ryan didn't know whether he should admire his friend's determination or if he should worry about him having a mental breakdown soon. Either way, he felt like he should check in on the poor pit bull that they had drugged and left unattended outside. He headed around to the back of the RV to the spot where the dog had been sleeping.

To his surprise, when he turned the corner of the trailer, Ryan came face to face with a wide-awake, and very angry, pit bull. He stopped dead in his tracks, just inches away from the snarling dog. In an attack position, the pit bull's fierce gaze was intensely focused on Ryan. The animal's ears shot stiffly upwards, its clenched teeth showed sharply through its gums, and a terrifying growl came from deep in its belly.

With no time to call for help, Ryan instinctively and immediately reached for the bear mace that was attached to his waist. But as soon as he felt the canister, he changed his mind, and he carefully moved his hand away from his waist and towards the back of his pants. Trying to be quick, but not make any sudden movements, he grabbed onto Dylan's second protein bar, and slowly pulled it out of his back pocket. Then, he held the bar up to the hungry animal. The dog instantly stopped growling and stared at the bar, licking its lips anxiously.

Ryan felt a deep sense of relief. "It's okay, buddy," he said with a shaky voice. "I just want to help you." He carefully peeled open the wrapper of the bar and then softly tossed the treat onto the ground in front of the dog.

All of the tension in the animal's body seemed to melt away, and it excitedly took the bar into its mouth and started to gnaw on the snack right in front of Ryan. Ryan hesitated a moment before deciding on his next move. Taking in a deep breath, he slowly reached his hand out towards the dog, and then petted the pit bull gently on the top of its head. When the dog seemed to not mind, Ryan continued to lovingly stroke the top of its head, and then moved to the back of its neck. The dog clearly enjoyed the attention, and after a few moments of petting, the animal curled up in a ball at Ryan's feet and continued eating its meal. Ryan crouched down low and gently scratched the dog's stomach and chest as it ate.

After finishing the bar, the dog hopped back up on all four legs and looked at Ryan, panting excitedly. The pit bull let out a loud bark that seemed friendly to Ryan and then turned and faced towards the back of the RV, letting out two more excited barks in the same direction. Ryan knew the dog was trying to tell him something.

Hearing the barks, and worrying that their friend was being eaten alive, Steve and Dylan came running around the corner of the RV fast.

Ryan turned to his friends and stuck his hand out. "It's okay!" he shouted. "He's not gonna hurt me."

Austin quickly slid out from underneath the RV, covered in dirt, and anxious to see what was going on.

The dog continued to bark in the same direction as before, and Ryan suddenly thought he knew what the poor animal was trying to say. "I think he wants to take me somewhere," he said, moving towards the dog. "What is it, boy? Where do you want to go?"

The dog moved forward in the same direction it was barking, until the chain, which was still hooked to the front of the RV, became taut. Yanking hard against its shackles, it let out a begging whimper and then looked back at Ryan excitedly.

Ryan approached the dog boldly and grabbed the collar around its neck. Without hesitating, he began trying to figure out how to release the animal from the chain.

"Whoa!" Dylan shouted loudly from behind Ryan as he

and Steve both tensed up in fearful anticipation. "What are you doing there, Ry?"

Ryan looked back at the boys. "Don't worry," he said calmly. "He just wants to show us something."

Austin quickly popped up to his feet. "Maybe he knows where the money is!" he shouted enthusiastically. "Let him go!"

Steve thought it was worth a shot, but looked at Dylan, wanting him to be the one to make the call whether or not they should release the seemingly dangerous animal.

Reluctant at first, Dylan soon caved in, figuring that they had come too far to not at least see where the dog was going. "Go ahead, Ry," he said hesitantly.

Ryan found the latch that would detach the chain from the collar around the dog's neck, and he looked back at Dylan, who was clearly still anxious about the dog being released. "You sure?" he asked. And Dylan nodded in approval.

Ryan unhooked the latch on the collar, and the mangy pit bull took off in a sprint as soon as it realized it was free. Not wasting any time, Austin ran off after the dog, with Dylan, Ryan, and Steve following close behind him. At the back of the RV, the dog scurried under a thick patch of brush and then disappeared into the foliage. One after the other, the Wendals forced their way through the deep bushes, and then popped out on the other side, where the dog was waiting for them excitedly. They were now in a small opening in the dense brush that was well hidden from the campsite's view.

After several anxious barks, the dog began sniffing aggressively all over the center of the opening, searching for a particular spot in the dirt. The spot it finally settled on was a patch of ground that looked as if it had been dug into very recently. Tossing dirt all around the clearing, the dog dug wildly into the ground.

"He found the cash," Austin cheered with a huge smile on his face. "I knew it was here."

Then, the same foul smell from earlier hit all four of the boys at once, but this time with a much stronger force than ever. The Wendals covered their noses and staggered backward in repulsion, realizing that they had found where the smell had been coming from all along.

The odor was so strong now that Steve felt like he was going to vomit. "It must be something buried in the ground!" he yelled.

"What's down there?" Dylan howled in anguish.

Ryan was covering his face with both hands. "I don't think it's the money," he lamented. "This must be where he buried the dead body."

The boys continued to wail and moan, resisting the urge to flee back through the bushes, while the dog dug deeper into the ground. Giving in to their curiosity, they reluctantly circled around the animal, ardently watching the spot where it dug. Something gradually began to peek out through the dirt floor below them, and it took them some time to make out exactly what that something was—their view being partially obscured by fluttering dog paws and a thick cloud of dirt. But slowly, it became more apparent to them that what they were seeing, poking out through the dark brown soil, were small white bones.

Austin's excitement about finding the money quickly vanished, and he felt sick to his stomach as he wondered if Ryan had been right, and that the Wendals were witnessing the remains of a human body being dug up from the earth. Dylan and Steve had similar fears as they watched the white fragments becoming clearer and clearer through the dirt.

Ryan was also afraid at first, but as he watched the dog dig further into the ground, he realized what the boys were actually looking at, and, lowering his hands from his face, he began to chuckle softly. Steve, Dylan, and Austin looked up at their friend in confusion.

As Ryan became more sure of what he was seeing, his chuckle turned into an all-out laugh, and he looked at his friends with a smile. "Those aren't human bones," he exclaimed.

Still confused, Steve, Dylan, and Austin waited for an explanation.

"Just like I told you, AP Anatomy," Ryan said, as he bent down and picked up a long sturdy stick from the ground. He walked over to the spot where the dog was digging and stuck the stick in the dirt, prying a roundish piece of white bone out of the earth. Then he cradled the piece of bone on the end of the stick and lifted it up for the others to see.

The other boys could now see clearly that what Ryan held at the end of his stick was definitely not from a human but was a tiny, fully intact, animal skull. "It's a cat!" Ryan shouted gleefully.

Steve let out a huge sigh of relief and then laughed to himself as he thought about how ridiculously panicked they had all just been. Dylan saw the humor in the situation as well, and a big smile came over his face. But, unable to smile with the others, Austin's feeling of relief was stifled by his disappointment that they still hadn't found the money.

"Why'd the dog want to show this to us?" Steve asked curiously.

"I don't know," Ryan responded. "Maybe it's a peace offering? Or a thank you for the protein bars." He shrugged his shoulders. "My neighbor had a dog that used to leave dead lizards on their doorstep all the time. Like a gift or something."

"That's just gross," Dylan said in disgust, looking closely at the cat skull. "Why would he have cat bones buried in the ground in the first place?"

The dog finished digging, and the boys could see many small bones of all different shapes and sizes lying in the shallow pit. Some of the bones were fresher than others and still had decaying flesh and hardened bits of muscle attached to them.

Fishing around the pit with his stick, Ryan sorted through the bones. "Must be at least six or seven different cats in here," he said. "Looks like a couple of birds too. Maybe this is all the poor dog gets to eat?"

"How would he even catch cats all the way out here?" Steve asked in bewilderment.

Austin suddenly remembered something. "The hermit brings them back for him," he responded, as he thought back to his stakeouts. "I didn't even think about it till now," he said. "But one of the nights that I was watching the campsite, the guy got out of his car with a trash bag. Something was moving inside the bag, and I thought I heard a meow." The boys thought for a moment about the strangeness of what Austin was saying.

"That's just weird," Steve said. "But I guess it goes along with everything else we've seen out here."

Dylan stared into the pit of bones. "He picked a lot of those things clean," he said, still in disgust. "Well, it's obvious this dog's got a taste for flesh. I say we get the heck out of here before he gets hungry again."

"Don't be such a jerk," Ryan said, feeling defensive of the dog. "I didn't see any kibble in that RV, did you?"

Austin shook his head, frustrated at how badly they had gotten sidetracked from their plan. "We're up against the clock," he exclaimed anxiously. "We gotta get back to the RV."

Steve looked annoyed. "Seriously?" he asked.

"Yeah," Austin said, confused by Steve's remark. "We need to find that money, fast."

Steve rolled his eyes and then turned around and aggressively pushed his way back through the brush until he eventually disappeared from sight. Now even more confused, Austin exchanged an awkward glance with Dylan and Ryan, and then quickly followed after Steve.

Back at the RV campsite everything was quiet and the midday sun was high overhead. Austin found Steve sitting alone on a large boulder near the spot where the boys had entered the campsite.

Walking up to his friend, Austin asked sharply, "What's your problem, man?"

Steve didn't move, but looked at Austin in silent disbelief.

"The money has to be here. We can't give up that easy," Austin continued. "It's probably buried in another spot around here." He started looking all over the dirt floor of the campsite. "We can find some good rocks and use them to dig."

Steve's frustration was building. "There's nothing here," he shot back. "Why would he bury the money right next to where he sleeps? It just doesn't make any sense."

Dylan and Ryan were back at the RV, but not wanting to get themselves involved in the heated exchange, they watched the two arguing boys from a distance. The mangy dog had followed them back as well and stayed close by Ryan's side.

"Okay," Austin responded, thinking about what Steve had said. "Well, then..." He quickly came up with another idea. "Maybe he got spooked when he saw our campfire last night?"

Steve put his face into his hands, embarrassed by his friend's insistence.

Austin kept going, "So then he took the money out of the RV... just in case we came snooping around...and he put it in the car for safekeeping." It was clear that he was speaking completely off the cuff.

Because they had heard Austin make so many excuses for his failed plans in the past, it was hard for the boys to take him seriously in the current situation.

"Let's wait until tonight," Austin pleaded. "After he falls asleep, we'll sneak back down here and search his car. The money's gotta be in the car."

Steve hopped down from his rock and stood up straight in front of Austin. "That's enough! You were wrong. Don't you get that? It's all in your head again," he blurted out in exasperation. "The hermit in the RV is probably just some loner with no job and no family who just wants to be left alone. But for some reason, you are incapable of leaving anyone alone. Why can't you just leave people alone?"

Austin felt deeply hurt by his friend's words and didn't know what to say. But his silence just made Steve even more upset. Pointing at the RV, Steve shouted, "The guy's not a bank robber, so just leave him alone!"

Dylan and Ryan continued to watch the tense argument,

neither one ready to step in, and figuring the two boys needed to get all their issues out in the open anyway.

Austin spoke back up. "I know what I saw," he said through clenched teeth. His hurt was now turning into his own frustration. "I wouldn't lie to you guys."

"Yeah, but you *would* drag us out here on a wild goose chase and ruin my last weekend in town," Steve said, shaking his head. "It's time to accept reality. Things change. Life goes on. Get over it."

"I was trying to help you!" Austin shouted back. "Why can't you see that?"

Steve stepped towards Austin and clenched both of his fists into tight balls. "You call this help?" he yelled, and his face started to turn red. "You must have lost your mind."

Austin took a step towards Steve, matching his aggressive posture and angry tone. "Forget it then!" he shouted. "We'll be fine without you anyway. Go live with your loser dad and forget you were ever a Wendal in the first place!"

Ryan's jaw dropped, unable to believe what he had just heard Austin say.

Surprised by the heated comment as well, Dylan stepped forward, wondering if it was time for him to do something before things got worse.

But before Dylan had a chance to step in, Steve charged at Austin angrily. Austin saw him coming but didn't have time to do anything except to brace himself for the impact. Lowering his shoulder, Steve spear tackled Austin right in the stomach and knocked him straight onto his back. Both boys fell hard onto the ground and immediately started to wrestle each other, rolling around in the dirt and swinging their arms wildly.

The mangy dog hopped up and down and barked excitedly as it watched the fight.

The dusty brawl didn't go on for long before Dylan broke it up. He grabbed Steve around the waist, and tossed him backward, away from his little brother. Then Dylan helped Austin to his feet, and stood between the two boys with his arms outstretched, preventing them from lunging back at each other.

Standing alone and breathing heavily, Steve dusted himself off.

Austin calmed down quickly, and it didn't take him long before he came to his senses and began to feel sorry for the whole argument. He looked at Steve and could see that his friend was still bursting with anger.

Still in a fighter's stance, Steve looked like he might be ready for round two. Breathing in huge gulps of air, he looked at each one of his friends, as if he was waiting to see what they would do. Then he abruptly turned around and stormed off up the cliff and away from the boys, in the direction of their campsite.

"Steve," Ryan shouted with concern. "Just wait for us!"

But Steve continued his march without acknowledging his friend, and the boys watched in silence as he disappeared into the brush.

Austin grimaced in pain and then limped over to a large rock and carefully sat down. Dylan and Ryan quickly huddled around him, with the mangy dog following close behind them. The wind was still calm, and the campsite was deathly quiet. Austin stared off into the horizon in deep thought.

Ryan broke the silence. "You gonna be alright?" he asked Austin compassionately.

"I don't know," Austin said as he rubbed the aching spot on his back where Steve had slammed him onto the ground. "He just gets so stubborn sometimes."

Dylan let out a sarcastic laugh. "Yeah, *Steve's* the only stubborn one," he said.

Austin's anger was now completely gone and he felt conflicted. "I probably shouldn't have said what I said, huh?" he eventually asked, with regret in his voice.

"Yeah," Ryan said, biting his lip and nodding his head. "That was pretty low."

Austin looked dejected. "I just feel like he's giving up on us."

"I don't think he's giving up on us," Ryan replied. "I just think he's a little lost and confused right now. Try and put yourself in his shoes for a minute."

"Yeah, man," Dylan joined in. "Steve was right. The three of us have no clue about the kind of stuff he's dealing with at home."

Continuing to rub his back, Austin looked down at his feet pensively. "I'm a bad friend, aren't I?" he asked sincerely.

Dylan opened his mouth, almost taking the opportunity for an easy jab at his brother, but somehow resisted, and stayed silent.

"No way. Steve knows you would do anything for him," Ryan said. "But maybe right now he just needs you to have some faith in him and to trust that he can figure this out on his own."

Austin looked up at Ryan with a devious smile. "You know that's really hard for me to do," he said laughing, and Ryan smiled and shook his head. "But I think you're probably right," Austin continued, his demeanor quickly changing as if he was realizing how wrong he had been. With a much more somber tone, he said, "I can try harder to be that kind of friend."

Dylan looked relieved. "Well now that we've got that figured out," he said. "Maybe there's time to have a little more Wendal fun before we head home?"

Austin excitedly hopped up from the rock he was sitting on. "Let's get back to the beach before it gets dark then," he said, starting to feel better already. He looked back at Ryan, who was now on one knee scratching the mangy dog affectionately. Knowing that Ryan was beginning to feel a connection with the animal, Austin hated what he had to say next. "We need to chain him back up," he said with great displeasure.

Looking back at Austin, Ryan begged, "Can't we let him go free?"

Austin shook his head. "The hermit would know we'd been down here."

Ryan's head fell forward in sorrow, knowing Austin was right. He gently grabbed the dog by the collar and walked it back towards the old RV. Once there, Ryan slowly reattached the chain to the dog's neck, gave the filthy animal a long hug, and then said his last goodbyes.

As Austin gave the old RV one final look, he felt an intense disappointment. It pained him to think of the mess he had made over the past couple of days and how badly he had been wrong about everything. It also hurt him to know that Steve's fate was completely out of his hands. He would now be forced to sit back and watch his friend leave, and all he could do was hope for the best.

Chapter 24

Austin, Dylan, and Ryan arrived back at their camp, after what they had hoped would be their last grueling hike up the hill from the old RV. Everything at the campsite was quiet, and at first glance, it looked as if nothing had been touched since they had left that morning. The afternoon wind was picking up, and the blazing sun was just starting to make its descent towards the western horizon.

Dylan quickly grabbed his backpack and pulled out a large bag of trail mix from inside and then plopped down on the small camp chair near the fire pit and enjoyed his snack. "Man, I really worked up an appetite this morning," he said, trying to get comfortable in the chair. "Is there any more leftover pizza lying around?"

Red-faced and covered in sweat, Ryan sucked in deep breaths of air as if he had just finished a heavy workout. He quickly found a plastic water bottle that had been left around camp and began chugging water as if his life depended on it.

Austin headed straight for the tent, assuming that Steve was taking an afternoon nap inside. He was eager to apologize to his friend for his harsh words at the RV and was hoping to make quick amends. As he thought about things on the long hike back up the hill, he had realized even more just how selfish his motives had been. He now saw how his insistence on helping Steve was more about what *he* wanted than it was about what *Steve* needed.

After unzipping the tent door as quietly as he could, Austin peeked inside and looked around. Sleeping bags, pillows, and other loose camping gear were scattered messily all over the tent floor, but Steve was not inside. *Maybe he went to take a leak?* Austin thought to himself. He pulled his head back outside of the tent and took a quick look around the campground, but there was no sign of his friend.

"Where's Steve?" Austin asked loudly.

Dylan shoved some more trail mix in his mouth and spoke as he chewed. "Maybe he went down to the water already?" Austin considered it, but he doubted that Steve would go down to the beach by himself.

"Would he take all his stuff down there with him?" Ryan asked from the other side of the campsite, still breathing heavily. He took another sip of water.

"What do you mean?" Austin responded, confused.

Ryan lowered his water bottle and took another deep breath. "His stuff's gone," he replied.

"All of it?" Austin was now starting to get worried.

"His bike isn't where he left it," Ryan said, signaling towards the pile of bikes lying in the dirt beside him, where there were only three bikes. "And his backpack's gone too," he said. "He left his skimboard though."

Austin gave Ryan a concerned look, knowing that Steve would never go down to the beach without his skimboard.

Realizing the same thing, Ryan started to worry. "Do you think he's coming back?" he asked.

Dylan didn't appear to be bothered at all. "I'm sure he just went somewhere to blow off some steam," he said. "Hopefully he goes back up to the main road for a food run while he's at it. I need some calories ASAP."

Lowering his gaze to the ground, Austin suddenly felt even worse about what had happened at the RV. "Do you think he's still mad at me?" he asked.

"He'll get over it," Dylan said nonchalantly. "Now let's get down to the beach and have some fun before it gets dark."

Austin was now feeling a bit distressed. "What if Steve comes back and we're not here?" he asked.

Dylan laughed. "Chill out, bro. Steve's a big boy. He can

take care of himself while we're gone."

"Yeah, man," Ryan said, trying to stay positive. "I'm sure he'll be here waiting for us when we get back from the beach. Then we can all go home together."

Chapter 25

Linda sat in an elegant business office inside the local California State Bank and Loan branch, nervously tapping her foot against the carpeted floor as she waited in silence. The office was large and clean, lavishly decorated, and filled with expensive-looking mahogany furniture. The walls boasted framed pictures of fishing trips and sporting events as well as important-looking award certificates and advanced college degrees. Through a large window on the side of the office, Linda could see into the main area of the busy bank, where customers filed into long lines, and tellers worked actively at their stations. This was not Linda's world, and it intimidated her quite a bit.

Linda looked like a completely different woman than the one who had been working at the diner the day before. Her hair was put up tidily in a professional bun, and her face was painted conservatively with make-up. She wore a clean white blouse, a long black skirt, and high heels that she usually only had occasion to put on for Sunday church. Her purse sat on the carpet next to her chair.

A man in his early fifties, wearing a three-piece navy blue suit and red tie, sat behind a large L-shaped desk in front of Linda, looking over a single white sheet of paper. His dark brown hair was parted to the side, his face was clean-shaven, and positioned at the front of his desk was a silver plaque that read *Chris VanHaaster, Bank Manager.* The man read the paper quietly with somewhat of a grim look on his face. After he finished reviewing the sheet, he put the paper down, looked at Linda, and forced a phony smile.

"Well," the bank manager said hesitantly. "You really

don't have any relevant experience for this job. No clerical experience, no prior work in a bank or financial institution. You've never worked in a professional business office of any kind for that matter." He paused a moment and contemplated his next words. "I actually thought you presented yourself very well in our first interview..."

Linda sat up in her chair and smiled back at the man hopefully.

"However, " he continued, "you didn't show up for the second interview." The man's smile disappeared as he looked at Linda. "Which looks very bad."

Linda's smile faded away as well and she began to feel even more uncomfortable in her chair.

The bank manager continued, "I'm really only meeting with you again at the request of a very good friend of mine who asked that I give you another chance."

Linda was very grateful that Paul had stuck his neck out for her, but she was starting to think that his help wouldn't be enough, and she began to wonder why she even came to the interview in the first place.

"So, I guess I'll just come out and ask you," the manager said, with a tone that was strictly business. "Why should I hire you?"

At that simple yet pressing question, Linda felt her body seize up on her completely, and she was suddenly filled with a debilitating sense of her own inadequacy. Opening her mouth, she found no power to speak. Her heart began to beat faster and faster until she thought it would burst from her chest. The room seemed to spin in circles, and she became so unbearably hot that she was worried she might faint. Negative thoughts flooded into her head, telling her that she wasn't good enough and that she should just leave before she embarrassed herself even more. And though Linda was very familiar with these feelings, she worried that this time her anxiety might overtake her completely.

Then something unexpected happened. A solitary

thought fought its way through the mess of antagonistic voices that she was hearing and arrived at the forefront of her mind. This new voice was quiet, yet powerful, and she was somehow able to force the other voices out of her head, making just enough room for this new idea. *You can do this!* the voice rang in her head. She quickly realized that she liked what the new voice was saying and decided to try and follow the comforting affirmation.

Linda took a deep breath, looked the bank manager straight in the eyes, and opened her mouth to speak. "Sir," she muttered out successfully. "I understand that I don't have anything on that sheet of paper that would qualify me for this...or any other real job." She paused again for a moment, collecting her thoughts.

The bank manager looked at Linda, grateful that she finally began to speak, but unsure where she was going.

Linda shuffled in her chair and then took another deep breath. "But that paper is not the whole story," she said, summoning her courage. "That paper doesn't tell you what I've been through in my life. There is no way to tell you on that sheet of paper about the blood, sweat, and tears that I have put into raising and providing for my son as a single mom." Linda started to shake a little as she was filled with emotion, but she kept her composure and spoke boldly. "I may not have experience in *this* field, but my life experience has taught me some very valuable lessons. It's taught me to fight, and it's taught me to be strong, and it's taught me that I really can do anything when my back is against the wall."

Sitting up in his chair, the bank manager was suddenly interested in what he was hearing.

Linda continued, "If you give me a chance, I will come in early, I will stay late. I will work weekends, and you will never hear me complain." She took a long pause and thought about Steve for a moment. "I will do anything it takes," she said resolutely. "I need this job for my son...and I need this job for myself. Give me a chance and you will not regret it." She delivered the last line with such surety that she couldn't help but smile after she said it.

The manager stared at Linda, both surprised and impressed. He looked down at her resume, and then back up at her.

Brrring! A large, black phone on the mahogany desk rang loudly.

"I'm sorry," the manager said. "Can you give me just a moment."

Linda nodded and smiled awkwardly, then grabbed her purse from off of the ground and headed out of the office as the phone rang once more. She heard the bank manager answer the phone with a friendly, "Hello," as she stepped out into the main lobby of the bank and closed the office door behind her.

As soon as the door was closed, her smile disappeared and her demeanor was reduced to one of disappointment and defeat. The brief shot of confidence she experienced was fading fast, and she now felt confused more than anything. Looking back through the large office window, she saw the bank manager leaning back in his chair, laughing and joking with whoever was on the other end of the phone.

Linda looked around the main area of the bank. All of the employees seemed so professional, confident, and capable. She wondered if a blue-collar girl like her could ever fit in in such a fancy place. She looked back through the window at the manager again. He continued his conversation, but with a much more serious tone, until he finally hung up the phone and signaled for her to come back in. Linda opened the door and entered the office.

The manager started speaking before Linda could even take her seat. "Listen," he said, sounding conflicted as he spoke. "I've got a lot of other applicants with much more impressive resumes than you."

Linda frowned.

"But frankly, I've never heard such a bold response to an interview question, as the one you just gave me," the manager said as he smiled at Linda. "I feel like you meant what you said, and I like you a lot more than I thought I would."

Linda felt a glimmer of hope.

"And honestly, it would be nice to have Paul Hartman owe me something for a change," the man said with a deep laugh, but then his tone quickly became serious again. "However, that was my boss on the phone. These robberies that have hit our bank branches recently have really forced us to tighten things up here."

Linda could instantly see where he was going.

"There's a lot of tension with upper management and a lot of pressure for us to cut back on expenses and make up for lost money," he said. The man then let out a sigh and looked at Linda apologetically. "I fought for you on the phone there, but I'm sorry. We just can't hire anyone else right now." He stood up from his desk and gave Linda his best genuine smile. "I really am sorry."

Forcing her own smile, Linda tried to hold back her tears of disappointment as she stepped forward and shook the manager's hand. "Thank you for your time," she said with a tremble in her voice.

"If anything at all changes, I promise I'll give you a call," he said.

Linda nodded and then turned around and quickly headed out the door.

Chapter 26

Steve was still very angry. But after spending the majority of his ride back up the cliffs thinking things over, he realized that the way he had taken his anger out on Austin had been all wrong. Coming to terms with the fact that Austin was only trying to help him, he suddenly understood how grateful he should be to have a friend who cared about him so much. And he imagined that very few people in the world had a friendship like he and Austin had.

Steve realized he wasn't angry at Austin. He was angry at life. He was angry that he never seemed to be able to get ahead. He was angry that his Mom had been dealt such a tough hand, and he was angry that it seemed like he was the one holding her back. And finally, he was angry that the best thing he currently had going for him, the Wendals, was now being ripped away from him so suddenly.

As he filled his styrofoam soda cup inside the highway convenience store, Steve was feeling extremely guilty for the way he had acted. He was also feeling extremely hungry. He put a plastic lid on his cup, inserted a straw into the slot, then headed over to the hot food rack to grab a bean and cheese burrito. The smell of the burrito made his mouth water.

The sun had gone down outside and the small convenience store was completely devoid of customers other than Steve. The same male employee from the day before stood behind the register, reading a magazine. Steve walked up to him and put his food on the counter. Then he fished through his pockets, pulled out a crinkled dollar bill and some coins, and handed them to the employee. Clearly annoyed, the man looked at the loose change and then looked at Steve.

The man counted the money reluctantly. "You're twelve cents short," he said impatiently.

Steve reached further down into his pocket, found a dime and two pennies, and handed them to the man. Then he grabbed his burrito and soda and quickly headed outside of the store.

Sitting on the curb outside, eating his meal alone in the dark, Steve thought about the Wendals and about his mom. He realized that if he decided to go through with his plan to run away, it could be one of the biggest turning points of his entire life. He desperately wished that he could talk to Austin one last time before he headed out on his own but realized that it wasn't possible. He promised himself that he would reach out to his friend, once he got to wherever it was that he was going, to let him know that he was all right and to clear things up.

As he stared at the pay phone at the other end of the dark parking lot, he decided that he at least needed to call his mom before he left. He owed it to her to let her know that he wouldn't be coming home, and to say goodbye.

Steve threw his garbage into the trash bin in front of the store and then grabbed his backpack from off of the ground and tossed it over his shoulders. Then he picked up his bike that had been lying on the sidewalk and rolled it alongside him over to the pay phone. The parking lot was completely vacant, and the outdoor lighting was severely lacking. He leaned his bike against the pay phone.

Now that he was at the phone, Steve began to feel nervous about making the call. He knew how hard the conversation would be on his mom, but he grabbed the black receiver from off the phone anyway, and searched through his pockets again. All he could find was a dime and a nickel, which left him ten cents short. He was about to put the phone back down and leave until he saw something shiny on the ground below him. He reached down and grabbed it from the dirt. It was a dime. Surprised by his unusually good luck, he smiled as he put the coins into the pay phone slot and dialed his home phone number.

The phone rang through the receiver and Steve waited nervously. It rang a few more times but no one picked up. Finally, he was sent to the family answering machine, and the sound of his mom's voice came through the receiver, telling the caller to leave a message after the beep.

Beep!

Steve took a deep breath. "Mom, it's me... I just wanted to let you know that I'm fine, but that I won't be coming home any time soon," he said solemnly into the phone receiver. "I know you are doing your best. And I know that you think sending me to Utah is the right thing to do. But I'm not going to go live with Dad." Steve paused for a moment, thinking. "And things will probably just be easier for you if you don't have to worry about taking care of me... so going off on my own seems to be the best solution for everyone. I hope you understand." Steve took another slow breath and then continued. "Please don't worry about me. I love you, Mom." There was more that he wanted to say, but he decided against it and hung up the phone instead. Steve stood next to the pay phone in the silence of the night, not quite sure what to do next. He almost didn't realize that a car was pulling into the parking lot until the headlights illuminated the area all around the pay phone.

The car parked in front of the convenience store entrance, the engine shut off, and an unkempt looking man wearing a baseball cap got out of the car and hurried into the store. Something about the man seemed familiar to Steve, but he couldn't figure out what it was. He turned his gaze to the car. Though it was hard to get a good view in the darkness of the parking lot, the four-door sedan also seemed oddly familiar. An eerie feeling suddenly came over him. He grabbed his bike and moved closer to the car to get a better view. Then he realized what it was that seemed so familiar, and the hair on the back of his neck stood up straight. The car in the parking lot was a green Ford Escort.

Although Steve had already decided that the man living at the old RV was nothing more than an anti-social hermit, something in that moment felt off to him. He looked through the large convenience store window and saw the disheveled man with the baseball cap speaking to the employee at the register. The employee handed the man a small wood plank with a key attached to it, and the man headed to the back of the store, entered the bathroom, and shut the door behind him.

Thoughts frantically raced through Steve's mind as he looked back at the Ford Escort. *What if Austin was right about the guy?* he wondered. *Could the money be in the car?* Steve contemplated taking a peek inside the Escort, but then he reminded himself that the whole idea was crazy. *Or was it?* he wondered. He could not shake the feeling that was telling him something was wrong. And after the way he had ended things with Austin, didn't he owe it to his best friend to look inside the car? Wasn't it the least he could do?

The temptation was too strong, so Steve laid his bike and his backpack on the ground right behind the car and looked inside the back window. The car was messy inside—as expected from the man living in that old RV—but he didn't see anything that resembled a sack full of money. The only thing that seemed remotely out of place was a dirty old shovel lying on the back seat, but he figured that the man probably used it to pick up the mangy dog's droppings. Then he made his way to the front driver's side door of the car. The window was rolled all the way down, so Steve peeked inside. The upholstery was stained and torn on the driver's seat, and a stale smell came through the window, but there was nothing unusual inside.

Looking back inside the convenience store, Steve saw that there was no sign of the man and that the bathroom door remained closed. He turned back to the car, stuck his head through the driver's side window, and searched all around the dashboard. After a moment, he found what he was looking for, and after pulling on a small black latch next to the steering wheel, a soft *clicking* sound came from the trunk of the car. Steve quickly made his way to the back of the car and then nervously glanced back through the convenience store window one more time, making sure he was still in the clear. Then he carefully opened the trunk, his heart racing with the anticipation of what he might find inside.

The trunk was even messier than the back seat of the car and was filled to the brim with trash, dirty clothes, jugs of water, and even a few rolls of toilet paper. But there was no money in sight. Foraging through the mess, Steve found a large roll of duct tape and some length of rope. These items initially seemed strange to him, but then he thought about all the ways they could be useful to someone who was living alone in the middle of nowhere.

Just when he was starting to feel ridiculous for searching through someone else's junk, he pulled a crumpled up black trash bag out of the mess and could feel that there was something oddly shaped inside it. The object inside definitely didn't feel like money, but for some reason, he felt a strong urge to take a quick peek at whatever it was. After uncrumpling the bag, he reached his hand inside and pulled the item out. Steve froze as he stared at what he now held in his hand, and his heart raced faster as he quickly tried to make sense of what he was seeing. In his hand, he held a yellow, rubber, Bart Simpson mask.

Shocked and confused, Steve tried his best to remain calm and to think rationally. Then he remembered something. He reached into his back pocket and pulled out the wanted poster printout he had taken from Austin the night before. Unfolding the paper, he compared the picture of the burglar's mask to the one that was in his hand. Without question, it was the same mask.

Steve dropped the mask back inside the trunk, and then quickly slammed the trunk door shut. He hastily grabbed his backpack, threw it around his shoulders, and picked up his bike. But just as he hopped on his bike and was turning around to leave, he heard the door to the convenience store open behind him.

"Hey, kid!" came a deep voice at his back.

Staying on his bike, Steve turned around where he stood and saw the disheveled man with the baseball cap staring back at him from the entrance to the store. The man let the door close behind him and took a few steps towards Steve. This was the first time that Steve had seen the man from the RV up close. He looked tired and angry, and in desperate need of a hot shower. Realizing he still held the wanted poster printout in his hand, Steve casually folded it up and then reached back and tucked it into the side pocket of his backpack.

"Were you messing around with my car?" the man asked sharply.

Steve tried hard not to panic. He thought about yelling to the employee at the store register for help, but he decided that it wouldn't do any good. He thought about taking off quickly on his bike but he knew that the man would easily catch up to him in his car. He thought about fighting, but the man was obviously much bigger and stronger than he was. Thankfully, Steve was always great at talking his way out of tough situations, so he tried that.

"Sorry," Steve said as calmly as possible. "I was riding my bike, and I wasn't paying attention, and I bumped into your car —on accident." He hoped that the man hadn't seen him with the trunk door open. "I hopped off my bike and was making sure that I didn't do any serious damage." Steve pointed to a spot on the back of the car. The car was already so banged up and scratched that it would be impossible to tell if anyone had made a new mark.

The man looked at Steve suspiciously.

Steve thought quickly again. "My mom's in the bathroom right now," he said pointing to the convenience store. "She'll be out any second, and you guys can exchange insurance information... if you're worried that I messed up the paint."

Continuing to stare at Steve, the disheveled man didn't speak.

"Really, let me go inside and get my mom," Steve said, selling the lie harder than he had ever sold anything in his life. "She'll know exactly what to do."

The man looked back inside the convenience store and

could see that the women's restroom door was shut, making it impossible to know if anyone was inside. Then he looked back at Steve and shook his head. "I don't need to talk to anyone. Just get away from my car," he said, extremely annoyed.

Steve nodded his head and then rolled his bike backward, away from the car, as quickly as he could. He continued to keep his eyes on the man as he went.

The disheveled man angrily trudged to his car and opened the driver's side door. As he bent down to get into the front seat, his t-shirt lifted upwards at his back, and Steve could see the silver handle of a handgun tucked into the back of the man's jean pants. A chill went down Steve's spine.

The car's engine fired up, and the Ford Escort backed out of the parking spot erratically. The disheveled man stared at Steve coldly through the driver's side window as he turned the car around and then peeled off out of the dark and empty convenience store lot. Steve watched as the car turned onto the main road and headed in the direction of the RV campsite.

After the car was long gone, Steve felt a sudden surge of anxiety fill his body. *Austin was right!* he thought. As this new reality set in, Steve felt both guilty and worried—guilty because he realized that he should have trusted his best friend, and worried because he knew that the Wendals might be in serious trouble. After being so close to the robber, Steve's gut told him that the man was seriously dangerous. And with how insistent Austin was on finding the robber's money, he worried that his friend might do something stupid, like head back down to the old RV. He had to warn the Wendals before it was too late.

Steve looked at the pay phone across the parking lot and contemplated dialing 911 first but made a snap decision against it, deciding that he didn't have the time. He could get down to the campsite to warn the Wendals a lot faster than the police would be able to. Then, once they were all safe from Bart the Burglar, they would call the cops together. He hopped on his bike and hurried down the road towards the campsite.

Chapter 27

The front door to the Andretti home opened and Linda walked inside the quiet house. She was still wearing her same dressy clothes from the bank interview, and it was clear from the runny makeup around her eyes that she had been crying. She slowly walked to the kitchen and placed her purse and car keys on the counter. Noticing that the red light on the answering machine next to the refrigerator was blinking, she shook her head in annoyance. She was sick of messages on her phone; they only seemed to bring her pain and disappointment.

Linda walked past the kitchen and into the hallway and poked her head through Steve's open door. "Steven," she called as she looked around the room. The room was still a mess and Steve wasn't there.

Linda headed back into the kitchen, took a cup from out of the cupboard, and filled it with water from a pitcher in the fridge. She looked at the light blinking on the answering machine again. After hesitating for a moment, she pressed the button on the machine that played back the messages.

"You have two new messages," the machine voice told her.

The first message started to play. "This is Tom Shinedling calling again from CAC collection agency..."

Linda quickly hit the delete button on the answering machine, wishing that the man would just leave her alone already.

The next message began, and she heard Steve's voice. "Mom, it's me... I just wanted to let you know that I'm fine, but that I won't be coming home any time soon."

Feeling an instant shot of panic, Linda continued to listen.

"I know you are doing your best. And I know that you think sending me to Utah is the right thing to do. But I'm not going to go live with Dad," Steve said.

Linda could hear the struggle in her son's voice.

There was a short silent pause and then Steve continued. "And things will probably just be easier for you if you don't have to worry about taking care of me... so going off on my own seems to be the best solution for everyone. I hope you understand"

Linda was starting to feel light-headed. She moved into the living room and sat down on the couch.

"Please don't worry about me. I love you, Mom," Steve said. There was another pause, and Linda could still hear Steve's breathing on the other end of the line, but then she heard the clicking sound of the phone being hung up.

Linda started to hyperventilate. She dropped her face into her hands and began to cry through her panicked breathing. She wasn't thinking about her own pain though. She thought about her son's pain. She thought about what he must be going through. And she thought about him being out in the world all alone.

Taking a deep breath, Linda quickly wiped the tears from off of her face, stood up straight, and headed back into the kitchen. With a sure feeling of resolution, Linda picked up the phone, pressed the *button, and then dialed 69. The phone rang on the other end and she waited. It rang three more times—she still waited. Linda didn't care what it would take; she was going to get her son back. Finally, someone picked up.

"Hello," a man with a Middle Eastern accent said from the other end of the phone.

"I just got a missed call from this number," Linda responded anxiously. "Can you tell me where this phone is located?"

Chapter 28

The trail that took the boys back up to their campsite from the beach had been a lot harder for Ryan, Dylan, and Austin to follow in the dark. The boys had lost track of time and had started their return hike back to camp much later than Austin would have liked, especially since he was anxious to make sure that Steve had returned to their campsite. At one crucial fork in the trail, Dylan had insisted the boys go left when they should have gone right, and just like that, they had gotten completely lost.

After several tense arguments, and an extra hour or so of wandering in the dark, they had finally arrived back at camp. The boys' hair and shorts were all still damp, and they were cold, hungry, and generally grumpy from the entirety of their long day.

As soon as Austin stepped into camp, he threw his wet towel down and quickly went about looking for Steve. He checked inside the tent and then called his friend's name out loudly several times, but it was quickly apparent to him that Steve wasn't there.

"Where could he be?" Austin asked the others with worry in his voice.

Rubbing his wet hair with his towel, Ryan said, "It is strange that he isn't back by now." He hesitated before his next question, knowing the gravity of what he was going to ask. "Do you think he went through with his plan?"

The boys looked at each other in silence, no one wanting to accept that what Ryan was suggesting was a real possibility.

"No way," Austin finally spoke up. "He wouldn't have left us without saying goodbye first."

Dylan tried to sound casual in his reply. "I mean, we're jumping to conclusions here. He could be a lot of places. Maybe he just went home?"

"Without us?" Ryan asked skeptically.

Dylan thought about it for a moment and realized that what he had suggested wasn't likely. "Well I'm packing up," he insisted. "I'm ready for a good meal and a hot shower." He grabbed his backpack and started shoving his belongings inside.

Ryan looked at Austin apologetically. "My parents are going to send a search party out if I don't get home before too long."

But Austin had a bad feeling about leaving without Steve. "You guys can leave, but I'm staying here," he said firmly.

Stopping what he was doing, Dylan said angrily, "No way. Mom and Dad would kill me if I left you out here alone. I'll drag you home in a headlock if I have to."

Austin looked at his brother earnestly. "We can't leave before we know Steve is okay," he said pleadingly. "Can we just wait one more hour?"

Dylan sighed.

"Please?" Austin begged.

"Okay, okay," Dylan finally gave in. "As long as Ryan's okay with it."

Ryan nodded his head and Austin smiled gratefully.

"At least get a fire going while I take down the tent," Dylan said. "It's freezing cold tonight."

Chapter 29

Pedaling as fast as his legs would allow, Steve sped down the empty main highway in the dark. It was hard for him to tell how much farther he needed to travel since nothing looked familiar to him in the night. Thankfully, the sky was clear of clouds, and the moon was large and bright, giving him just enough light to maintain a sliver of hope that he might be able to find the entrance to the trail.

He felt like he had been riding down the road for longer than it should have taken though, and at the pace he was going, his legs were quickly becoming exhausted. Fearing he had already passed the trailhead by accident, he started to worry that he wouldn't make it back to the Wendals before something terrible happened.

Steve saw headlights in the distance, coming down the road directly towards him. He thought about waving the car down and asking the driver to call the police for him. At this point, nothing really mattered to him other than keeping his friends safe, and calling the police suddenly seemed like it might be the best way to do that. Then he remembered that Austin's Dad knew exactly where the boys were camping. If the person in the car could get a hold of Sergeant Kenney, maybe the police could meet them at their campsite and arrest the burglar before the Wendals got themselves into trouble.

Steve waived one arm frantically in the air in the middle of the road. The car was getting so close to him that the brightness of the headlight beams was almost blinding. But instead of slowing down, the car appeared to accelerate. Steve panicked, thinking that maybe the driver didn't see him on the road, and he quickly swerved his bike off the street and stopped on the shoulder.

Finally, the car slammed on its brakes and came to a screeching halt in the middle of the road. Then the car started moving forward again, and slowly pulled up right next to Steve. Steve stared at the car, his vision still partially impaired due to the bright headlight beams. When his sight finally came back to him in full, he realized that the car that was in front of him was the beat-up green Ford Escort.

The driver's window of the car was rolled down, and the disheveled man with the baseball cap stared back at Steve. Steve's entire body went stiff.

The disheveled man looked at Steve for what seemed like an eternity before he finally spoke. "You following me, kid?" he asked in a hostile tone.

Steve didn't speak or move a muscle.

The man continued to stare. After several tense moments, he opened the car door and slowly stepped out onto the asphalt. With the car engine still on, the man moved towards Steve.

Steve knew that he should run, or scream, or fight—but at the moment, he couldn't do any of that. Instead, he stood on his bike, scared completely stiff. Soon, the man was so close to Steve that he could smell the staleness of his breath.

"Where you headed?" the man asked.

Steve knew it was too late to run, now that the man was close enough to easily reach out and restrain him. He quickly decided that his only chance was to continue to play it cool, so he did his best to sound confident. "Just heading home," Steve replied, trying to hide the tremble in his voice.

Looking down the road in the direction Steve was riding, it was obvious to the man that there were no homes that way for many miles. Definitely a further trip than any kid would make on a bike, especially that late at night.

"Must be a long ride home," the man said with a nasty snarl. "What happened to your mom?" he asked skeptically.

"My mom?" Steve was confused.

"Yeah, your mom!" the man snapped back. "The store down the road. You said she was in the bathroom."

Cringing, Steve suddenly remembered the lie he had told the man back at the convenience store.

The disheveled man reached his hand behind his back and Steve braced himself for the gun that he knew the man was carrying in his pants. But instead, the man pulled out a large wad of crisp one hundred dollar bills that were folded in half, and then carefully unfolded the bills, and grabbed a small plastic card from the middle of the wad. Steve watched, confused at what the man was doing. After folding the wad of money in half again, and sticking it back in his pocket, the man squinted and looked at the small card in his hand.

In the dark, it took Steve a minute to realize what the plastic card was. Then it hit him, and his feeling of panic skyrocketed. The disheveled man held in his hand Steve's missing school ID. Steve instantly remembered how Ryan had accused the man of coming into their camp and rummaging through their belongings, and he knew he was in trouble.

The man looked at Steve, and then at the card, and then at Steve again. A look of both surprise and rage came over the man's face. "You're one of those kids that's been camping out next to me," he said.

Seeing this as his last chance to escape, Steve sat back on his bike and pressed his feet down on his pedals quickly, trying to take off down the road. But the disheveled man was ready for him, and he swiftly grabbed Steve with one arm and held him in his place. Steve tried to squirm free, but the man was strong, and Steve was certain he was trapped.

No longer resisting, Steve protested, "Yeah, so what if I am?"

"You boys been snooping around my RV, haven't you," the man said, as more of a statement than a question.

Steve's confidence was waning fast, and he now sounded like a child who was defending an obvious lie. "No way!" he rebutted. "Of course not."

The man glared at Steve. "What were you boys hoping to find?" he asked.

"What are you talking about?" Steve continued to play dumb. "We came out here to have some fun at the beach." He tried again to pull himself free of the man's grasp, but the man didn't give him any slack.

Breathing slowly, the disheveled man held Steve in his place. The look of uncertainty on the man's face told Steve that the man wasn't quite sure what he wanted to do with him yet. Then the man noticed something on the side of Steve's backpack. Seeing where the man was looking, Steve suddenly remembered the wanted poster that was sticking out of the backpack's side pocket, and he quickly turned his body in an attempt to hide that side of the bag from the man. But it was too late. With great force, the disheveled man twisted Steve's body around, and aggressively tore the giant orange backpack from off of his shoulders. The man then pulled the sheet of paper from out of the side pocket, tossed Steve's bag backward towards the car, and unfolded the poster and looked it over.

If there was ever a time in his life to be terrified, Steve knew that this was it. He waited anxiously for the man's reaction. But the look of rage that Steve expected to see on the man's face never came. Instead, the man nodded his head calmly and quietly. Steve thought he even noticed the man smirk subtly. Having no idea what to expect from a dangerous criminal like the one that stood in front of him, he wondered what was going on inside the man's head. Then, in a flash, the man pulled the silver handgun from out of the back of his pants and pressed the barrel firmly against Steve's cheek.

"Where did you get this?" the man asked in a quiet but intense voice as he held the paper up in front of Steve's face.

Steve trembled as he stared down the barrel of the gun. The metal felt cold on his cheek, and he felt like he might faint— his young life flashing before his eyes.

"I had a bad feeling about you kids," the man snarled.

Then he quickly flipped the gun around in his hand, gripped it by the barrel, and hit Steve hard over the head with the gun's handle.

Everything suddenly went black for Steve.

Chapter 30

The boys were in a dull mood as they sat around the campfire, quietly contemplating the events of the day. It had been some time since anyone had last spoken. Dylan sat on a log, chomping down intensely on his last bit of trail mix, thinking about how badly he wished he had a hamburger and a cold soda instead. Ryan lay on top of his beach towel and stared up at the large moon and twinkling stars above him. He tried to not think of how much trouble he would be in when he arrived home late that night and his parents inevitably realized that he had lied to them about the camping trip.

Leaning forward in his camp chair and staring into the fire, Austin was hypnotized by its flickering flames. He was starting to accept the fact that Steve wasn't coming back, but he struggled to figure out exactly where everything had gone wrong that weekend. What should have been one of the most triumphant adventures in Wendal history had turned out to be a weekend that could destroy the Wendals forever. If only he could go back in time, he would have accepted Steve's fate from the start and would have spent the weekend enjoying the last bit of time he had with his best friend.

The fire crackled and popped, and Ryan sat straight up and looked at Austin, and then at Dylan. "Hey," he broke the silence excitedly, as an idea came into his mind. "We've still got plenty of fireworks. We haven't even touched the big ones yet." Intentionally speaking with extra enthusiasm, he tried to lighten the mood. Dylan smirked and shook his head as if to say, "Now's not the time." Ryan slunk back down on his towel, and there was silence once again. He thought for a moment and then decided that someone needed to address the elephant in the room. "What do you think things will be like without Steve?" he asked.

Austin continued to stare into the fire as if he hadn't heard Ryan.

As he chewed another bite of trail mix, Dylan pondered on the question before responding somberly, "Life will definitely be different."

Ryan looked at Austin, waiting for a response, but when it didn't come, he tried to answer his own question. "There'll be a lot less girls hanging around us, that's for sure," he said, and then he chuckled to himself.

Dylan smiled. "Maybe for you two nerds," he replied.

Ryan acted offended for a moment, but then laughed.

But Austin wasn't in a laughing mood, and he kept his stoic gaze on the fire.

Ryan couldn't stand seeing his friend so down. "Come on, buddy," he said cheerfully to Austin. "We did everything we could, so there's no use dwelling on it now. Think about all the good times we had instead. Steve was a huge blessing in our lives." He continued to look at his friend, and Austin finally returned the glance. "I don't know about you guys," Ryan said. "But I wouldn't trade the past few years that we've all had together for anything in the world. Even if I had known it would all end like this."

Dylan nodded in agreement, and even Austin finally tried to internalize what Ryan was saying.

Ryan went on, "I, for one, can't be angry. Steve did more for me than I could ever thank him for." He smiled fondly as the words came out. "He helped give me the courage to stand up for myself, and he made me feel like a real somebody. My self-confidence has never been so strong in my life," he said assuredly. "I'm much better off for having known Steve Andretti, so I'm just going to be grateful for his friendship while I had it."

Austin couldn't help but crack a small smile as he listened to his friend. He knew what Ryan was saying was true, and he was definitely aware of how much Steve had helped not only Ryan's self-esteem, but his own as well.

Dylan stared into the fire and continued to nod his head. It was obvious that he had something to say, but he was never very good at expressing his emotions. After a minute or so, he finally spoke up. "I guess I should just be grateful too," he said. "The Wendals have always been there for me. Even if you guys are total goobers half the time." A big snarky grin came over his face. "Steve is the one who brought us all together. All the crazy stuff he convinced us to do over the past few years...Those are times I'll never forget."

As his sulking expression melted away, a genuine smile came over Austin's face. He agreed with everything his brother had said, and as he sat there around the fire, with two of his closest friends, he started to feel that maybe everything would be okay after all. Sitting up straight in his chair, he looked at his friends gratefully. "Maybe you guys are right," Austin finally conceded. "All three of us really are better off for having known Steve. I guess we should just take everything we've learned from him and move on to our next adventure," he said confidently. "I mean, we're pretty darn lucky that we still have each other."

Dylan and Ryan nodded in agreement.

"Besides," Austin continued. "It's not like Steve's dying. I guess I'll just have to learn to do the long-distance friendship thing."

"Wow, is my little brother finally starting to grow up?" Dylan asked, laughing.

Ryan chuckled. "Maybe you guys can figure out how to use that new AOL internet email stuff my Dad uses all the time," he said.

Dylan gave Ryan a confused look.

Smiling, Austin admitted, "I was wrong, guys. The Wendals are here to stay."

Ryan became excited and eagerly shouted, "Wendals for life!"

Dylan laughed. "Absolutely," he said. "Wendals for life."

Standing up from his chair, Austin declared, "I guess we can get home now. No point hanging around here any longer."

Dylan jumped out of his seat as well. "Who's game for a burger on the way home?" he asked excitedly as he rubbed his stomach.

"Ryan's in a hurry," Austin responded. "I don't want him getting in any more trouble."

But Ryan was quick to respond. "I'm game to grab a bite. I'll deal with the consequences when I get home. You guys are worth it," he said boldly.

Dylan and Austin both looked at Ryan in surprise, and Ryan shrugged his shoulders. "What?" Ryan asked. "I stood up to Tyler and a vicious dog this weekend. I can handle my parents."

"That's my boy!" Dylan shouted as he started grabbing his belongings from around camp.

Austin smiled contentedly at his friend's confidence, and then he turned around to grab his backpack. As he did, he saw headlights in the distance, up near the main road. He knew it was the Ford Escort, heading back down the trail to the old RV— like it did every night—but he immediately realized that something was different with tonight's descent. Instead of the car's usual slow movement down the cliffside, it was speeding down the hill erratically.

Continuing to watch the car, Austin was confused by what was going on. He had never seen the hermit fly down the path in such a hurry—and for good reason. The trail down the cliff was very treacherous, especially in the dark. With the car moving so fast, Austin knew that something had to be wrong, and his imagination began to run wild again.

Ryan and Dylan noticed the situation and were now by Austin's side, watching the car along with him. "What's going on?" Ryan asked.

The green Ford was already halfway down the mountain. "I'm not sure," Austin said in bewilderment. "But whatever it is, I've got a bad feeling about it." He went to his backpack and quickly searched through the main pouch, pulling his binoculars out from deep inside. Then he went to the edge of the cliff that overlooked the old RV and lay down on his stomach, as Dylan and Ryan ran back to the firepit and hastily started to put out the blazing fire.

Through the binoculars, Austin watched the car as it arrived at the bottom of the hill and came to a brake-squealing stop next to the old RV. With the engine still running, the front door of the car opened abruptly and the disheveled man jumped out of the car and swiftly headed towards the RV. Austin quickly realized that the man appeared to be stressed-out.

Once Dylan and Ryan had finished putting out the fire, they rushed back to Austin's side and knelt down next to him at the edge of the cliff. They tried to see what was going on at the campsite below, but the darkness and the distance made it impossible for them to get a clear picture without the binoculars.

"What's he doing now?" Dylan asked impatiently.

"Do you think he knows we went through his stuff?" Ryan cried out nervously.

Still confused, Austin apprised his friends on the situation the best he could. "He went into the RV," he said with a bit of a tremble. "There's definitely something wrong though. He's in a serious rush and he seems upset. I don't think he's planning on sticking around here tonight." Austin continued to observe.

When the disheveled man finally emerged from the old RV, he carried a small plastic grocery bag in one of his hands. Though Austin couldn't completely make out what was inside the bag, it looked to be full of random contents from the RV. With his other hand, the man grasped the collar of the mangy dog and aggressively pulled the animal towards the running car. The dog wasn't going without a struggle though. Austin watched the pit bull howl and kick and twist its body, trying to break free of the disheveled man's grip. Annoyed and irate, the man eventually pulled the gun out from the back of his pants and pointed it at the pit bull.

Gasping in horror, Austin was sure that the clearly psychotic man was going to shoot the poor creature.

But the dog immediately stopped its struggling, lay on the ground submissively, and trembled as it looked up at the gun. The disheveled man appeared to calm down only slightly, and after a moment, he lowered the gun and tucked it back into his pants.

Anxiously choking on his words, Austin reported to the others, "He's loading the dog into the car. He's definitely getting out of here."

"Where's he taking the dog?" Ryan asked furiously.

"Maybe he's moving on? Gonna go hide out somewhere else?" Dylan suggested. "Maybe he didn't like us encroaching on his turf?"

But Austin's original suspicions started to reemerge—that the man's erratic actions were in line with those of a criminal—and he continued to spy on the scene below.

Austin watched the disheveled man quickly yank the back door of the car open, and he saw something large and neon orange tumble out of the back seat and onto the ground. Then the mangy dog hopped into the back seat of the car.

Austin's attention immediately shifted to the bulky orange object that had fallen onto the ground. With all the excitement of the moment, it took Austin some time to realize what the object was, but once he did, his heart stopped cold in his chest. He didn't know how it was possible, but he knew without a shadow of a doubt, that the object on the ground was Steve's large orange backpack.

The fear brought on by this new revelation was almost crippling to Austin. But, now believing that every detail he viewed was of life and death importance, he tried to remain focused on what he was seeing. Still watching through the binoculars, Austin saw the man take the backpack to the back of the car, open the trunk door, and toss the backpack inside. With the back of the car facing away from Austin, there was no way for him to see what was inside of the trunk, but somehow, deep down inside, he knew that Steve was there. Trembling at the horrible thought, he prayed that Steve was still alive.

The man slammed the trunk door shut with a crash that echoed through the canyon and made all three boys jump. Then the man hopped into the driver's seat of the car and peeled out of the campsite, heading quickly back up the steep trail.

Lowering his binoculars, Austin faced his friends.

Ryan and Dylan stared at Austin in eager anticipation. "Tell us what happened!" Dylan shouted tensely.

Austin stood in dreadful silence for a moment, gathering his thoughts. He felt sure of what he had seen, but as he repeated in his mind what he wanted to say to his friends, he knew that it would sound completely ridiculous.

Ryan could see the look of turmoil on Austin's face. "What is it?" he begged his friend to speak. "Just spit it out."

Austin forced himself to say it. "Steve's pack," he said quietly, almost to himself.

A look of total confusion came over Dylan and Ryan's faces.

Austin took a deep breath and spoke with slightly more force. "He had Steve's backpack."

Now Dylan and Ryan were even more perplexed as they tried to comprehend what Austin was saying.

"What are you talking about?" Ryan asked.

After a moment of silence, Dylan started to laugh, and then he playfully slapped Ryan on the shoulder and looked at Austin with a smile. "Nice one man. That's really clever."

Austin's face was ghost white. He stood still, speaking to himself in half sentences, and trying to put all of the pieces together. "How did he...? Why would he...? Steve..."

Dylan stopped laughing. He knew his brother well enough to know when he was messing around, and he was beginning to realize that something actually was wrong. Now feeling stressed out, he grabbed Austin by the shoulders and shook him aggressively. "Get it together bro!" he shouted. "Now's not the time for paranoid thinking! I need you to be straight up with us. What did you see?"

The shaking seemed to jolt Austin out of his stupor, and

he knocked Dylan's hands from off of his shoulders and looked into his brother's eyes. "The hermit," he started in a much steadier voice. "He opened the back door of his car, and Steve's backpack fell out onto the ground."

Ryan was still confused but was becoming panicked as he realized what Austin was trying to say. "There's no way he could..." Ryan paused, unable to comprehend how it was possible. "Are you sure it was Steve's backpack?" he finally asked.

Becoming more worked up, Austin spoke frantically, "Unless the guy has his own giant neon orange backpack. It's pretty hard to mistake that thing."

Dylan's mind was trying to work out the tangled web of information he was hearing. "Well, what could it mean, then?" he asked, perplexed. "Did the guy take it from our campsite while we weren't here?"

Ryan was also working hard to connect the dots in his mind. "No way," he chimed in, trying to recall earlier events from the day as he spoke. "Steve's bag was here when we went down to look through the RV this morning. And then it was gone when we got back to camp, along with Steve's other stuff."

"Exactly," Austin jumped in. "So Steve definitely took the backpack with him when he left here today," he said. "That means that the hermit must have taken it from Steve."

"Where would he have run into Steve?" Ryan asked.

"And why would he steal a camping backpack from a kid?" Dylan was puzzled. "There was obviously nothing of value in there."

Austin paused for a moment, his mind drawn to the trunk of the Ford Escort, and to his worst imaginable fears. When he spoke, his words came out with an eerie stoicism. "What if he wasn't after Steve's backpack?"

Dylan stared at Austin in confusion. But Ryan was starting to understand, and his eyes opened wide with worry. "You think he did something to Steve?" he asked bleakly.

"I couldn't see inside the trunk," Austin replied. "But something is telling me that Steve was in there." He shook his head. "It's hard to explain."

Ryan wasn't sure why, but he didn't question what Austin was saying. Something told him to trust his friend. "Maybe you were right. About the robber, I mean," he said. "Maybe he figured out that we were on to him, so he attacked Steve when he was alone?" He thought for a moment. "And that's why he's in a rush to get out of here?"

No longer pushing back against Austin's story, Dylan knew that even if there was a small chance his brother was right, then they needed to act fast. "Well, what do we do then?" he asked restlessly.

Ryan was quick to answer. "We could ride back to the convenience store and call the police?"

"There's no time for that," Dylan responded in frustration. "This guy has been evading the police for weeks. If we lose sight of him now, he may disappear forever."

"Well, what then?" Ryan shouted in a panic.

Dylan quickly looked at Austin. "You're the one with all the plans!" he yelled. "What do we do?"

All of a sudden Austin felt like someone had opened up the floodgates, and he was hit with a debilitating tidal wave of fear and doubt, and he began to feel completely unsure of himself. "I don't know! What if I'm wrong?" he shouted back, as his mind spun in circles. "What if I'm just being paranoid and imagining things again?"

Dylan and Ryan went silent as they listened to Austin battle with himself.

"I mean, we didn't find anything at the RV," Austin said, thinking out loud. "So maybe this guy's not the robber, and there's a logical explanation for all of this. Like, what if Steve just dropped his backpack on the trail, and this guy picked it up...or maybe Steve saw the guy on the main road and felt bad for him, so he gave him his bag? Could be a million answers, right?" he continued to ramble. "Steve's always telling me to mind my own business, so maybe that's what I should do right now?"

Dylan nodded his head. "Yeah, you could be right," he said. "Maybe it's nothing."

The boys took a moment to silently contemplate the many different possible scenarios.

Ryan was the first to break the silence. "But what if it's *not* nothing?" he asked gravely. "What if Steve is in that trunk? Or the guy hurt Steve in some way?" Dylan and Austin listened quietly. "What did you ask us all the other night, Austin? How far would we go to save our friends?" Ryan took a deep breath. "Maybe this is the time to really answer that question."

Ryan's words pierced through Austin's self-doubt like a dagger pricking his soul, and he began to feel like himself again. "You're right," Austin said with assurance. "I know we would all do anything for each other. And there's a chance our friend is in serious trouble." He looked Dylan and Ryan in the eyes. "And Steve would do it for us." Then he stuck his right hand out in front of him. "We do this together?" he asked.

Ryan smiled and immediately put his hand on top of Austin's.

Following right after Ryan, Dylan put his hand in the middle, and said confidently, "I'm with you brother."

"Wendals for life," The boys all said together with a sense of determination and optimism.

"So how do we do it then?" Dylan asked eagerly.

Austin had a plan. "The shortcut we found," he said emphatically. "It's still going to take him a bit to get up that hill." Austin turned his gaze to see the car still climbing up the rough trail in the distance. "He's moving fast, but we might be able to catch up to him if we take the new trail. We'll cut him off at the main road."

Dylan and Ryan nodded their heads quickly. "Well, what are we waiting for?!" Dylan shouted. "Let's follow that car!"

With adrenaline rushing through their bodies, all three boys moved swiftly to their bikes. "Leave anything behind that you don't need," Austin yelled as he picked up his bike, and slung the strap of his binoculars over his head and across his chest. "But, Ryan, take your backpack."

Ryan looked back at Austin as he hopped on his bike. "What for?"

"Just trust me!" Austin shouted back.

Chapter 31

Dylan was the first to burst through the last bit of brush and arrive at the main road, with Austin and Ryan close behind him. All three boys were completely out of breath after their intense climb up the steep trail. Ryan wondered if he had ever physically exerted himself so much in his entire young life, and he was slightly angry that he was the only one carrying a heavy pack on his back. The shortcut trail was a bit rougher in the dark than Austin had anticipated, but the boys had still made the trip in pretty good time. Finally at the main road, they stopped their bikes and tried to catch their breath as they looked around in the darkness. The road was completely devoid of cars, and there were no signs of life anywhere around them.

Breathing heavily, Dylan struggled to speak. "Did we get here first?" he asked hopefully.

Austin looked all around in a dizzying frenzy and took in a deep breath. "I don't know," he exclaimed in frustration. Staring up the road in the direction of the original trail entrance, he couldn't see any headlights or other signs of the Green Ford.

"Well...what do we do?" Ryan shouted. He looked like he was hyperventilating with how fast he was breathing.

"Yeah," Dylan said, quickly looking back and forth down each direction of the road. "Which way do we go?"

Feeling an extreme amount of pressure, Austin tried to think quickly. He had no clue which way the man went, and the fear that they would never find their friend was welling up inside of him.

Then, piercing through the dark black of the night, the boys saw headlights in the distance coming towards them from the direction of town. As the lights got brighter, the hum of a car engine grew louder and louder.

Soon the boys had to shield their eyes from the brightness of the approaching light. "Is it them?" Dylan shouted over the sound of the engine. The boys waited nervously, standing their ground in the middle of the road, blocking the car from passing by.

The vehicle came to a stop in the middle of the road, right in front of the boys. Through the blinding brightness of the headlights, Austin could vaguely tell that the car was a green four-door sedan, similar in shape to the hermit's car. But, as his vision focused, he realized that the car was not an old Ford Escort, but a shiny new Honda Accord.

Moving his bike carefully towards the driver's side of the car, Austin tried to peer through the darkly tinted window. The car sat still for a moment, with the engine idling, before the front window started to roll down.

"Josie!" Austin shouted in complete surprise as soon as he realized who was inside the car. He quickly dropped his bike to the ground and ran to the driver's window. Dylan and Ryan threw their bikes down as well and quickly headed to Austin's side.

Sitting in the driver's seat of the car, Josie was very surprised by the boy's frantic reaction to seeing her there. Her blonde hair was tied up in a bun, and a black bathing suit was visible under her light blue tank top and jean shorts. In the passenger seat of the car sat Josie's popular friend from school, the tall one with the short, dark hair, who was also wearing a bathing suit underneath her clothing. Both girls looked sunburnt from spending the weekend in the sun. "Jumper," by Third Eye Blind, played loudly from the car stereo.

Austin grabbed onto the bottom of the window frame and spoke frenziedly. "Josie!" he shouted again, loud enough to be heard over the music. "What are you doing out here?"

Josie smiled at Austin condescendingly and turned the stereo music down. "We just got back from the lake and wanted to go for a drive," she said calmly.

Looking excited, the dark-haired friend immediately leaned over Josie to get closer to the window. "And we're looking for Steve!" she shouted aggressively. "He can't dump Josie like..."

Josie slapped her friend on the shoulder and shot her an angry look before she could finish her sentence. Immediately embarrassed, the girl quietly sat back in her seat.

Austin had no time for their adolescent drama. "Listen," he said eagerly. "It doesn't matter right now. We need your help."

Josie smiled and spoke calmly again. "Really?" she asked with extreme smugness. "You need *my* help? What's going on?"

Speaking quickly, Austin responded, "There was a car...A green Ford...It came down this road..." His words were choppy and stressed. "Did you see where it went?" Dylan and Ryan stood behind Austin, fidgeting anxiously and hoping the girls could help.

Josie looked at her friend, and the two girls smiled at each other deviously. Then Josie looked back at the boys with the smile still on her face. "We saw the car. What's it to you?"

Dylan let out a sigh of frustration and Ryan smacked his forehead with the palm of his hand. They wondered if they were wasting valuable time with Josie and her friend while the hermit was escaping with Steve.

"Now's not the time, Josie!" Austin shouted angrily. "Please just help us!"

Josie's smile went away and she laughed vindictively. "What about all the times I asked you for help with Steve, huh?" she asked in a stern tone. "You *Wendals* never cared to help me out. Ever!" She cranked the stereo back up, and Third Eye Blind blasted through the car speakers, even louder than before.

The boys' frustrations were boiling over. Trying to be heard over the loud music, they argued with and begged Josie, while she yelled back in protest. "Just tell us where the car went!" Ryan shouted. "This isn't a game, Josie!" Dylan exclaimed.

Finally, sticking his upper body inside the car window, Austin reached for the dashboard, and smacked the car stereo, turning the music off abruptly. Everyone went completely silent, and Josie and her friend looked at Austin, startled. "Listen to me," Austin said, now that he had their attention. "Steve is in serious trouble."

Josie looked at Austin for a moment, but then scrunched her face up in disbelief. "Yeah, right! You Wendals and your stupid pranks. How am I supposed to believe anything you say?" she asked.

Taking in a deep breath, Austin put his hands together in a pleading way. "Josie," he said in the calmest tone he could manage. "I am so sorry for how I treated you. I was wrong." Josie looked at Austin, surprised at how sincere he suddenly sounded. Austin continued, "I've tried to keep Steve to myself, and I see now how selfish that was. If you help us out, I swear to you that I will fully support you and Steve hanging out whenever you want."

Josie and her friend looked at each other again, both completely taken off guard by Austin's new tone. Josie looked back at Austin. Her contentious demeanor had changed and she now looked concerned. "Something really is wrong, isn't it?" she asked.

"There's no time to explain," Austin replied gently. "I need you to tell me where that car went."

Now eager to help, Josie pointed back in the direction that the girls had come from. "He went that way," she said anxiously. "He was driving fast and he almost hit us. But I saw him turn off the highway and onto a dirt trail that went back into the hills." She looked at her friend. "Maybe a quarter mile down the road?" she asked, and her friend quickly nodded.

The boys looked at each other with wide eyes, and then they all hurried to grab their bikes. Getting to his bike first, Austin immediately started up the road speedily. Dylan got on his bike but paused and looked at Josie before he took off. "Go down to the convenience store and call the cops!" he shouted. "Ask for my Dad, he'll know exactly where we are. And tell him Steve was taken by a man with a gun!"

A look of shock and panic came over Josie's face. "What?" she shouted in terror. "What's going on?"

"Just go!" Dylan shouted, and then he and Ryan took off on their bikes down the road.

Chapter 32

Austin stood with his bike on the main road and stared at the entrance to the dirt path where he believed the green Ford Escort had gone. The trail looked similar to the other brush-covered paths they had taken that weekend, except that instead of going west towards the ocean, it headed east into the hills. A deep shiver went through Austin's body, and he wasn't sure if it was because of the coldness of the night, or if it was because he was afraid of what they might find if they followed the trail. He saw Dylan and Ryan heading towards him on their bikes, moving as fast as they could. Coming to a stop next to him, they looked down the dark trail themselves.

"Is this it?" Dylan asked, out of breath again.

"About a quarter-mile down the road, just like the girls said," Austin responded. "And it definitely looks like someone came through here recently." He pointed to the dirt floor at the entrance of the trail.

Ryan quickly pulled a flashlight out of his backpack and shined the beam at the ground. With the help of the light, the boys could see a fresh set of tire tracks in the soft dirt. They also saw other sets of tracks that weren't so fresh but looked like they had been made by the same car.

"I don't think this is his first time out there," Ryan said, and then he pointed the flashlight further down the path. The boys could see that at least the beginning of the new trail was windy and bumpy and covered in brush. "Looks like another rough one," Ryan said. "But with the hills back there, the trail can't go very far, and there's nowhere else for him to go."

Austin nodded in approval. "No lights on the trail," he

said as he put his right foot on his bike pedal and gripped his handlebars tightly. "I don't want him to know we're coming." And at that, Austin took off on his bike down the dark path. Ryan put his flashlight back in his backpack, and then Dylan and Ryan headed down the trail right behind their friend.

In complete silence, the boys traveled down the windy path, over the bumps, and through the brush. The further they got from the main road, the more wild and overgrown the wilderness around them became. In this new area, the brush and foliage were taller and thicker, and the terrain became dense with massive trees. They had gone two miles or so down the trail when Dylan finally signaled for the boys to stop, and all three of them put on their brakes together.

"Look over there," Dylan whispered as he pointed further down the road and off to the east. About two hundred yards away, the boys could see the faint glow of car headlights through the thick brush. "It looks like he's stopped down there."

Looking nervous, Ryan said, "We should get off the path and cut through the bushes if we don't want him spotting us." Austin and Dylan nodded in agreement, and all three boys got off their bikes and quietly hid them in the thick brush. Then they headed into the bushes in the direction of the headlights.

The boys travailed through the brush on foot as quietly as possible. They eventually arrived at a location that appeared to be close enough for them to watch what was happening at the car, but far enough away to not get themselves noticed. They climbed up the side of a small hill overlooking the spot where the car had stopped, hid behind a couple of trees with wide trunks, and spied the situation from their new lookout spot.

The car had stopped at a small clearing in the brush— about forty yards from where the boys were hiding—and was parked so that its headlights pointed into the clearing, lighting up the area all around it awkwardly. In the distance, the boys could see a shadowy figure that appeared to be digging aggressively into the ground in front of a large gray boulder. Next to where the figure was digging, the boys saw a body lying on the ground. The face of the body was covered in a dark shadow, making it hard for the boys to tell if the body on the ground was Steve's.

Grabbing onto the binoculars that were strapped around his chest, Austin pulled them up to his face, and peered through the sights, focusing the best he could on the body that lay on the ground. Even with the terrible lighting, it was clear to him that it was Steve.

Austin could see that his friend had a thick rope tied around his upper body and his arms and that his wrists and ankles were bound tightly together with duct tape. Another large piece of the tape also completely covered his mouth, keeping him from crying out for help. Austin watched Steve flounder and twist his body violently on the ground, fighting to break free of his restraints, with clearly no chance of escaping on his own. The expression on Steve's face was one of pure terror and exhaustion, and a thick line of red blood ran from his forehead all the way down to his chin. His usually suntanned face was now a pale white color.

Seeing Steve like this made Austin sick to his stomach and gave him an intensity of anger that he had never felt before. Every muscle in his body tensed up. Austin tried to quell his rage, knowing that he would need to be as level-headed as possible if he was going to help his friend.

With a grim look on his face, Austin handed the binoculars over to Dylan. "It's Steve," he said quietly. Dylan took the binoculars and viewed the scene for himself.

Even though Ryan had already assumed the worst, it still stung him to have his fears confirmed. "Is he okay?" he asked in a whisper.

"He looks pretty bad off," Austin responded glumly.

Ryan watched the hermit from the distance. "Is he digging a hole?" he asked.

Austin nodded his head.

Feeling his throat tightening up on him, it was hard for Ryan to swallow. He stared down at the ghastly display in the clearing. A shiver ran down his spine as he thought of several different terrifying reasons why a kidnapper would dig a hole out in the middle of nowhere.

Dylan continued to look through the binoculars, watching as the hermit dug into the ground aggressively. After the hole had gotten to a certain depth, the hermit threw the shovel to the side and crawled down into the hole. Exerting himself, the man lifted a large and dirty duffel bag out of the pit and heaved it onto the ground next to the hole. As the bag landed harshly in the dirt, Dylan saw two stacks of crisp twenty dollar bills spill out of the slightly unzipped opening and tumble to the floor next to the bag.

Dylan gasped, almost unable to believe what his eyes were seeing. Until that point, he had never really considered the possibility that his brother might have actually found Bart the Burglar. "You were right," he whispered in a voice that rang of total shock. "He's digging up the money."

Ryan was surprised as well, though not nearly as much so as Dylan. At this point in the weekend, he felt like he was mentally prepared to accept almost anything as a possibility.

Grabbing the binoculars back from Dylan, Austin watched again as the robber continued his work. Now there was a second bag full of cash lying outside of the hole, next to the first one. Austin saw the man bend down into the hole again, and after lifting a third heavy bag out of the ground, the man tossed it next to the others. Then the burglar did the same thing a fourth time. Even though Austin had been sure that the man was Bart the Burglar from the start, he still felt a bit of surprise at his accusations actually being vindicated. But their current situation didn't allow him any satisfaction in his being right.

"I think he got the last bag out," Austin whispered as he watched.

"Good," Ryan responded hopefully. "Maybe now that he's got his money, he can leave Steve alone and run off to Mexico."

Austin continued to watch the burglar, who had finished digging and was standing inside the hole. The man paused for a moment and stared at Steve long and hard as if he were sizing up his body's dimensions. Steve kicked his legs and contorted his body, fighting with all his strength in an attempt to escape his certain fate. Then the burglar grabbed the shovel from off of the ground and began again to dig aggressively.

Feeling an immediate sense of urgency, Austin said, "I don't think we're getting off that easy. I think that if we don't do something quickly, Steve is going to end up in that hole." He put down his binoculars and looked at his friends. "But I've got a plan," he said as confidently as he could. "Ryan, give me your backpack."

Chapter 33

Linda burst through the convenience store door in a hurry and looked around the small shop in distress. The store was completely empty, except for the man at the register with the tan skin and the dark hair. Practically running to the register, Linda almost twisted her ankle as she stumbled in her high heels. She hadn't had time to change out of her interview clothes, being in such a hurry to leave the house and hoping to find Steve before it was too late. She reached down and quickly pulled her heels off of her feet, and held them in her hand as she continued towards the register.

"I'm looking for my son," Linda blurted out as soon as she arrived at the counter. The man gave her a strange look. "He's fifteen years old, with short, spiky, dark blonde hair. He was probably wearing a backpack and riding a BMX bike." Linda was speaking quickly, but the man nodded his head as if he was understanding, so she continued, "He made a call from the pay phone outside, maybe forty minutes ago." She took a deep breath. "Have you seen him?"

With a look of irritation, the man spoke to Linda slowly. "A boy like that has been here a few times this weekend," he said in his thick accent. "He and his friends caused a real scene yesterday." Now the man looked extremely annoyed. "They got in a fight with some other kids right outside there. Made a huge mess for me to clean up."

"That's gotta be him!" Linda shouted hopefully. "Do you know where he is?"

"I have no idea," the man responded. He obviously couldn't care less about helping her. "All I worry about is what happens on my property."

Linda's excitement was slightly deflated. "Did you see anything else at all?"

The store employee thought for a moment. "There was a man," he finally said. "A dirty, smelly, man. He's been coming in here a lot lately to use the restroom. The man was yelling at your son outside, not too long ago. He seemed pretty angry about something your boy did to his car."

Linda didn't know if that information could help her at all. "Did you at least see which direction my son went after he left?" she asked, and the man shook his head. Linda tried to think of more questions she could ask, but she came up blank. "Thanks anyway," she finally said.

Frustrated, Linda turned and hastily headed outside of the store and back into the dark parking lot. A feeling of despair came over her as she strained to figure out what she could possibly do next. She looked across the parking lot and she saw two young girls finishing up a call at the pay phone on the other side of the lot, and she quickly noticed how distraught they appeared. Then, she realized that she knew one of the girls.

"Josie?!" Linda shouted, breaking the silence of the night.

Josie and her friend turned to see Linda running towards them. "Ms. Andretti?!" Josie shouted back, both surprised and relieved. "What are you doing here?" she asked excitedly as Steve's mom arrived at the pay phone.

Linda caught her breath. "I'm looking for Steve," she quickly responded, fighting back her emotions. "He's run away. Do you girls have any idea where he might have gone?"

Josie and her friend looked at each other apprehensively, and then both looked back at Linda. Josie felt a horrible knot in her stomach as she thought about how she would break the news about Steve to his already tormented mother. She tried her best, but could only speak incoherently. "We saw them... up the road...the Wendals," she said through her heavy breaths. Josie's friend trembled hysterically next to her as she spoke. "He's in trouble. A man with a gun...kidnapped..."

The chunks of phrases that Linda could understand turned her worry into complete dread. Trouble? Kidnapped? Gun? Her anxiety skyrocketed and she felt faint. But she knew that there was no time for panic and that all that mattered was finding her son.

Doing her best to stay composed, Linda tried to calm the young girls. "It's okay, just slow down," she said as she put her hand on Josie's shoulder. "It's all going to be okay. Just slow down and tell me where they went." But Linda was definitely not feeling like it was all going to be okay.

Finally regaining enough control over herself, Josie pointed up the road in the direction of the boys. "They were up the road...a few miles...and turned onto a trail...towards the hills," she barely muttered out through her heavy sobbing.

"We called the cops. They're on their way," Josie's friend cut in, completely beside herself.

Linda stared up the ominously dark road and knew she didn't have any time to waste. "You girls stay here and wait for the police!" she shouted resolutely as she headed for her car.

Chapter 34

As Bart the Burglar continued to dig in the light of the car's headlights, his body cast an ominous shadow against the large gray boulder behind him. He breathed heavily as he took one last shovel full of dirt from out of the ground, and tossed it onto the fresh mound of soil next to the hole. The robber stopped for a moment to examine his pit. Satisfied with his work, he placed the dirty shovel on the ground outside of the hole and climbed out.

The man walked over to the four duffel bags that he had just unearthed and examined each one, unzipping them one by one and inspecting the contents inside. A contented smile came over his face as he closed the bags back up. The total earnings of his haul would be enough to last him several comfortable life-times, especially if he lived out the rest of his days in a cheaper country like Mexico. And he knew that he would have a much higher chance of spending the rest of his days outside of a prison cell if he headed across the border.

He also knew that it would be unwise for him to leave any witnesses behind.

Completely exhausted, Steve lay still on the ground, watching the robber's every move and wondering what would happen to him. His forehead continued to bleed, and he felt the pool of blood trickle towards his left eyelid. He quickly closed his left eye and held the lid shut, trying to stop the blood from getting inside. Through his right eye, Steve saw the burglar turn away from his pile of money and head straight towards him. Steve felt a resurgence of adrenaline fill his body, and he began to kick and twist and fight again. He tried his hardest to scream, but with the tape still on his mouth, nothing audible came out. The man grabbed him by his tightly bound legs and began to drag him through the dirt, towards the freshly dug grave. Steve fought even harder, but it was pointless, and he felt his body move closer and closer toward his certain doom.

Then, something shattered the silence of the night. *Bang, bang, bang!* The sound of a nearby exploding firecracker startled both Steve and Bart the Burglar.

With quick reflexes, the man dropped Steve's legs and pulled his gun from out of the back of his pants. He turned around and aimed the gun fiercely in the direction of the sound of the small explosions, ready to fire his weapon without a second thought, but he saw no one there.

The mangy dog popped his head up from inside the back seat of the parked car where it had been resting. Spooked by the tiny explosions, it began to bark ferociously out of the car's half-rolled down rear window.

Steve watched the commotion from his spot in the dirt, next to the menacing hole, unsure as to what was going on.

Now very much on edge, the robber cautiously and slowly moved in the direction of the noise. When he finally spotted the flickering lights of the firecracker in the brush ahead of him, he stopped in the middle of the clearing, aiming the gun steadily in the direction of the firework. He watched as the firecracker's explosions began to fade and eventually stop altogether. The night was silent again, and the man stared into the darkness of the brush in complete confusion.

Bang, bang, bang! The same firecracker sound went off again, but this time behind the robber, and the already startled man anxiously jumped at the loud noise. Spinning his body around quickly, he aimed his gun towards the new explosion. His finger rested on the pistol's trigger, ready to pull at the first sign of threat. He strained his eyes to see in the darkness of the night—the awkwardness of the lighting that came from the car headlight beams not helping—but all he saw was a second lone firecracker popping and flickering in the brush.

With its paws pressed against the glass of the window, the pit bull angrily yapped and bellowed from inside the car. Its head stuck out of the small opening, and it struggled to see what was going on outside.

A third firecracker erupted into small explosions to the left of the robber, and the man spun around quickly again, looking for anything to shoot at. He was furious to find that he was without a target once again.

Then something whizzed past the man's face in a flash, missing him narrowly, and exploded in the bushes behind him with a loud *Pop!* The man turned and saw a burnt-out bottle rocket firework lying on the ground under the brush, just below where the small explosion had occurred. He stared at the firework, bewildered as to what was going on around him. Another bottle rocket zoomed by him and landed on the ground next to his feet with a startling *Pop*, and the man jumped again. A third and fourth bottle rocket flew through the air and exploded almost simultaneously.

Becoming more irate, the robber headed back into the center of the clearing and angrily pointed the gun in all different directions around him, paranoid by the threat of his attacker. He peered into the thick brush and the large trees that surrounded the clearing but saw nothing. The dog continued to bark loudly from the car, getting more and more excited with the sound of every explosion.

The firecrackers finally ceased, and for a moment the night was silent again, except for the sound of the yelping dog. A faint smell of sulfur and potassium nitrate wafted through the air. The man guardedly began to walk in the direction where he thought the bottle rockets had come from, with his gun pointed straight out ahead of him in an attack position.

Boom! A new and more terrible sound broke the night's silence. It was a much louder explosion than all the previous ones combined, and it shook the ground around the disheveled man. The entire clearing, and the sky all around it, lit up in a brilliantly bright red hue, and the man reeled back in terror and braced himself as if he were expecting the impact of a powerful blast. But no such blast came. He looked up into the sky, and through the trees, he saw the dazzling red sparkles of a professional-grade firework high above him, and he heard the *fizzling* sound as the firework faded away. After a few moments, the night turned black again.

Boom! Boom! Boom! A second large firework painted the night sky with an awesome blue, and then a third with a brilliant green, and a fourth with a dazzling white. The large fireworks continued to erupt relentlessly, one after another, and the dog's barks became even more excited and angry.

With wide eyes, Steve stared up at the night sky from his position on the ground and watched the spectacle that, to him, rivaled anything he had seen at any Fourth of July celebration. He was now one hundred percent sure of who his rescuers were. And though he was still convinced that his fate was to end up in that hole, he suddenly and strangely felt a remarkable sense of peace and pride as he thought about his friends coming to his aid.

Chapter 35

Driving speedily down the dark road, Linda frantically looked out the windows around her, searching for any sign of her son, or the trail that went into the hills that Josie had spoken of. So far, all she had seen was asphalt, dirt, and brush. Her feelings of anxiety and fear were almost to a breaking point and the voice inside her head was telling her that she would never see her child again. But she pressed on, hoping against hope that maybe she still had time. If there was something in her life worth fighting for, Steve was it, and she had decided on that terrifying drive that she would bring her son safely back home, or else she would die trying.

Linda saw something shimmering on the side of the dark and empty road, and she slammed on her brakes and came to a quick stop. Leaving the engine running, she hopped outside and ran towards the item. It was a silver BMX bike, lying in the dirt all by itself. Picking up the bike and examining it, she confirmed that it was Steve's, and instantly felt an inkling of hope. She anxiously looked all around her for any other sign of her missing son, but when she found nothing, her hope started to fade again.

Boom! The sound of a loud explosion in the distance almost gave Linda a heart attack. A red firework lit up the sky all around her. Her heart racing, she turned and saw the luminous flames of the firework sparkling in the night sky, back at the foot of the hills to the east of the main road. She stared in awe, trying to recall something from the day before.

"The Wendals," she whispered to herself as she suddenly remembered the fireworks that the boys had stashed in their backpacks before the camping trip.

At her best guess, Linda estimated that the firework had been launched only a mile or so away from where she currently stood on the road. Without another second's hesitation, she dropped Steve's bike and ran back to her car. She wasn't sure how she would find her way to the source of the firework, but somehow she knew without a doubt that she would find her son there.

Chapter 36

Ryan had moved away from the boys' hiding spot and was now about thirty yards or so from where Dylan and Austin continued to watch Bart the Burglar from behind the large trees. The field that Ryan was now in was more open and clear of trees and generally much more conducive for the launching of his firework show. He had situated the mortar launching tube on the ground in front of him and stabilized the base of the launcher with two large rocks. Ryan held another ball-shaped mortar firework in his hand and loaded the shell into the launching tube as carefully as he could. The fact that he was working in the pitch dark, combined with the pressure of their current situation, had him worried that he might make a mistake and blow off one of his fingers or set fire to the dry brush around him—but he was willing to take those risks tonight, for the life of his friend.

The twinkling light of his last aerial explosion was just fading away when Ryan used his Bic lighter to ignite the long fuse that was attached to the ball-shaped mortar and was sticking outside of the launching tube. The tip of the fuse sparkled wildly as Ryan quickly turned and sprinted across the field, back in the direction of his friends.

Fizz! The sparkling flame moved fast along the fuse and disappeared into the tube. Moments later the firework shot high into the air and then exploded in the sky with a loud *boom*, and the field around the boys was bathed in a hot orange color.

Rejoining his friends at their hideout spot behind the trees, Ryan said in an intense whisper, "That was the last one."

Dylan had three filled-up water balloons in his lap and

waited anxiously for Austin to fill up another. Austin was using Ryan's plastic water bottle with the squirt top nozzle to fill up another balloon, just as Ryan had taught him. As soon as the balloon was the right size, Austin pulled it off of the water bottle and quickly tied the end shut.

"We only have four balloons left," Austin said to Ryan, worried about his plan working out.

"That'll be enough," Ryan assured him, knowing they needed to stay positive.

After pulling the water balloon launcher from out of Ryan's open backpack, Austin handed it to Ryan, who took the launcher and nodded approvingly as he searched for the handles at either end.

Dylan laid the water balloons from his lap carefully onto the top of Ryan's backpack and then grabbed one end of the water balloon launcher. He gave Austin a grave look. "Are you sure we can do this?"

Looking back at his brother, Austin took a nervous breath. "We have no choice."

Still standing in the middle of the clearing, the robber aimed his gun around angrily as he cursed to himself. The glow from the final firework had faded away, and once again the clearing was left with only the light from the robber's car headlights. The mangy dog had stopped his barking, and the night had become silent again.

The disheveled man looked back at Steve and then stared at him for a moment. Then he noticed something strange. The look of sheer terror and confusion he had seen in the boy's eyes moments earlier was gone, and now his prisoner almost seemed...hopeful? Then, realizing what might be giving the boy his false sense of hope, Bart the Burglar smiled.

The robber turned and looked all around him, into the thickness of the surrounding brush and trees. "I know who you are!" he shouted aggressively into the darkness. His voice was tense and slightly hoarse. "You're the kids who've been camping out next to me!" He lowered his gun and seemed to at least pretend like he was trying to be reasonable. "I know you've been snooping around my trailer, and I know that you know who I am!" He waited a moment for a response from the brush, but nothing came. "I know you're probably all just as scared as your little friend here, so I'm going to make you a deal," he shouted again, trying to make his voice sound friendly and enticing. "If you come out now, I'll let your friend go." Then he pointed the gun backward at the bags of money that were piled in the dirt next to Steve. "And I'll even share some of this money with you. You can have as much as you want, but you have to come out now!" Continuing to stare into the trees, he waited patiently. The night was painfully silent, and he heard no response or indication of any movement from within the brush.

When his patience began to run out, the robber moved the gun sideways, until it was pointed directly at Steve, and he snarled into the brush. "Have it your way then," he yelled angrily. "If you don't show yourselves right now, then I guess I'll just have to put a bullet in your little friend's head!"

Steve's heart began to race again as he stared up at the barrel of a loaded gun for the second time that night. Although he was convinced that this was the end for him, all he could think of now was the safety of his friends, and he prayed that they would leave him and get as far away from this madman as they could. He thought about how devastated their families would be if they didn't return home that night, and he thought how he couldn't bear to be the reason they never saw their loved ones again. He felt lightheaded and dizzy, and the clearing seemed like it was starting to spin in circles around him.

Ryan and Dylan stretched their ends of the water balloon launcher out wide on each side of Austin and held their handles straight forward. They spread their legs and bent their knees to give themselves a stronger launching stance. Both boys were deathly anxious as they looked down into the clearing, where, in the sharp light of the car headlights, they could see the robber pointing his gun straight at Steve.

Dylan looked back at his brother, who was loading a water balloon into the launching pouch. "We've gotta go now," he said urgently.

Once Austin had the first balloon secured in the pouch, he pulled back on the pouch's grip, stretched the water balloon launcher into a firing position, and bent down on one knee, lining up his aim. His eyes strained as he stared down into the clearing and at his distant target. The conditions were not great, with the poor lighting, and the brush and tree branch obstacles that could potentially impede his shot. But somehow, Austin felt like his vision was beginning to work for him at a heightened level, and he could see his target clearly through the dark.

Austin made a small adjustment to his left, and then lowered the pouch towards the ground by a half an inch. He fought off the nervous thoughts that pressed into his mind. He knew he needed to think positively, but at that moment, he wished that it was Steve who was taking the shot instead of him.

Ryan held his end of the launcher tightly, as sweat rolled down his forehead. "You gotta take the shot, man," he whispered to his friend.

Austin made his final adjustments and knew that it was now or never. "Come on, Austin," he whispered to himself. "For the Wendals. For Steve."

The robber continued to hold the gun aimed at Steve with his finger resting on the trigger, and he looked up into the brush once again. "I gave you your chance," he yelled at the top of his lungs. "Say goodbye to your friend!" He looked back at Steve and hesitated for a moment. Then he tightened his finger around the trigger and slowly began to pull.

Zoom! Something flew past the robber's head in a flash and crashed against the large boulder behind him. The robber jumped backward, startled and annoyed. He looked at the boulder and saw a wet stain in the middle of the rock. Then he turned back around and stared into the dark brush again.

Whoosh! Another water balloon shot out through the brush, this one missing him on the opposite side and crashing onto the back window of his car. The mangy dog hopped up and down in the back seat, barking angrily as he looked through the back window of the car.

Reacting quickly, the robber swung around and faced the bushes where the balloons had come from. His eyes were filled with an indignant rage as he raised his arm and aimed the gun in the direction of the boys. Then he pulled the trigger and the gun exploded, firing a shot into the dark forest ahead of him. He fired a second shot, and then a third. Each shot from the small hand-gun sounded like the blast from a canon as it resonated through the quiet clearing.

Before the disheveled man could fire a fourth shot, another balloon came flying from out of the dark woods. Like a heat-seeking missile, this one made a direct hit on its intended target, exploding onto the disheveled man's stomach, and stunning the man with a powerful force. The man bent forward in pain, the impact having knocked the wind completely out of him.

Collecting himself, the man tried his best to shake off the blow, and he slowly lifted his gun back up towards his attacker—now more angry than ever. But before he could steady his shot, another balloon flew out of the brush, this one crashing straight into the man's face.

The robber's arms flew outward in painful shock and agony, and the tight grip that he had had on his weapon was loosened, and the gun was tossed to the ground wildly. Somehow, the man managed to stay on his feet, and he stumbled forward in the clearing, covering his stinging face with his hands.

Then, like one of his favorite professional wrestlers charging into the ring, Dylan burst through the dark wooded foliage and into the clearing, sprinting as fast as he could towards the disoriented robber. By the time the man saw him coming, it was too late, and Dylan speared the confused man with his right shoulder and tackled him backward. The two of them slammed onto the ground hard and rolled violently in the dirt, kicking up a large cloud of dust. Realizing that this was his chance, Dylan scrambled to his feet as quickly as he could and searched the ground for the missing weapon. He quickly spotted the handgun lying alone by the back tire of the car and he made an immediate move towards it.

Dylan didn't get far before he felt two hands grab on to his right ankle with powerful force. The robber pulled Dylan back down onto the ground in a single heave, and the two commenced a vicious wrestling match. There were flurries of punches, kicks, chokeholds, and armbars, all inside the cloud of dust that now filled the clearing. Dylan fought with all he had, but the robber, being slightly stronger than he was, began to overpower him.

Austin and Ryan finally broke through the brush and into the clearing, eager to know what was going on. They saw the wrestling match taking place and immediately knew that Dylan was losing. Instinctively, the boys ran to help their friend right away. But before they could get to the brawl, they heard a loud and terrible growl coming from inside the Ford Escort. Stopping dead in their tracks, the boys watched as the mangy dog squeezed its body through the half-open back seat window of the car, and landed on the ground, right in between them and the wrestling match.

Shaking violently, the dog barked and snapped at the two boys, holding its ground in the middle of the clearing. The angry animal's muscles were tense and its eyes were glassed over, looking especially worked up and irritated by the commotion that had been made by the fireworks and gunshots. There was no way around the ferocious guard dog. Petrified with fear, and not knowing what they could do, Austin and Ryan stayed right where they were.

The robber finally rolled on top of Dylan, gaining a clear advantage in the fight, and he angrily threw several powerful punches until he landed one that connected squarely with

Dylan's left temple. Dylan was dazed, and for a moment was unable to fight back. Taking advantage of Dylan's temporary incapacitation, the robber scurried through the dirt and grabbed a hold of his loaded handgun. Then he slowly rose back up onto his feet and pointed the gun at Austin and Ryan.

Austin and Ryan looked on in horror, terrified of both the raging dog and the man with the gun.

Lying in the dirt, all alone, Steve watched the terrible scene helplessly.

The mangy dog continued to howl savagely at the boys. However, when it saw the disheveled man standing with the gun in his hand, the dog turned and began to howl at him as well. Confused, the dog went back and forth between the man and the boys, barking, and yapping, unsure as to who was the bigger threat for the time being.

Dylan finally recovered from his stunned state and scrambled backward, away from the robber and the dog. He got to his feet and watched the standoff fearfully.

The robber snarled at the boys, and then walked towards his dog confidently, believing he could control the animal, as he always had. But as the man got closer to the dog, the pit bull let out a deep growl, as if it was warning the man to stay back. Stopping for a moment, the man stared at the dog. "Don't you bark at me like that," he shouted authoritatively. The dog went quiet and then looked back at the boys with a look that said it was still confused as to what it should do.

The disheveled man took another step towards the dog, and the dog immediately began to growl again, this time more aggressively than before. Bart the Burglar quickly became irritated at the animal's disloyalty. "Shut up!" he yelled cruelly. Stepping forward, the man raised his arm and viciously smacked the dog across the face with the barrel of the handgun.

The dog whimpered in pain and immediately cowered down to the ground, again fearful of the man's power and rage.

Gasping in horror, Ryan glared at the robber resentfully. Then he looked down at the trembling dog and could see in its eyes the torment that comes from a life filled with abuse and neglect. Even in that moment of crisis, Ryan felt for the poor animal. The mangy dog looked back at Ryan pitifully.

"Don't worry," Ryan whispered to the dog. "It's all going to be okay."

The robber started to laugh and looked up at Austin and Ryan. He raised the gun again and pointed it at the boys, with a murderous smile on his face.

Closing their eyes tightly, the two boys braced themselves for the shot of the gun.

But instead of the sound of a gun blast, they heard a completely different sound—the sound of Bart the Burglar screaming in agony.

Austin and Ryan opened their eyes and saw the mangy dog hanging from the robber's arm, with its jaws firmly clamped down around the man's bicep. Trying to break free of the dog's painful bite, the man flailed his arm wildly, sending the gun flying through the air and into the nearby bushes. The dog continued its aggressive attack, until the robber fell backward, hitting his head violently on the hood of the green Ford Escort. The man tumbled to the ground and his body went completely limp.

Waiting to see if the robber would make another move, the mangy dog stood over the man's idle body, growling defensively.

The boys could hardly believe what had just happened, and it took them a moment before they realized they were safe. Once they did, Ryan ran to the mangy dog and fearlessly wrapped his arms around its neck. The dog was instantly pacified, and it excitedly licked Ryan's face.

Running quickly to check on the robber, Dylan made sure that the threat truly was neutralized. Once it was clear to him that the man was out cold, he started searching all around for the gun.

Austin went straight to Steve and, kneeling by his friend's side, he eagerly tore the duct tape from off of his face. "Steve!" he yelled frantically. "Are you okay?"

Steve was trembling, both from the pain of the tape being pulled from his face, as well as from the horror of the events of the last couple of hours. He breathed in heavily through his mouth, savoring every bit of fresh air, and trying to calm himself down. Then he looked up at his friend, still in complete shock, and replied, "Yeah, I think so."

Austin gave Steve a contented smile and then quickly began to loosen the rope that was wrapped around his body. Dylan and Ryan came running over to join the two and eagerly began to help Austin untie their friend.

"Steve!" Ryan shouted enthusiastically as he tore the duct tape from his friend's ankles.

Dylan worked on breaking the tape from his wrists. "Another mess I had to get you out of!" He exclaimed, laughing gleefully.

The mangy dog had followed right behind Ryan and sat down next to the boys. Its tongue hung loosely from its mouth and it panted excitedly.

Still feeling nervous, Austin looked at Dylan and anxiously inquired, "Bart the Burglar?"

"Unconscious," Dylan said as he tore at the tape.

"What about the gun?" Austin asked.

"We couldn't find it," Ryan responded. "Must be somewhere in the bushes."

The boys pulled the last bit of tape and rope from off of Steve and then sat him up against the large boulder. Steve was visibly shaken. His forehead was bruised black and purple where he had been hit by the gun, and the blood in his open gash was starting to clot. The color was just starting to come back to his face, but he still looked grayer than usual.

Ryan knew he should give his friend a moment to calm down and breathe, but he couldn't control himself. "What happened?!" he shouted impatiently.

It took Steve a moment, but he eventually smiled faintly at the boys. "Wouldn't you like to know," he said sarcastically, his voice still weak. The boys were glad to see that he still had his sense of humor, even after all that had happened. Then his smile faded again. "It's a long story," he said dismally, and Ryan didn't press him any further. Steve looked at Austin. "You were right. I should have believed you," he said. Austin could hear a deep remorse in his voice.

But Austin no longer cared who was right and who was wrong. He was just glad to have his friend back—at least for the time being. "I got lucky," he said with a smile. "And if it wasn't for my insistence on this stupid plan, you never would have been in danger anyway."

Steve shook his head quickly, then cringed as he felt a sharp pain from within his skull. He pressed firmly on his right temple with the palm of his hand, trying to relieve the pain. "No," he said, still cringing. "You were just trying to help me. It's not okay how I treated you. You're the best friend I've ever had...I should have trusted you." He lowered his hand from his head as the pain subsided and looked around at his friends. "The Wendals are the best friends I've ever had. I guess I've just hated knowing it couldn't last."

Austin looked over at the large duffel bags full of cash sitting unattended in the dirt. "It could last a little longer if we wanted it to," he said, nodding towards the money. "It's ours for the taking."

The Wendals all stared at the bags of money together. They would probably never see that much money again for the rest of their lives, and the boys were certain that no one would ever know if they took just enough to get Steve's family back on their feet. And after all they had been through, why shouldn't they take a reward for their trouble?

Austin looked back at the Wendals with uncertainty. "I'm not making that decision though," he said. "It's Steve's life, so it's Steve's call." He looked at Steve with a sly and sarcastic grin. "I should really just mind my own business when it comes to this sort of thing anyway."

Steve laughed softly and took a moment before he finally

responded. "No," he said firmly. "It's not our money. We should turn it all in to the police." The boys all looked surprised at what Steve was saying. "My mom and I need to work out our problems the right way, or else we'll just end up back in the same type of mess a year from now." Looking confident in his decision, he took a deep breath. "I'm gonna go live with my dad. That way my mom can have some time to figure her stuff out. Who knows, maybe I'll end up back here someday," he said with a smile. "We'll still be Wendals, regardless of where I'm living, right?"

Austin, Dylan, and Ryan all smiled and nodded in quick agreement.

Though he still dreaded the thought of giving up Steve, Austin was ready to do what was best for his friend. "No matter what happens, you will always be a Wendal," Austin said proudly. "And you'll always be my best friend."

"Wendals for life!" Ryan shouted loudly.

Dylan joined in, "Wendals for life!"

A large smile came over Steve's worn-out face. "Wendals for life," he said with the little energy he had.

Click! The boys heard the gut-wrenching sound of a handgun being cocked behind them.

Feeling a suffocating terror, Austin turned around to see the robber, standing on his feet, with his gun pointed back at them. The horrid man had a disturbing look of both pain and indignation on his face as he rubbed the back of his head with his free hand and stumbled forward dazedly.

The mangy dog hopped up on its paws and immediately started growling in fierce anger at its former master.

The man glared back at the dog. "I should have put you down a long time ago!" he yelled angrily and then pointed the gun at the pit bull.

"No!" Ryan shouted as he quickly jumped in front of the animal, shielding it from harm. His heart raced in his chest as he thought his life was about to end.

Seeing what Ryan had done, and making a split-second decision, Dylan and Austin both jumped in front of Ryan. The two brothers wrapped their arms around their friend, protecting him from the bullet that they were sure was coming their way. Then they stared back at the robber determinedly.

Surprised, the robber lowered the gun and looked at the boys. "All so eager to die?" he asked, still rubbing his head. "Have it your way." He raised the gun again and pointed it at the cluster of bodies, ready to shoot.

Vrrrrrrrmmmm! The low hum of a car engine vibrated through the night air, coming from just outside of the surrounding brush. Keeping the gun aimed at the boys, the robber quickly turned his head, startled by the unexpected sound.

Just as surprised as the robber, the boys fixed their gazes on the bushes as well, wondering what could be happening. The engine sound grew louder and louder and appeared to be heading straight for their clearing. Then, in a flash, a pair of headlights burst violently through the thick foliage, illuminating everything around them. The car's engine roared as the vehicle flew into the center of the clearing and slammed on its brakes just in front of a startled Bart the Burglar. Stumbling backward, the robber shielded his eyes from the blinding light of the car beams.

Immediately, the Wendals recognized the car as Linda Andretti's white Dodge Neon—covered in dirt and tree branches—and they saw Steve's mom sitting in the driver's seat of the car, with a look of total shock and alarm on her face. The car engine idled as Linda took in the scenery around her, trying to decide what was going on around her.

Linda's attention quickly went to the filthy looking man in the dirty baseball cap standing right in front of her and looking just as confused as she did. It was several moments before Linda realized why the man looked so familiar. *The dirty customer from the diner!* she thought. *What is he doing here?*

There was a brief standstill, the man staring at Linda, and Linda staring back at the man. Then the robber raised his arm and pointed the gun at Linda. His expression was deliberate, and his eyes were cold.

From that point on, everything seemed to happen in slow motion for Linda. She saw the gun being aimed at her face. She felt her foot lift off from the brakes and slam down onto the gas pedal. She heard the engine roar and the tires spinning wildly in the dirt. A gunshot was fired, and Linda saw the bullet break through the glass windshield. A second shot was fired and Linda felt the car lurching forward. Then there was a collision. The man's face slammed onto the windshield, and soon he was rolling on top of the car. Then there was a second collision. This one was louder and harsher than the first, and Linda felt her face against the car's airbag. The Dodge Neon had stopped moving, and everything in the clearing was quiet again.

Looking on in horror, the boys hoped that it was all finally over. They had witnessed Linda drive straight into the robber, sending him flying over the top of the car, and crash landing back down onto the dirt in the middle of the clearing. He once again appeared to be unconscious, but this time, after the hit he had taken from the car, the boys doubted he would be getting up any time soon. After hitting the disheveled man, Linda's car had crashed straight into the green Ford Escort. The boys stared at the car, praying that Linda was all right.

The driver's side door to the Dodge Neon flew open, and Linda Andretti stumbled out of the car. Her face was scraped and bruised, but she appeared to be otherwise in good health. Standing up quickly, Dylan and Ryan ran to her aid, just in case she was worse off than she looked.

Linda's eyes immediately locked onto her son.

Still lying against the boulder, Steve looked back at his Mom, unsure as to how she would react to seeing him there.

Linda's eyes filled with tears. "Steven!" she shouted as she ran to her son. Falling down at Steve's side, she quickly wrapped her arms around him, trembling with both terror and joy.

Steve had never been so happy to receive a hug from his mom.

Wanting to give them some space, Austin stood up and

backed away from the two. He smiled as he watched the warm embrace of mother and son.

Dylan quickly went to the unconscious robber and grabbed the gun from off the ground next to where he lay. He could hear the faint sound of police sirens in the distance, and he imagined they were on the main highway now and would be at the clearing soon.

After kissing Steve's forehead ecstatically, Linda looked her son in the eyes. "You had me so worried," she said with a shaky voice. "Your phone message...the bike in the middle of the road...those fireworks..." she hugged her son tightly again, and Steve hugged her back. Then she pulled back and looked at her son again, with a terrified expression. "Why did that man have a gun?!"

Steve smiled, absolutely content at the moment. He had never seen his mom so worried about him, and it felt really good. "I'm okay, mom," he said confidently. "Everything is okay now."

Linda smiled and continued to cry joyfully. "Well, that's all that matters," she said. Then she looked around at the Wendals. "That's all that ever really matters." She signaled for the boys to come in closer to her, and the Wendals and Linda all shared an emotional embrace.

Austin knew that Linda was right. They were all safe, and for the moment they were all together, and nothing else really mattered at all.

Chapter 37

The once dark and isolated clearing was now teaming with noise and activity. Ambulances and police cars filled the open spaces, bathing the area in red, blue, and yellow flashing lights. Young police deputies patrolled the grounds, writing reports, and collecting evidence. An older detective with a mustache chatted with a young man in a business suit, pointing excitedly at the large bags of money that still laid next to the grave-sized pit in the ground.

Standing next to the Dodge Neon in his full police uniform, Sergeant Kenney listened intently as Linda animatedly described her run-in with the robber and the car crash that followed. He jotted down notes on a clipboard while she spoke excitedly.

Steve sat on the tail bumper of a large ambulance with a thick, white bandage wrapped around his head, while a young female medic checked his vitals. Huddled around Steve, the other three Wendals laughed and joked as they recounted the events of their crazy weekend. The mangy dog sat calmly in the middle of the boys, while Ryan affectionately scratched its head.

"We've never had a Wendal mascot before," Dylan said to the group playfully. "What should we name him?"

Ryan looked down at the dog with a smirk and then looked up at Dylan. "Well, I'm sorry to break it to you," he said, now laughing unabashedly. "But the newest member of the Wendals is not a *he*. It's a *she*!"

Looking at Ryan, Dylan patted his friend on the shoulder affectionately. "Well, that's just really great," he said in a sarcastic tone. "I knew you would eventually find yourself a girl-friend."

The boys all laughed together at the remark.

"Actually, I think it would be refreshing to finally have a female Wendal in the group," Austin said excitedly. "We're breaking new ground!"

"Well, what do you call a female Wendal?" Ryan asked, partly in jest.

Amused by their conversation, the young medic smiled at the boys as she finished up with Steve. "You're all set," she said to him. "You may have a bit of a headache for the next couple of days, but other than that you should be just fine."

Steve smiled back and thanked the young lady. Then he noticed the name tag that was pinned onto her chest, right above her left shirt pocket—it read *Wilma.* Steve smiled and laughed to himself as the medic walked away, thinking it was just too perfect to be a coincidence. As soon as she was gone he quickly looked at the boys. "Wilma!" he said excitedly. "You call a female Wendal a Wilma."

Looking impressed, the other boys nodded in approval.

"Okay, Wilma it is," Ryan said as he bent down and gave the mangy pit bull a hug. The dog licked Ryan across his face. "You're my dog now, Wilma, whether my parents like it or not." Wilma's tail wagged excitedly and she gave a loud howl of approval.

A smile came to Austin's face as he thought about how much Ryan and the dog both deserved each other.

Sergeant Kenney handed his clipboard off to another officer in full uniform and then left the officer to finish taking down Linda's report without him. Then he headed over to the Wendals, who all suddenly quieted down as soon as they saw him coming. The sergeant settled into the group and then looked at Steve sympathetically. "We're almost done here," he said. "And then we can get all of you home." Looking at his sons, his expression became more serious. "Just from the pieces of the story that I'm putting together so far, it doesn't appear that you guys listened to me *at all* when I told you to stay out of trouble." He gave Austin a particularly stern glare.

The Wendals all looked guilty and apologetic.

Sergeant Kenney relaxed his glare. "I guess we'll deal with that later though. I'm just glad you're all okay," he said with a smile. Then he chuckled as he looked at Dylan and Austin and exclaimed, "Your mom is going to kill you guys when she finds out the whole story." He continued to laugh for a moment, but then, looking at Ryan, he immediately stopped his laughter, and his expression changed to one of pure pity. "And *your* mom," he said softly to Ryan. "Gosh, I don't think I'd go home if I were you."

As he thought about how angry his parents were going to be when they found out that he had lied to them, Ryan's throat suddenly felt tight.

Sergeant Kenney smiled at the boys and then left the group and started yelling out orders to the uniformed police officers around him.

After finishing her report with the young policeman, Linda headed over to the boys and joined in on their huddle. Her white blouse was dirty, and her hair and makeup were messy. She looked at Steve affectionately. "I sure am grateful Steve has the Wendals," she said, sounding as if she was holding back tears again. "I promise I'll never complain about you guys raiding my fridge again."

Dylan became especially excited at that promise.

But Austin looked at Linda, disappointed. "But we won't even be able to take you up on that offer now," he said with a raspy voice.

Seeing a look of discouragement on all four boys' faces, Linda became confused. "Well, what do you mean?" she asked, very concerned.

Steve looked at his mom, now confused as well. "Because I'll be living in Utah, starting tomorrow," he said, without any hint of strife or resentment.

In the chaos of the evening, Linda had completely forgotten that she had ever even considered abandoning her son, and her eyes went wide. The idea seemed so foreign and awful to her now. "Oh wow, I forgot to tell you!" she said enthusiastically. All four boys perked up and listened with anxious anticipation. "I called your dad, and I told him not to come down here," Linda exclaimed.

Steve couldn't believe what he was hearing. "Really?" he asked with a bit of skepticism.

A confident feeling came over Linda, as she had never been so sure of any decision in her life. "I realized that whatever we need to do to get out of this mess, we need to do it together," she said. "So, yes, really."

Steve shot off the back of the ambulance and abruptly wrapped his arms around his mom in an exuberant bear hug, burying his head into her neck. Linda was taken aback by this, not used to such a blatant showing of affection from her son. She liked it very much, and she held her son tightly in her arms. "You belong here with me," she said passionately. "And with the Wendals too."

Barely able to contain their enthusiasm at the hugely important news, Austin, Ryan, and Dylan looked at each other excitedly. Austin felt very sure that everything would work out if they all stuck together and that Steve and Linda would find a way to fix their financial problems.

Another police officer in a full uniform and hat walked towards the group, escorting a middle-aged man wearing a dark suit and tie. After pointing to the Wendals, the officer left the man's side and went back to his work on the crime scene. The man in the suit approached the group, and the boys and Linda turned to greet the new visitor.

Linda immediately recognized the man as the bank manager that she had met with earlier that day.

"Ms. Andretti, is that you?" the manager asked, surprised to see Linda.

Linda was starting to get used to the day's constant surprises. "Well, hello," she said with some awkwardness. "What are you doing here?"

Smiling, the man looked around at the boys again. His crisp and clean business suit was in stark contrast to the pandemonium of everything the boys had been around that night and brought with it a small sense of order. "The police phoned me, and I had to come right away to thank these brave young men in person," he said proudly, still looking around at the boys. "As you know, we've been spending a lot of valuable time and resources trying to help the police catch this criminal and recover our stolen money, and I was elated when I heard that this nightmare was finally over!" The man started to laugh arrogantly. But when he quickly realized that his audience wasn't finding the humor in the situation, he became serious once again.

"Anyway," he continued, clearing his throat awkwardly. "We've kept very careful accounting of every dollar that was stolen from us. And from the preliminary numbers my guys have given me, it appears that the full amount will be accounted for in the bags that you have given back to us!" Clasping his hands together, the man's face beamed with excitement. When he didn't see a similar reaction from the boys or Linda, he threw his arms out to his side and exclaimed, "You boys are heroes in the bank's eyes!"

Linda nodded her head slowly as the man finished speaking. "Well, I'm glad you guys got your money back and all," she said stoically. "But I'm not so sure I would celebrate what happened tonight. These boys could have been killed."

The banker's smile faded and he shook his head quickly. "I completely understand that," he said in a humbled tone, and he looked at the Wendals sympathetically. "Well, it might not make up for everything you boys have been through, but hopefully the bank's reward will help compensate you for some of your pain and suffering?"

Completely surprised and confused, Steve, Dylan, and Ryan all looked at Austin.

Austin shrugged his shoulders as he looked back at his

friends. He was just as surprised as anyone else at the mention of a reward, and he turned to the banker. "What are you talking about?" he asked sincerely.

At first, the banker was taken aback by the boys' confusion, but when they continued to stare back at him blankly, he began to laugh heavily. "Well, of course!" he said with a voice that boomed through his laughter. "The fifty-thousand dollar reward that the bank announced a couple of days ago. You must have known about it? Why else would you be out here looking for the robber?" The man's face was red from his laughter.

Austin's jaw dropped open and he looked at his friends in complete amazement. As the amount of the reward started to sink in, ear-to-ear smiles came across the boys' faces.

Thinking she must have heard the man wrong, Linda asked in amazement, "Fifty *thousand* dollars?!"

"Absolutely," the manager said boastfully. "That amount is nothing compared to what that criminal took from us. Not to mention all of the cash we were spending trying to track him down." He smiled proudly. "I'd like to present the money to you first thing Monday morning—in front of the local media, of course," he smiled sheepishly. "That should help with the PR crisis we've been dealing with. I'm assuming you would like four checks, split evenly between you boys?" he asked, and then waited for a response.

Austin looked at both Ryan and Dylan. The two boys could somehow read Austin's mind, and they smiled and nodded to their friend.

"It all goes to Steve and Linda," Austin replied to the bank manager with certainty.

Linda was speechless.

Shaking his head, Steve said soberly, "You don't have to do that." Then he looked at Linda. "My mom and I will be okay. We're going to figure things out."

Linda nodded in quick agreement. "That's too much, boys, we can't accept that," she said. "You deserve a piece of that money too."

"No way," Dylan piped in. "I won't accept any of it," he said, and then looked at the bank manager. "It all goes to Steve and Linda."

Ryan smiled. "I don't want any of it either," he said emphatically, and then his smile faded. "Trust me, my parents wouldn't let me take any reward anyway... after they find out what went down this weekend."

Austin looked at Steve and shrugged his shoulders again. "You found the money all on your own," he said laughing. "I was totally wrong about where we'd find it."

Steve puffed out his chest and put his arm around Austin. "Yeah, I guess you were *way* off, as usual," he said sarcastically, and the Wendals all laughed.

The bank manager smiled at the boys and then turned his attention to Linda. "One last thing before I go," he said. "Seeing that our big issue at the bank is now resolved...and that you had a hand in resolving it." Linda looked on, eager to hear what he had to say. "I'd love to officially offer you that position as a part of our team at the bank," he said. "That is, if you still want it?"

Tears began to well up in Linda's eyes, and it took her a moment before she could speak. "Yes," she finally said, her voice tight with emotion. "I would like that very much." She smiled at the manager. "Thank you."

"Excellent," the manager responded. "My assistant will give you a call Monday morning to finalize things then." He looked around at the Wendals one last time. "Thanks again, boys," he said, and then he turned and headed back towards his car.

Linda and the boys stood in their circle, all of them speechless and quite amazed at how everything was turning out.

Suddenly becoming very excited, Steve looked at Austin. "I just had a great idea! About how we can spend some of the leftover reward money," he said with his typical smirk. Then he looked at his mom. "After we pay off all our bills first, of course."

Linda smiled and nodded.

Without Steve having to say another word, Austin felt a rush of adrenaline fill his body. He didn't even need to ask what his friend had in mind. If it involved all of the Wendals together, then he already knew it would be great.

Epilogue

Two Weeks Later

It was a perfectly sunny morning in San Diego, California, and the Del Mar outdoor amphitheater was packed tightly with enthusiastic punk rockers. The raucous crowd was adorned in mohawks, baggy shorts, studded belts, and t-shirts of their favorite bands—*The Vandals, Pennywise, Rancid,* and *Face to Face.* Large signs and banners all over the venue read *WARPED TOUR '98.*

Hordes of grungy concert-goers pushed their way towards the main stage where Blink-182 was in the middle of an energetic set. Tom, the band's guitarist, quickly picked at his guitar strings, playing the intro to their popular song, "A New Hope." The crowd jumped up and down and bobbed their heads to the sound of the fast-paced music.

Dylan, Ryan, Steve, and Austin rocked out from their spots backstage, feeling like they had died and gone to heaven. They had figured that after everything they had been through, they could afford to splurge on the punk festival's most expensive VIP passes.

From where they were standing, the music coming out of the large speaker system was so loud that Ryan wondered if his eardrums would burst. They were so close to the band's drummer, Travis, that Austin could see each bead of sweat that dripped from his forehead and splashed down onto the large drum in front of him. Steve's gaze was fixed on the bass player, Mark, as he danced around the stage and showed off to the crowd. When the guitarist, Tom, began to sing the lyrics of the song, the boys sang right along to every word.

Behind the boys, a little further back, and away from the booming speakers, Linda and Josie smiled as they watched the Wendals singing and dancing together.

Not quite able to understand the appeal of the distorted music that the band was playing, Linda had foam earplugs fastened into both of her ears. She had gladly agreed to take the boys to the concert, knowing that she owed the Wendals more than she could ever repay them. She also wanted to soak up every moment she could with her son.

Josie had been ecstatic when Steve asked her to join the Wendals at the event, and she was even more excited when she found out that Austin was the one who had recommended that she come along.

As the band's song came to an end, Austin wrapped his arm around Steve. There was a look of ecstasy on both boys' faces. "I can't believe we're really here!" Austin exclaimed.

"I'm just glad that we're all here together," Steve responded, smiling excitedly.

The crowd went wild with cheers for the band to play one more song, and the three band members took in the roaring applause and then signaled for the audience to quiet down.

Tom approached the microphone covered in sweat but looking lively. "Before our last song, we want to acknowledge some very special guests that are here with us today," he shouted to the crowd. "Some crazy kids who have been through a whole lot together!" His voice boomed throughout the entire amphitheater.

The Wendals all looked at each other, wondering if their favorite rocker could possibly be talking about them.

"You may have seen them on the news. They became local heroes for capturing Bart the Burglar," Tom continued as the audience cheered loudly. "They call themselves by a super silly name. Please make some noise for *the Wendals!*" Thunderous applause erupted from all over the enormous crowd.

The boys froze in complete shock, none of them having had a single clue or warning that they were going to get this opportunity. Looking back at his mom in awe, Steve knew that she must have had a hand in the surprise. Linda smiled and winked at her son, and then signaled for him and the others to get moving. Tom, Mark, and Travis were all turned to the Wendals, waving their arms wildly and encouraging them to come out and join the band. Together, the Wendals took in a calming breath of air, wrapped their arms around each others' shoulders, and exuberantly ran out onto the stage.

Tyler and his two bully friends stood in their spots at the very far end of the crowd and watched the show from a distance in total disbelief.

"No way," Tyler's friend mused, in complete astonishment.

Confused, the other bully friend looked at Tyler and shrugged his shoulders as he spoke hesitantly, "Maybe the Wendals aren't complete nerds after all?"

Tyler's face turned red with anger and he raised his arm and smacked his friend hard in the back of the head. Then he continued watching the show, straining his eyes to see what was going on at the distant stage.

Back on stage, Tom and Mark were greeting the Wendals and giving them all high fives. Then the boys followed Tom back to his microphone and huddled up all together. The encouragement of the crowd gave them an unbelievable feeling of energy.

Tom approached the microphone again. "This song is for the Wendals," he said to the crowd and then picked up his guitar, ready to strum. "Let's go!" he shouted as he started to play the intro to one of the boy's favorite songs, "Carousel."

The Wendals went wild—rocking out with all of their energy, jumping up and down, and singing together at the top of their lungs—as if they didn't have a care in the entire world.

ACKNOWLEDGEMENTS

I would like to thank my wife, Natalie, for allowing me the time and space to write this book while she managed our four young children, along with everything else in our home. And for being my first reader. I love you, Nat.

A big thank you to my brother, McCain, for his awesome cover design. I hope everyone judges this book by its cover.

And thank you to Amy Otteson, for working her magic on this second edition, and fixing so many of my grammatical errors.

Made in the USA
Las Vegas, NV
05 March 2021